Lies That Stalk Us

"Moms Who Lie" Psychological Thriller Series - Book 4

Brett Monk, McKenna Langford

Big Why Media

FOREWORD BY BRETT MONK

Welcome to *"Lies That Stalk Us"*! This is the fourth book in the 5-book *"MOMS WHO LIE"* series. As in the first three books, McKenna and I are just having a blast working together to bring you this story.

In addition to the five full-length novels in the series, there's also a special FREE bonus novella called *"The Lying Begins"* that's not available on Amazon or anywhere else other than the link below. It tells the story of just what happened twenty years ago, the night of the prom when Maddy and Amelia were in high school together. Once you're thoroughly hooked on this story, you're definitely going to want to read it, too.

When you join my reader's community, you will not only get free books and other content by me and some of my friends, but you will get the inside scoop on discounted products and upcoming releases. Plus, I share some personal thoughts and "behind the scenes" photos and notes about my life, media adventures, and favorite grilling recipes. :-)

Community members also get to vote in polls and make suggestions for upcoming books and projects. You might even want to consider being a "beta reader" or an "advance review reader", both of whom get to read the books before they're available to the public.

https://www.brettmonk.com

But for now, enjoy *"Lies That Stalk Us"*.
- Brett

CONTENTS

Chapter 1

Amelia

As I cross the tiled flooring, it is cold under my bare feet. When I get to the vanity in my bathroom, I grip the edge of the counter for a moment to steady myself.

I'm disoriented. Everything is groggy. I'm still half asleep. I sort of still think that I am dreaming.

And when I realize that I'm not, I wish that I was.

I brace myself to look in the mirror at my reflection. Sunken eyes. Dull blonde hair with gray and brown roots showing. Skin stretched tightly over my cheeks. Worry creases on my forehead. And no color to me whatsoever.

I open the medicine cabinet and pull out the orange pill bottle. I don't even need to read the label before I pop the lid off and dump a pill into the palm of my hand. Then I stare at my open hand, noticing it trembling. I have no idea why other than a side effect of my crippling anxiety.

When I toss the pill back, I don't even need water. Still, it might be good to splash some on my face, so I do. Then I dab myself with a hand towel, and when I check my reflection in the mirror again, I see no changes. I don't look any better.

This is not the Amelia Bailey that I spent years building.

Carson Price kidnapped my daughter, and even though I have her back now, he has still stripped me of myself. He still has this hold over me. He still tormenting my dreams and my wakeful state.

And that's because Carson Price is still out there.

And it's even worse because people don't believe me.

I find myself in my sister's shoes, when she was fifteen years old. Way back in 1998. When she was just a sophomore at Blackfell High, head over heels in love with Carson. And then, in the blink of an eye, he was gone. No matter what she did, no matter who she talked to, there was still a massive sum of people who didn't believe a word out of her mouth. And where did this lead to her ending up?

Institutionalized.

The reason I am in her shoes now is that people don't believe me. The police won't even release it to the press that I saw Carson in those woods after he burned down the shed he was keeping Lyla in and subsequently, the old A-frame cabin he had been camping out in as well. And when I told Nora what I saw, she didn't believe me either.

Because she believes Carson to be dead.

A lot of people believe him to be. He's been missing for over twenty years. What is the more likely explanation?

I used to be one of those people who believed he was dead.

Because I used to think I had killed him.

I pushed him over the rotting balcony on the second floor of that A-frame cabin. I watched him fall into the pool. I saw the blood spread darkly over the pool lights as he hit his head on the side of it. Then when I pulled him out of the water, I shook him hard and he did not stir.

For over twenty years I was keeping that secret. And the guilt of it crippled me. But now I know I don't have to feel as guilty anymore. Because he survived. And I know this because I saw him—whether people believe it or not.

Sick of seeing how ghastly and disgusting I think I look in the reflection, I turn my back to my mirror and lean against the countertop. I cross my arms and pull my phone out of the pocket of my gray faux-fur robe. I go to Dean's contact and give him a call.

It rings six times. And instead of picking up, I am left with his voicemail.

"Dean, hi." I don't even really know where I'm going with this. "Please just talk to me. I have to tell you something. And it's important. I just... I don't know what happened that night. I don't get why you're mad and why you're ignoring me. Can we please just...?"

I'm thinking of how to wrap this up when I glance out of the corner of my eyes and jump away from the counter in fright. My husband, Gentry, has rounded the corner and scared the crap out of me.

I don't know how much he heard, but I'd rather him not know I'm trying to get Dean to stop ignoring me.

"Just call me back," I say quickly, then I finish the voicemail.

Gentry clears his throat and goes over to his vanity, which is separate from mine. He looks at me only through the reflection of his mirror as he begins running a toothbrush under the tap. He has complete bedhead, with strands sticking up in every which direction—something I used to find endearing and cute about him. Now, I'm just wondering why he doesn't cut his hair shorter like most men his age do.

"So..." he starts off slowly. I think for a moment he's going to ask me about who I was just talking to. But it's not really any of his business anymore." I think that I'm going to get my own place."

It's not at all what I had been expecting him to say.

"What?"

I heard him clearly. I just can't comprehend it well.

"Yeah." He shrugs and puts toothpaste on his gray and white toothbrush. Then he turns the sink off and stands there, not putting the toothbrush in his mouth. I watch the toothpaste on it carefully, wondering if it's going to slide off and fall down his sweatpants or onto the tile. "I just think it's time. The kids all know. The secret's out. I don't want to be in the guestroom another night. The kids don't like it. I think it would just be easier for everyone if you and I got some space and I had a place of my own."

It takes me a moment to reply. It's a lot to digest. I don't know why I'm so caught off guard and why I feel slightly offended. This is what I want, too. It's a good thing that Gentry wants to leave. I've been sick of him for a long while now. At first, when we decided we no longer loved each other and only wanted to stick it out for the kids, Gentry and I still got along great and had a good relationship as friends. He still comforted me and gave me advice and helped a great deal with the kids. But then, he grew more and more distant... not just from me, but from the kids as well—going on long work trips and retreats, which ended up not really being work trips at all but instead were visits to see a new girl he had met outside of town. Once I learned that he had started another relationship, things just got worse from there. Recently, it had gotten to the point where I couldn't even stand the sound of his breathing in the bed beside me.

So it's good that he wants to leave.

"All right," I say, shrugging back.

"Yeah?" He raises an eyebrow like he's surprised that I am agreeing so willingly.

What—does he think I'm in love with him after all, and that I want to make this work?

Not a chance.

"Yeah," I say. "I think that would be best."

He nods, and I assume the conversation is over because he finally begins brushing his teeth. I was going to get ready for the day as well, but I don't want to be in the same bathroom as him, so I'll give him his privacy and I'll just get ready later.

I turn to leave, but he calls my name softly.

"Hmm?" I ask when I turn back to him.

He's pulled a toothbrush out of his mouth halfway. His mouth is full of white foam. "And just another thing—I think I should take Joey."

CHAPTER 2

LYLA

The feeling of smoke filling my lungs and nearly pulling me under is what makes me wake up this morning coughing and sputtering in my bed.

It seems that from the moment I got home until who knows when, I'm only going to be dreaming about that night. Not about all of the other horrible things that happened when I was kidnapped, but specifically the night of the fire. That's all I've been able to dream about so far since I've been back, anyway.

Gulping in fresh, clean air and sitting up so that my head is tilted back and the fan is blowing cool air on my face, I try to leave the dream behind and focus on the present. I am home and I am safe. Carson Price isn't going to come for me and lock me in a building burning ever again.

At least I sure as heck hope not.

I take a moment to look around at my room and feel extra appreciative of everything inside of it. My furry blue rug on the ground. My record player on top of my dresser. My flatscreen TV mounted to the wall with every streaming service that's out there logged in on it. My comfortable bed, which is king-sized and massive. My large walk-in closet, stuffed to the brim with clothing of all different styles. The top drawer of my dresser, which is overflowing with different pairs of warm, fuzzy, or colorful socks.

I never really appreciated before how lucky I am to have everything I do.

I guess getting locked in a shed and having to sleep on the dusty, cold, bug-infested ground really puts things into perspective.

I stretch and get out of bed. For some reason, my body aches slightly. Like it had started to get used to sleeping on the floor of the shed. Like it's not accustomed to the soft way my mattress fits into every curve of my body no matter what position I'm lying in.

There's no school today, and even if there was, Mom and Dad told me that I wouldn't have to go. Not until I'm ready.

But of course, I'm ready. I have to go to school. I have to do lots of things.

Because I have a list.

A list of all the things I promised I would do if I got out of that shed.

My main focus on that list is to just be a good daughter and student. Among other things.

For example: step one is what I'm going to be focusing on today:

Step 1) Talk to Trinity's parents.

I promised I would. I promised that I would come clean. That I would apologize for the fact that I had been texting and driving that night of the car accident that killed Trinity Cruz. Yes, we were hit by a drunk driver, and it was presumed to be his fault, but it doesn't change the fact that I could have prevented the accident from happening if I had just been paying better attention instead of excitedly texting Wrigley Hall back—while I had a boyfriend, not to mention.

Old Lyla—the me before the accident and before all of this went down with Carson Price and all of his torments—would dress in something cute and trendy. She would put the effort into how she looked every single day, just like her mother and twin sister did.

New Lyla—who I became after the accident—would hardly have given a crap about how she looked and would have just either let Audrey pick stuff out for her or threw on whatever looked comfortable and helped her blend in.

It takes me some time to figure out what a trendy outfit would be now. So much so, that I even go on Pinterest to get some inspiration. Sure, I could bug Audrey to help me again, but then that would involve her asking what I'm getting ready for. And I'm not exactly ready to tell her about what I'm doing.

Pinterest informs me that cardigans seem to be a huge hit again, so I find my pastel green one and put that on over a simple white tank top. Then I throw on some straight-leg high-waisted jeans and white sneakers. Then in the bathroom, where I have it to myself because I don't think Joey or Audrey is awake yet, I run a straightener through my hair and curl the ends of it. I also go as far as putting makeup on—that's something I feel like I haven't done in ages.

"See?" I ask myself in the mirror as I fluff up my blonde hair and pretend like I'm posing for a selfie. "You can be the old Lyla. Easy peezy."

I tiptoe down the stairs carefully because I don't want to have a run-in with any of my family members. With my father, who has suddenly become our roommate sleeping in the guestroom down the hall. With my mother, who still looks at me like she's staring straight at a ghost. With Audrey, who will be nosy and won't want me to do anything without letting her know first. And even with Joey, who acts all weird around me now and doesn't try to tease me or flick me anymore. He's actually... nice to me. And I hate it.

Thankfully, it's a quiet morning in our house, and I have an easy enough time making it into the garage. Once I'm inside, I turn to the workbench next to the door I've just stepped out of to pick up an unfamiliar set of keys off of a key hook. These keys belong to me. They go to the white Toyota 4Runner that's been sitting in the garage untouched since it was bought.

The old Lyla wasn't afraid to drive her car. So I shouldn't be afraid to drive this new 4Runner.

I open the garage and take a couple of steps toward the vehicle. I grip the keys tightly in my hand.

Come on, Lyla. You've gotten this far.

I stop when I'm only a couple of steps to the driver's side door. My chest is tight. My palms are sweaty. Every time I blink, I catch a glimpse of Trinity's unmoving body in my mind. I hear myself screaming.

I shakily reach my hand out toward the handle, but at the last second, I snatch it back. I run back over to the workbench and throw the keys down. Then I grab my bike, kick up the kickstand, and pedal as far away from my car as I possibly can.

Maybe next time.

It's chillier out than I thought it would be, so I'm glad I have the cardigan on. And despite the cold weather, I enjoy the bike ride. I'm cautious about it, too, eyeing down every single car that passes me, determined to turn my bike right around and go right back home the moment a car slows down next to me. I won't be captured again.

My parents don't even want me going anywhere by myself, which is understandable considering that Carson hasn't been caught yet, and I know it's on my list to start obeying them and listening to their requests more, but this is something that I just have to do. That's why it's first on my list.

When I roll up outside of Trinity's house, my stomach knots up. The last time I was here was when I sleep-walked and woke up in the woods in their backyard. I had hoped to escape the premises without being seen, but Marty and Hilda Cruz had been on their back patio when I emerged from the trees.

I remember them trying to call out to me, but I hightailed it out of there anyway.

When I look at the front of their older Victorian-style home backing up to the woods, a little montage plays in my head of all the times I walked up those porch steps to knock on the door with a big smile on my face, waiting to see my best friend. Then after she died, I told myself I was never going to be knocking on that door ever again.

And yet, here I am.

I don't want to do this. But I know I have to. Because of that awful promise.

I take a few soothing breaths, get off the bike, put the kickstand down, and fiddle with the tips of the sleeves of my cardigan as I slowly ascend the few steps of the front porch. It's early, and I wonder if they're even awake.

I hope they're not. I hope they don't even hear me knock and I stand there for a few minutes and have to give up and go back home.

My hand hovers over the knocker for a long time before I finally grip the cold metal and clank it three times.

My heart is pounding ferociously. My mouth is dry. I can't believe I've actually done it.

I wait for what feels like an eternity but has probably only been a couple of seconds, and then the door slowly creaks open. It's Marty Cruz, tall and lanky and in a pink polo with a gold chain bearing a cross around his neck. His big brown eyes stare down at me and his bushy, dark eyebrows furrow.

"Lyla, is that you?"

Of course, he's unsure. I have an identical twin, after all. One who recently cut her hair short to look just like me again.

"Yes," I say nervously.

"What are you doing here?"

"Did you just say Lyla?" Hilda's voice calls from somewhere inside the house. Then suddenly, she's standing beside Marty at the door. She looks beautiful, even if she looks tired. Her brown hair is up in a messy bun, she's wearing a simple black jumper, and her feet are bare.

"You did say Lyla," she says, answering her own question.

"Um, hi," I say nervously. "I was wondering if it would be okay if I talked to both of you."

They look at each other. It feels like they're never going to answer my question. I get to stand there and worry that they're going to start screaming at me to get the heck off of their porch before they call the police.

But finally, Marty sighs. "Come in." And he and his wife step away from the door and I enter the small foyer in front of the staircase as Marty closes the door—and locks it, I can't help but notice—behind me.

"Let's go into the living room," Hilda says, directing me where to go as if I haven't been here a million times before. I nod, swallow, and lead the way into it. I take a seat in the oversized armchair, just at the edge of it where my feet still touch the ground. If I backed all the way into it, the cushion would stop at my mid-calf and I would feel like a child.

Marty and Hilda sit on the sofa together adjacent to me and mute the TV, which had been playing, to my dismay, the news.

"How can we help you?" Marty's voice is stern and demanding. I notice that neither of them is saying anything about my recent return home after the great ordeal I went through. But why am I even expecting them to?

"I just..." I don't know where to begin.

"It has taken you a long time to finally come here," Hilda points out. So they've been expecting me. They've been waiting for this moment.

I nod my head and look into my lap. "I know," I say. "And I'm so sorry. I should have come a long time ago."

"Yes, you should have," Marty agrees. It makes me feel even worse.

I force myself to look up at them. It hurts. A lot. I see so much of Trinity in her mother. And if I just focus on looking at Marty, I am almost overwhelmed by the look of disdain he has for me.

"Right," I say. "But, I finally made it. And I want you both to know that I am sorry."

There. It's out. I've said it. I'm sorry.

A lump forms in my throat. I'm so, so sorry.

"What exactly is it you're sorry for?" Hilda asks, straightening in her seat and staring me down intensely.

"For what happened to Trinity."

"And what did happen, Lyla?" Marty asks.

Great. I am sure they've heard already—all about how it's my fault. But they want me to confess directly to them. I should have expected this.

Just do it, Lyla. They already know what you did. It's not like it's anything new to them.

"I was driving Trinity home from the movies when we were hit by that drunk driver. But..."

"Yes?" Marty asks deeply.

"But the reason the driver hit us was that I hadn't been paying attention to the road. I was texting and driving. It's... it's all my fault. And I am really, really sorry."

I quickly wipe the tears that fall. I don't want them to see me crying. I don't want them to think that I'm trying to make myself look like the victim in all of this. I just want to take full responsibility. I just really miss Trinity and I really wish I hadn't taken their daughter away from them.

Suddenly, Hilda crumbles and puts her head in her hands. Marty leans forward and clasps his hands together, his elbows on his knees as he glares at me. They don't say anything.

"I wish I could bring her back," I try.

"But you can't," Marty says. "You made the decision that night to take that risk with our daughter's life. You had no regard for it. You didn't care what happened to her. You weren't a friend at all."

"I know," I say, my heart breaking. All of the horrible things I think to myself about what an awful human being I am because of that night, are being said straight to my face. "You're right. You're so right. I wasn't even thinking. And I am—I was careless and reckless and stupid."

Hilda removes her hands from her face. She used to always be so kind to me, whereas Marty was always a little more on the strict-father side.

"You killed her," she says, taking me by surprise. "You killed my daughter, Lyla."

Then she gets up and storms out of the living room.

I sit there, not knowing what to do. Marty is still glowering at me. I feel stuck in this chair. I want to run for it. I hate the way he's looking at me.

And where did Hilda even go? To call the police? To go get a knife out of the kitchen so she can get her revenge?

My heart starts beating faster the more I think about it.

What if Marty and Hilda have been waiting a very long time to get me inside of their house so that they can finally avenge their daughter?

What if they don't let me leave?

"I know that nothing I say can make this any better," I say cautiously. "I just wanted to finally let you guys hear it from... from me." I slowly get to my feet.

"You know, Lyla?" Marty asks as I slowly start backing toward the front door. "I try to find peace in the fact that you've received your karma."

"I-I did," I stammer. "You're so right. I absolutely did."

I deserved to be locked in that shed.

"Like I said," Marty continues. I'm nearly at the door. "I try to find peace in it. But somehow... it's just not enough."

"I am—I'm sorry." It's all I can think to say before I spin on my heel, fumble with the deadbolt, and run out of there. I get on my bike and I pedal as hard and as fast as I can the entire way home, too terrified to ever look back.

CHAPTER 3

MADDY

"**S**o are you gonna tell me what's going on or not?"

Steven Hall's words replay in my head as I sit on my crappy, old, sunken-in sofa and absent-mindedly braid my long brown hair while I watch the news about Lyla's kidnapping on my small TV. I notice how no one is mentioning Carson Price's name anywhere. On any news station. The only place I can seem to find information about how Mia claims she saw Carson Price in the fire is when I Google it and find different blogs and social media posts talking about it.

I already tried to tell Detective Fritz that Carson Price is alive and that he did this to Lyla. But he didn't believe me. He thinks the only murderers in Toxey are me and my son.

After Steven had been jumped in his house and robbed, I could only think of one culprit. Carson. He must have immediately left that fire, and then went on to fulfill his next plan. To do his next torment. I think that it's been him all along. That it's been one single man messing with not only me, not only Lyla, but Warner, Mia, and her other daughter, Audrey, as well. All to get his revenge over how Mia and I nearly killed him all those years ago.

I remember staring back-and-forth between Steven, with his killer smile, sandy blond hair, and dimply chin, and the note he had received as we stood out front of his house after the police drove away. The note had said...

Stay away from Madeleine Carpenter. Far away.

How could I even begin to explain any of this to him? How would he understand? How would what happen to Lyla in those woods tie in with me? The only way I could explain everything to him plainly would be is if I admitted what Mia and I did all those years ago when we were teenagers. If I told him the truth about how we kept it a secret for all these years. And I just had this feeling that if I did that, I would lose him for sure. And it just wasn't something I was willing to do.

I'm still not.

"Steven, I am so sorry," I had said to him with big, apologetic eyes, trying to sound as sincere as possible.

"Sorry for what?" he had asked, taking the note back and shoving it in his pocket. Why he wanted to keep it, I had no idea. "What is this, Maddy?"

I let my shoulders sag and I looked at my shoes for a moment. "I... I should have told you sooner," I said to him, "I think that note is from my ex-boyfriend."

It was the quickest lie I could come up with.

"An ex-boyfriend?"

I nodded repeatedly and sighed. "Yes. I thought that he was finally going to leave me alone. But apparently not. Apparently, he found out about you somehow. I... I never meant for this to happen, Steven. I'm so sorry."

When I snuck a peek at him, he looked a little less angry. But still, it was clear he was upset. Confused. And hurt—literally.

"Who is he?" he asked, making my stomach flip.

"I—you wouldn't know him," I made up. "He doesn't live in Toxey. And... I don't want to tell you who he is because I don't want you doing something stupid. I'm too afraid of him."

"Afraid of him," he repeated.

"Well... yeah. I mean... you saw what he did, Steven! He's danger-ous. I... I'm an idiot for ever getting involved with you. I'm sorry. And your son was in the house..." I put my hand over my mouth and looked away from him.

I almost felt like I was living out of some sort of soap opera. I was standing outside of his incredibly expensive white mansion while he stood in front of me in his expensive silk pajamas, his face and knuckles bloody and bruised.

"I..." Steven trailed off. "I guess I don't really know what to say."

I nodded understandingly. "I can pay for any damage that he did. For anything that he stole, too, I'll replace it."

He shook his head and gave me a slight eye roll. "Don't be ridicu-lous."

"It's not ridiculous. This is my fault."

Did he think I was being ridiculous because he knew I likely didn't have the money to replace the stolen items? Because he had been to my small, rundown house and he had seen the old Jeep Wrangler I have to share with my son since my Hyundai exploded?

"Look," he said, "it's been a long night. I'm just gonna go back inside. I just thought you should know that it happened."

"Is there anything I can do?"

But I knew without him answering that it was hopeless.

"I'll just... talk to you later," he said instead of answering my question. "Okay?"

I bit my lower lip which was trembling. "Okay," I agreed.

After that, I waited for him to text me or call me. It's been a couple of days and he still hasn't. And I miss him terribly. I know that my being with him put him in danger and put his son at risk of being hurt, too, but it's not fair. Just because some psychopath wants to ruin my every bit of happiness, I'm supposed to just not go for what I want anymore?

When Lyla's face shows up on the TV screen again, I turn my attention back to the news.

"It is still not known yet who did this to her and where they are now," the news anchor is saying.

"What a bunch of baloney!" I say, rolling my eyes. "It was Carson Price!" I want to hit my TV, but I know that it would just be stupid to do so. It wouldn't solve anything. And I don't need anything else to go breaking in this house. With Warner out of a job and no longer helping me with bills, and with me continuously not showing up for work or leaving early, we are stretched thin. I want to get people to believe us. Mia saw him in the woods. Mia watched his mask drop off of his face.

Maybe I should have just told Steven the truth. Maybe I was just overthinking it and he wouldn't really have been mad at me for what I did so many years ago.

But the maybes are pointless. Because I already said what I said. I created this lie and now I have to stick with it.

I'll admit—I thought my story would have made him feel a little sorry for me. I thought he would have told me it was not my fault and put his arms around me, even. But it seems like no matter what story I told him, truth or not, he was still going to want nothing to do with me after.

Well, you know what, Steven?
I'm not letting you get away that easy.

CHAPTER 4

WARNER

I can't seem to get myself to do anything other than lie in bed and toss my football up in the air and catch it, hardly even paying attention and getting dangerously close to letting it just bounce off my chest or hit me in the face. But hey, what's another fat lip? Probably nothing compared to what I've already received from my fight with Jackson outside the house yesterday.

I'm miserable about it. For multiple reasons. I hadn't meant for Jackson to see Lyla and me, for one. Not that that's okay—I know the almost kiss with Lyla shouldn't have happened at all. She's his ex-girlfriend, and he's supposed to be my best friend. And he's heartbroken over her—anyone can see that. And I also told him that I'm not interested in Lyla. Or... more that I was interested but that I would never let anything happen and that Lyla made it clear she wasn't interested in me anyway.

Apparently, I had been lying about that.

I'm also upset because the kiss didn't happen. I had wanted it to. Badly. Lyla and I had been inches away from each other. I had been inches away from doing something I have wanted to do for a long, long time. Probably even longer than I even realize. When I thought I had lost Lyla forever, it made things much clearer for me. I'm crazy about her. I want to be with her. I want her to be with me. I would make a good boyfriend for her. I would take care of her. I would treat her better than Jackson did. Jackson always resented the fact that she changed after her car accident. I wouldn't be that way. I like the new Lyla. And I like being there for everything that she's gone through. I understand that she can't have gone through what she went through and not changed as a person.

Heck, even I've changed as a person. I've been run off the road, called a murderer, and nearly blown up.

And I think it was possibly by Carson Price—my mother and Lyla's mother's old enemy from years ago.

The fight with Jackson has gotten messy fast. Lyla and I had immediately jumped up to our feet when he yelled at us and started storming across his yard to get to my yard to get to us.

"Jackson!" Lyla had gasped out in surprise.

I held my hands up like someone who was clearly guilty and was giving himself up. "Dude," I said quickly, my stomach lurching. "I'm sorry. Nothing happened."

But it didn't stop him from storming up to us, his fair-skinned face twisted with rage, his black hair blowing back in the breeze. And it didn't stop his fist from flying into the side of my face.

"Nothing happened!" I tried again, my face pulsing and throbbing.

Still, he said nothing and kept swinging. Jackson likes to work out as much as I do, and he's on the football team, too, so he wasn't exactly an easy fight.

I had to defend myself at some point. So I tried pushing him off of me. And... fine. He repeatedly hitting me was getting on my nerves, so maybe I threw a punch or two back. It all happened so fast—Lyla screaming in the background for us to knock it off—but I don't really remember a whole lot. All I know is that my mom had burst through the front door of our house and jumped off the steps to separate us. When Lyla had Jackson away from me and my mom had me away from him, I got a look at Jackson and saw that he had a red spot on his cheek, but otherwise looked unharmed. I could taste blood in my mouth. And my entire face throbbed. It still does.

"What is the matter with you two?!" My mom had shouted at us as we stood there trying to get out of the grasps of the ladies holding us back.

"He's being a total jerk for no reason!" I shouted. "Jackson, nothing happened!"

"Yeah, because I stopped it!" he yelled back.

"Knock it off!" Lyla snapped. "Both of you! Do you seriously think this is something I can deal with right now?!"

I immediately felt like a jerk myself. I hadn't even been thinking about Lyla. It was kind of hard to when a fist was getting slammed into my face repeatedly.

"I'm sorry," I said to her. But it didn't matter. She had tears in her eyes as she spun quickly on her heel and marched away from the house.

"Warner, get inside the house, now," Mom said in her angry voice. "Jackson, go home."

Jackson shook his head, glared at me like this wasn't over, and then finally went back to his house.

I haven't talked to Lyla since. I've tried texting her and calling her but she hasn't replied. I hate that she's mad at me. It wasn't even my fault. She has to know that. She was there. Jackson attacked me and I was defending myself. still, I can see how it might've been sort of triggering for her with everything she had just recently escaped from. I have no idea what happened to her when she was locked in that shed. She won't talk about it. It kills me to think about the possibilities.

"Warner!" my mom calls from somewhere inside the house. "Get out here, please."

I drop the football and roll out of bed with a heavy sigh. I know why I'm being summoned. I know who has come to the house. I already hear their deep voice talking to my mom in the living room.

Dean Reeves is here.

My old English teacher.

My current football coach.

And my biological father.

I trudge down the hall, regretting agreeing to this meeting. Dean had apparently asked my mom if we could all sit down and talk... as a family. He asked if, for just once, we would hear him out. My mother has been snubbing him for years.

When I exit the hall and make myself known in the living room—which is already crammed even with there only being three people in here—Dean looks at me and gives a slight smile. It's crazy to think about how much our relationship has changed in such a short amount of time. He used to be my favorite teacher at Blackfell High. I used to feel like I could talk to him about anything and confide in him for whatever I needed.

I could tell I was his favorite student, but I never put any thought as to why that was. I guess it had been pretty stupid of me to not see it. Even as I look at him now, I can see the resemblances.

"Hi, Warner," he says, sounding a little bit formal.

"'Sup."

Mom rolls her eyes at me and motions for us to sit down. I sit on the couch next to Mom and Dean takes a seat in the armchair. It's weird having him in my house like this. Any student would think it was weird having their teacher visit their home. But it's even weirder for me because now I have to deal with the fact that he's also my father and I have been kept in the dark about it for nearly eighteen years.

"Thank you for letting me come," Dean says.

"Yeah. Well... you've been persistent," Mom says, sounding annoyed.

"And I would have kept persisting," he points out. "I would've done whatever I needed to to get this to happen. I've been wanting this for so, so long. Neither of you even realize."

"How long, exactly?" Mom asks. "Because eighteen years ago, you definitely didn't want this. It was the last thing you wanted." Then she laughs sarcastically.

I feel secondhand embarrassment for Mr. Reeves. Dean. Whatever I'm supposed to call him.

He shifts in the chair. "Well... I was only a little bit older than Warner is now when I found out. How do you think Warner would react to finding out he was going to be a father right now?"

I shake my head dramatically. "Can we not?"

"How do you think I felt?" Mom asks, the both of them ignoring me.

"I know I made a mistake," Dean says. "I should have manned up, and I've regretted it ever since."

"Right." Mom is apparently not any happier that this is happening than I am.

"I didn't come here to argue with you, Madeline. I'm trying to make things right. I really am."

She takes a moment to gather herself, inhaling a deep breath and slowly letting it out. I just sit there next to her silently, feeling completely uncomfortable.

"So..." Dean trails off after a long while of silence. "Do you want to talk about what happened to your face there, Warner?"

"No," I say quickly.

"He and Jackson got in a fight outside because Warner tried to kiss his ex-girlfriend." Mom clearly doesn't care about whether or not I wanted to talk about it.

"Mom," I complain.

"Lyla Bailey?" Dean asks, raising his eyebrows.

"That's the one," Mom answers. "Trouble seems to follow her, doesn't it?"

"It seems to follow all of you," Dean points out.

"Yeah," I say, leaning forward. "And why is that, exactly?" I know Dean has some involvement in everything that's going on. Have I figured out exactly how? No.

But I'll figure it out. I'm determined to.

"I... I don't know," Dean says, shaking his head. "There are weird things going on around here. That's for sure."

I roll my eyes.

Mom slaps her palms to her knees. "Anyway," she says quickly, clearly wanting to get off of the topic of Carson Price and what has been happening to us. What he's been doing to us. I don't even know if Dean thinks Carson Price is the one behind this or not. I don't know of anyone that is on our side about it.

Sometimes I wonder if I'm even on our side.

I hadn't seen him in the woods, after all. Mia had been the only one who recognized him.

"What is it you wanted to talk to us about, Dean?" Mom asks.

Dean clears his throat. "Right. I'll just... I'll get right to it then."

"That would be great," I say bitterly.

"Okay. Warner, I know things have probably been put on a bit of a hold with what's been going on. But I'd still like to help you apply to those colleges in Florida. And... more than that, I would also like to help you pay for whatever one you go to. I've had over seventeen years where I haven't contributed a dime to your upbringing, and so I have a lot to make up for. I want to help in any way I can. I don't have a lot, but I'm comfortable. Comfortable enough to where I can definitely contribute."

I've never had anyone offer to pay for my college before. Or to help my mom and me with money at all, for the matter. I stay silent and let Mom handle this one.

"He doesn't know for sure if he's going to go to college in Florida," she says. This makes me roll my eyes again.

"Yes I do, Mom," I say. She and I were fighting for a while, and even though we're starting to get back on the right track of being in a better relationship, it hasn't changed the fact that I still want to get the heck out of Toxey when I graduate high school. I want to go to Florida. I want to be in the sunshine.

"I think getting out of here and experiencing someplace new would be great for him," Dean says.

"I'm sure you do," Mom sneers.

"I don't... I don't want you to help," I say uncomfortably.

"I get that," Dean says. "And I honestly figured you would react that way. But, just think about how much I owe it to you. After all of these years of not helping. Let me do it now."

"I'm sorry," Mom says, looking up at the ceiling. "I'm just having a really hard time wrapping my head around all of this right now."

The two of them continue talking, but I've tuned them out because I've received a text from Lyla.

Lyla: Hi. I'm sorry I've been ignoring you. I've been trying to work things out in my head and... I really do think we need to just be friends. I'm really sorry.

I gnaw on the inside of my sore cheek and reread her words over and over again. To say I'm disappointed is a gross understatement. It's not what I want. I don't want to be just friends with Lyla.

But she's made her choice, I guess. And I know that there's nothing I can do about it.

CHAPTER 5

AUDREY

I hate that we've become the family that has formal meetings in our kitchen at our big farmhouse table.

I also hate that I am a part of a broken family. And that I never saw it coming. I never knew that my mother and father weren't in love anymore. Sure, they have been fighting a lot lately and not seeming like they really care to be around each other, but I had always assumed it was because of Lyla's disappearance. That would put a lot of strain on any relationship, I think.

But no. They've been keeping up this façade for forever now. They've been pretending to still love each other and pretending like this marriage is working just for the sake of us kids and for the fact that they're fostering Joey.

Now Dad stays in the guestroom upstairs and it's completely weird. I've cried a lot over it, but I haven't let anyone see it. In front of the family, I need to be a certain way. Brave and put together. I see myself as the glue that holds us all together. That keeps us all from falling apart.

"So," I say with my head held high, flicking my ponytail behind my head. "What is this all about?"

I'm at the table with Lyla, Joey, Mom, and Dad. Joey has his phone out, but my father, who is sitting next to him, reaches over and slowly takes it away from him. "Family meeting, Joe," he says.

Joey leans back in his chair and crosses his arms. His bowl haircut is turning out to be more of a shag cut now. It's been a while since he's gotten to go to the hair salon. It's been a while since any of us have. I'm still rocking the choppy haircut I gave myself to look like Lyla when Warner and I went searching for her in the Boldosa redwoods.

Lyla, who is sitting next to me, is being silent. She doesn't look moody or annoyed, she just doesn't look like she wants to say anything.

"Your father and I wanted to talk to you guys," Mom says.

"Again," I say. We already had one of these meetings in the living room after Lyla got home when I let it slip, out of a moment of anger and frustration at my parents, that I knew they were both cheating on each other. If I had never said anything, we wouldn't be having this meeting now. We wouldn't have had the meeting we did the other night when they finally told us about how they're not in love anymore and how this is all one big fake arrangement between them.

In a way, it's my fault that our family is broken.

"Right," Mom says slowly. "Again." Even though she got ready today, she still doesn't look like her normal self. She looks like it took extra concealer to hide her puffy eyes. And she still looks tired. Like she half-heartedly put her hair back in that bun. And Mom never does things half-heartedly. Or at least, she used to not.

"We're really sorry about how your mom's and my relationship has been affecting all of you," Dad says. "Especially with you, Lyla, after you've gone through such a hard time. I know it can't be easy coming home and having to deal with this."

She shrugs. "It's okay."

"But it's not okay," he says, shaking his head. "I feel horrible." He's avoiding looking at me. I know he's thinking in his head that he wishes I had never said anything about knowing about him and Mom cheating. Not that they really were, anyway—Mom already knew that Dad apparently has a new girlfriend. And even though she's gotten on a dating website, she hasn't used it yet.

"We do," Mom agrees quietly. She reaches across Dad, toward Joey, and holds out her hand for him to take. He stares at it for a while, looking like he doesn't want to do it, but eventually, he caves. She gives him a weak smile. "I know change isn't easy."

"It's not," Joey mutters.

"But it also can't be easy having me living upstairs with you guys," Dad says. "It can't be easy seeing your mom and me living under the same roof knowing what you know. So... I've made a decision."

"You're moving out?" Lyla asks.

Joey's head snaps to Dad. "What?"

"Is it true?" I ask.

Mom and Dad look at each other. Then they both nod their heads. "It's true," Dad says.

"He's going to get his own place," Mom explains. "He's just going to move into a temporary rental for now. And you guys will take turns seeing him and seeing me. He's not going to be far at all. So you don't have to worry about getting to school and all of that."

"Yeah," Dad agrees. "I'll be just around the corner."

I hate this. I hate it so much. I hate the way my chest is constricting and I'm feeling sweaty and things around me seem a little hazy. I hate that their voices have started sounding far away and I hate that I feel like I want to run to a toilet and vomit up dinner.

"Wow," Lyla whispers.

"But I don't want you to move out," Joey says.

"When are you leaving, then?" Lyla asks.

"Tomorrow." Dad looks heartbroken to be spreading the news.

I am heartbroken to hear it.

"Audrey?" Mom asks softly.

"You okay, sweetheart?" Dad asks, turning his attention to me.

Snap out of it, Audrey. It's fine. Everything is fine. Do not let them see how you're feeling.

I roll my shoulders back. "I suppose I wasn't expecting it to happen so soon," I say. "But I guess it does need to happen at some point, doesn't it?"

Mom smiles at me. "You're so mature."

I try to smile back. I don't know if it worked or not.

So what if Dad is moving out? I have a lot bigger things to deal with right now. I shouldn't even care about this. It's not like I'm never going to see him again. What is it that kids say about divorced parents? That it rocks because they got two birthdays and two Christmases?

"This is dumb!" Joey suddenly shouts. Everyone turns their attention to him. He has tears streaming down his cheeks. "This wasn't supposed to happen! Audrey, you ruined everything!" Then he gets up from the table.

"Joe," Dad calls. "Please don't go."

"Leave me alone!"

He runs up the staircase and is out of sight.

Mom sighs.

"I guess the family meeting is adjourned," I say, getting to my feet as well.

"I'll go talk to Joey," Mom says. Then she looks back and forth between Lyla and me. "Again, we're really sorry. And we appreciate you both being so understanding about this."

"Of course," I say.

"Sure," Lyla says. "Whatever you guys need to do." Then she and Mom head up the staircase together.

I am about to walk in that direction, too, but then Dad calls out, "Hey, Audrey, wait up."

I freeze in my step, my stomach dipping. When I turn to face him, he's wiggling his finger, signaling that he wants to have me follow him out back really quick.

Great.

I put on a brave face and go outside with him. I already know what it is he wants to talk to me about.

"How you holding up, kiddo?" he asks.

"I'm fine," I say, hoping that will end the discussion.

"You sure?" he asks.

"Yeah. Fine."

"And you're... you're still on board with not telling your mother what happened the other night?"

He doesn't have to say the specific moment he's talking about for me to know for sure. He's referring to Friday night when that random man came up to me outside of the house claiming to be Carson Price's father. I had been afraid of him at first. Lyla had just been kidnapped, after all, and Mom claimed to see Carson in the woods. But this man being Carson's father could've looked a lot like him. And it made me worried that maybe he was the kidnapper for some reason.

"I'm Carson Price's father," the fifty-something-year-old buff man had said to me. "And I think he's alive, too."

I stood there and stared at him for a long while. I didn't know what to say to that.

"Do you know where he could be?" he asked me.

I slowly shook my head. "I... I don't," I said. "Probably still out there somewhere in those woods." But what I wanted to do was scream at him.

Do you have any idea what your son did to my sister?! What he's done to me?!

"Look, I know he's put you through a lot. You and your family. I... I'm sorry for any trouble he's caused. I just want to help him. That's why I want to track him down."

"Help him do what?"

"Audrey?" Dad's voice came from inside the garage. Then in a matter of a millisecond, he was suddenly by my side. When he saw the man staring at us on the driveway, he quickly moved in front of me, holding onto my wrist tightly.

"Can I help you?" he asked in an intimidating voice that I hadn't heard before.

"I'm sorry," the man said. "I'm just looking for Carson Price."

"Well, what are you doing looking for him here? You're not going to find him. Why are you interrogating my daughter at our home, on my property, at this time of night?"

"I'm sorry," the man, who told me his name was Eric, said sincerely. He slowly started backing away from the both of us. "I'm just trying to find him."

"Why?" Dad asked. "Are you a cop?"

"He's his dad," I answered for him.

Dad looked back at me for a second with a disgusted look. Then he turned back to Eric. "You need to leave."

Eric nodded quickly. "I'm sorry to interrupt your evening."

After he left, my dad, still holding my wrist tightly, pulled me back into the garage. I went to go open the door to the inside of the house, but he held me back.

"What?" I snapped.

"I don't think we should tell your mother about this," he said.

"What? Why not?"

"Look. Your mom is going through a lot right now. It's best if we just keep this between us. Okay? I don't think the guy is going to bother us again. And it will just be added stress for her."

"So you want me to keep it a secret?" I wasn't okay with it. I didn't like being asked to hide something from Mom. And I didn't like knowing that Mom and Dad were the types of people who kept secrets from each other. Or at least Dad was.

"It's just for your mom's sake, Audrey. Please."

"Fine."

He let go of my wrist to give me a tight hug. Like it sealed the secret.

And I guess, in a way, it did. I haven't told Mom. I haven't even told Lyla or Warner.

And I get the feeling that Dad is wrong.

I don't think we've seen the last of Eric.

CHAPTER 6

LYLA

The next morning, I'm startled a little when I look in the doorway of my bedroom and see Audrey lingering there.

"So, you're really going?" she asks as I finish doing my makeup in the mirror on top of my dresser.

I shrug and straighten up. "Yeah, why?"

"It's just that... Ly, I don't think anybody would judge you or think less of you for wanting to take some time off. You just went through something really scary. No one is expecting you to be able to just bounce back."

I stare at my reflection in the mirror and finger-comb through my hair some more to make sure it's soft and silky. "It's fine," I say. "Seriously. It's not a big deal. I took some time off after the accident, and catching back up on that schoolwork nearly killed me. I'd rather just go to school, catch up on the week that I missed, and get things back to normal as soon as possible."

She nods slowly, but she's still looking at me like I'm some sort of alien.

"I haven't seen you wear that shirt in a while," she comments.

It's a slightly baggy gray sweater with a giant pink heart in the center of it. I've paired it with some light-wash blue jeans and my white sneakers again.

"Is it still cute?" I ask.

"Yeah," she says, nodding. "Totally."

She looks ready to leave, too. Her hair is pulled back in a ponytail—a short one—and she's fiddling with it as she talks to me. "I had to throw my hair up," she says, noticing me staring. "I haven't had time to go to the salon and get it fixed since I cut it myself."

"You didn't have to do that, you know," I remind her. She loved her long hair.

"And you didn't have to go and get yourself kidnapped pretending to be me."

Touché.

I say nothing to that and grab my backpack. "You ready to go?"

She purses her lips in a way of saying yes.

When we pull into the school parking lot, she puts her Mini Cooper in "Park" but doesn't move.

"Are we getting out?" I ask.

"Are you ready?"

I furrow my eyebrows. "Yeah. Really, it's no big deal."

And it's not a big deal. If I just stick to my list, everything is going to be okay. In fact, I'll be so busy that I won't even have time to think about my experience inside that shed. I won't even have time to think about Carson Price. Before I know it, I'll forget all about him and my life will be totally back to normal.

"Okay..." Audrey trails off like she thinks this is going to be a huge failure. Like I'm not going to even make it through thirty seconds of being back at school.

I'll show her.

I get out of the car and walk confidently through the parking lot toward the front of the school.

Yes. Eyes are on me one hundred percent.

People are calling my name and waving to me. I smile big and wave back.

Audrey trails a little bit behind me, running to catch up.

I get hugs from several people, a lot of them telling me that they're so glad I'm okay. I keep the smile on and tell them I'm thankful that they've been thinking about me. By the time I've even reached the school stairs, I've been approached by ten different people. I have even been given cards from some of them.

I have to admit, I don't know what I have been expecting coming back, but I hadn't expected such a warm welcome. After all, I'm still the girl who killed Trinity. I thought I'd get maybe some mixed reactions to my return. But so far, everyone is smiling big and acting pleasant.

The only time my stomach really twists in a knot is when I catch sight of Warner getting out of his jeep. He has sunglasses covering his face and a hood up. He's starting to build a reputation for coming to school bruised and injured.

I feel horrible for the text I sent him about us needing to stay as just friends, but it had been necessary. It simply had to be done and it's for the best.

When I go inside with Audrey, I am surprised that she's still walking with me and hasn't disappeared to go hang out with her friends.

"Lyla!" A couple of steps in front of me, Wrigley is closing his locker door and grinning at me. He approaches me and throws his arms around me tightly. I hug him back with a big smile on my face. It does feel good to be in his arms. This is who I agreed to go on a date with. That means Wrigley is the one I chose. Not Warner. The fact that I nearly kissed him had been an accident. It had been a heat-of-the-moment thing that could've really screwed things up for me and Wrigley. I'm glad it didn't happen.

I just wish the fight between him and Jackson hadn't happened, either.

"I can't believe you're here," Wrigley says.

"Neither can I," Audrey says, shaking her head and crossing her arms.

He smiles at her briefly before turning back to me. "How are you?" he asks.

"I'm good," I say. I hold up the cards I've been given. "Everyone's being really nice."

It's weird to be hugged by Wrigley in the hallway like this. Before, our friendship had always been more secretive. We acknowledge each other with secret glances and then Snapchatted each other about it after. Now, mysterious, keeps-to-himself Wrigley Hall doesn't care about being seen hugging and talking to me.

"That's good," he says. "And you're back on social media, too?"

That's another thing. I reactivated social media. I showed a lot of people my return by liking a lot of my classmates' posts and watching their stories on Instagram and their videos on TikTok. If

I'm going to be my normal self, I need to be social. I need to be involved with my peers.

"I am," I say.

"Cool," he says. Then the bell rings. "I'll Snapchat you later, then."

I smile at him and wave goodbye.

Audrey makes a big deal about walking me to class, telling me that she just wants to make sure I'm okay.

"Why aren't you meeting up with Sophia and Danielle and Olive?" I ask, suspecting something is up. I haven't seen any of them, and usually, Audrey always meets up with them in the mornings.

"You're not the only one who sort of fell out of touch with them," she says.

I crinkle my forehead. "In a week?" I ask. "What happened?"

"Just... go to class. We'll talk about it later. Sit with me at lunch."

We hug and I go to my first hour with Warner's dad, Mr. Reeves. He smiles at me when he sees me. I hope he doesn't make a stink about me being back, so I quickly nod my head at him and take a seat at my desk. When everyone is done talking to me and greeting me and telling me that they're so glad I'm back, I get an alert on my phone and pull it out, glad to have a momentary pause where I'm not smiling at everyone and telling them how happy I am to be here.

It's a TikTok notification.

An unknown user has sent me a video in my inbox.

I watch it with the volume super low. The class is too busy talking loudly anyway for them to really hear it.

The videos of a person in front of a green screen depicting them being in the middle of the woods. They have a filter on their face of an animated cat taking up their whole head so I have no idea who it is.

And when they talk, their voice is completely masked by some sort of voice changer.

"Looks like Lyla Bailey has decided to show her face at Blackfell High today. After what she went through, why come back? What does she have to prove? And are we going to be able to find out who really kidnapped her? Is she going to tell anyone what happened to her? What do we think? Was it Carson Price who kidnapped her or not?"

"What the...?" I mutter to myself. Then I go to the TikTok users' page. The username is Toxeydramaenthusiast. And my heart nearly flies out of my throat when I see that they've gained Nearly four-thousand followers and have already over a million views on the videos.

Who is this person?

I swipe to another video. It's a recap of the press release Mom and Dad gave when I went missing. And the poster still uses that animated cat filter on their face and a green screen behind them to mask their location.

I can't bear to look at the heartbroken expressions on Mom and Dad's faces, so I skip that video and go on to another. This one is a recap of the day I got kidnapped and everything that had happened before it. This person is just telling the world information about me and Audrey. And people are eating it up. People that don't even live in Toxey.

There are over ten videos already made. And people are going nuts over them.

Too terrified to even read the comments, I shove my phone in my pocket and get up to use the restroom. I grab the hall pass and don't even ask Mr. Reeves if it's okay before I dive into the hall that is empty now that the final bell has rung. I sprint to the bathroom, the pain in my chest starting. I fly into a stall and slam it shut, the door echoing loudly through the tiled room. I tug at my hair and try to breathe, but it feels like I can't. It feels like I'm literally dying. I sit on the toilet seat and put my feet up. I hug myself tightly and rock back and forth. I know I'm having a panic attack. Over the stupid TikTok account. Over someone narrating the events happening in our small town and making it out like some sort of dramatic movie for everyone to take part in. And the anonymous poster... I hate that I don't know who it is. I hate that it could be the very person who kidnapped me.

They are still out there. And this new TikTok account could just be their next way of tormenting us.

CHAPTER 7

AMELIA

I am sitting in my Range Rover at a stoplight on my way to work, reflecting on how this morning had gone with a bad feeling in my stomach. I don't understand why I have this bad feeling, which is why I keep thinking everything over; trying to see if there is something I did wrong. I feel guilty and anxious even though I already had my meds.

This morning, the first thing I did when I woke up was take more pills. Then I splashed more water on my face. Then, just as I had done yesterday, I gripped the edge of the counter and stared at myself hard in the mirror. I wanted to try and understand why I couldn't just get myself back to normal. So what if Gentry and I were finally separating? It was supposed to be a good thing. And I had my daughter back. And everything could finally start going back to normal.

But it just didn't feel like normal was happening yet.

Joey had made it down the stairs first. Gentry was already not here because he finalized things last night with his rental and headed over extra early this morning to scope things out. So it left just me to see the kids after school. It was like it was my first official day of being a single mother.

"Hey, sweetie," I had said to Joey as he wandered into the kitchen with his hair still a mess from sleeping. He opened the cabinet and pulled out a box of cereal.

"I can make you breakfast," I tried. I was in the middle of making a cup of coffee.

"Cereal sounds good," Joey said in a flat voice. I think that's when I got my first surge of worry. I became worried that he hates me. Worried that all my children do.

But with Joey, it was different. I was worried—and I still am— that he had started to wish he was with a different family. That he was no longer happy with this one.

"How are you this morning?" I had asked.

Joey shrugged and said nothing.

My stomach dipped again.

I didn't want to press Joey to keep talking to me, so I gave up and sipped my coffee, and then a few moments later, Audrey and Lyla came down the stairs, fully ready for school. I looked at the clock and saw that it was nearly time for them to need to leave already.

"Did you guys have breakfast?" I asked, thinking maybe they ate before I left my bedroom this morning.

"No," Lyla answered. "But I'm not hungry."

"I have a protein bar in my bag," Audrey said.

That was when another bout of anxiety ran through me. It made me cold. It made my hands clammy. I hadn't been out of my bedroom early enough. I'm already failing at this single mother thing. I should've had breakfast ready before they even entered the kitchen. I made a mental note to set an alarm clock earlier for tomorrow.

"Lyla, you really should eat something," I suggested. "Just give me three minutes I can whip you up a bowl of oatmeal or something."

"It's really okay, Mom," she said. "I just wanna get to school so I can get this day over with."

"You don't... you don't have to go," I said. I wondered if she felt that I was pressuring her to do so. Or if she would just rather endure school than endure being here another second with me. Would they prefer to be staying with their father over me?

"I know," she said, sounding slightly exasperated. "Audrey already told me this. But I'm going."

"Okay."

They started passing me and making their way to the mud room.

"Well, have a good day!" I called to them. I would've liked hugs goodbye or at least a smile, but they apparently did not feel like doing either.

And it made me feel worse.

So. There are lots of reasons why I feel off about how the morning went. Mainly because I'm overthinking every little thing and feeling like I'm failing as a parent.

And then there was the other thing I kept doing that even Joey noticed. After the girls left.

"Why are you checking your phone so much?" Joey asked as he put his bowl in the sink.

Have I been checking it that much?

"I'm... I'm not," I said, feeling stupid.

"Yes you are," he said. "Are you talking to somebody?"

That was a thing—I wanted to be talking to somebody. I wanted to be hearing back from Dean.

"No. It's nothing."

"Whatever," Joey said, his voice tinged with attitude as he put his bowl in the sink. "I'm going to go get changed."

So, Joey had noticed how much I was checking my phone. And I'm still checking it a lot now—even as I sit at this red light. And I check it again even as I'm driving, too. I would've thought I would've learned a lesson about looking at my phone while driving after what happened with Lyla, and usually, I'm good about it, but I'm just feeling desperate and anxious.

I want to hear from Dean. I don't want him to be mad at me anymore. I'm still confused over why it is he's even mad in the first place.

How am I supposed to work like this? How am I supposed to sit at my desk and try to talk to my clients and focus on giving them the interiors of their dreams?

It's not going to happen.

The light ahead turns red, and as I pull up to it, I should be getting into the left lane. Instead, I get into the right one.

I've decided to take a last-minute detour.

CHAPTER 8

WARNER

I know the simplest way to get over what happened with Lyla and everything going on with Carson—or whoever is tormenting us—is to distract myself. And I can distract myself by getting back into football, focusing on applying to colleges, working out, fixing up my Jeep, and being more invested in school.

But I don't feel like doing any of that. That's the problem. Everything sucks too much.

As I walk through the halls at school, everyone is still staring at me and whispering. Maybe I'm being paranoid, but I still feel that people think I'm a murderer even though I'm not the one who kidnapped Lyla or killed Sydney. The thing about that is that no one is really certain who was the one who kidnapped her. So everything is still up in the air about it. And I had been there that night when she was found. So people are making their own conclusions in their heads about why that is.

Then, I see Lyla across the way. As soon as it happens, I duck out of sight and go into the nearest classroom, where there happens to be a tutoring session going on that I completely interrupted. I awkwardly apologize, fiddle with my shoelaces, and then leave the classroom when I think it's safe. My heart is hammering and my palms are sweating. Then I felt stupid because Lyla still wants to be friends so I shouldn't be avoiding her. Still, I just don't know if I'm ready to face her.

At lunch, I know I'm going to run into her again. Or I at least expect to see her in the cafeteria.

I feel conflicted about where I'm supposed to sit after I get my food. Do I try to sit with Lyla and Audrey and talk to them about everything that's been going on? Or do I sit with the football team even though Jackson is at their table talking loudly and joking around, getting everyone to laugh like he always does?

I'm supposed to be distracting myself.

So I opt for the football table. I sit at the other end of the table on the same side as Jackson so that he can barely even see me. Across from me is Cody Lawson, and on either side of me are Austin Booth and Brandt White. They don't notice me right away —no one does—because they're all busy laughing at something Jackson just said.

I silently dig into my burrito.

"Oh, what's up, dude?" Cody says when he notices me across from him.

"Not much," I say, my mouth still a little bit full of food.

Everyone seems to quiet down upon Cody addressing me. They all look in my direction, realizing that I've joined the table. I haven't exactly been a part of the team lately even though I'm the captain. It's a miracle that I still even am.

"Awkward," Chance says over at the other end of the table by Jackson.

"Why?" Jackson asks, sounding irritated. "Who cares? Who cares about Carpenter?"

I shake my head and keep my eyes on my burrito as I eat. It's tasting blander than ever.

"If anything, he should've been sitting here a while ago. And he calls himself our captain." Jackson, down at the other end, evidently still feels like talking smack. And what sucks even more is that I hear some of my teammates muttering in
agreement with him.

"So, are you good?" Brandt asks me.

"What do you mean?" I reply. "I'm fine. Why wouldn't I be?"

"There's just some crazy... stuff... going down lately. And that shiner you got..."

"I'm good," I say again. Then I glare at him a little bit so that he knows how serious I am and how much I want him to drop the subject. I don't want to talk about what's happened with Lyla. And I don't want to talk about what happened with Jackson—even though I'm sure they all have already gotten to probably hear his side of the story.

Thankfully, they all move on and talk about other things so I can sit there in silence. But while I do so, I find myself scanning the cafeteria in search of Lyla. I don't see her, which surprises me. And it makes me wonder where she's gone.

Then I get mad at myself for wondering where she is, and it takes away the last of my appetite so I get up from the table and toss the rest of my food, then I leave wordlessly.

During practice, I go as hard as I would if it were a real game. I put my all into it, wanting to focus on football and football only. I want to be so busy running plays and doing drills that I don't even really have time to talk to Coach.

It works out well for a while, but then as luck would have it, Dean Reeves calls me over to stand alongside him and help determine if one of the plays he wants to use is going to work out or not.

After, when he calls for a water break, I go to walk over to the sideline to grab my water bottle, but Dean doesn't let me get too far.

"So, uh, Warner," he says, stopping me in my tracks. I slowly turn to face him. "You're doing good out there today. It's good to see that you're all healed up and have your head back in the game."

"Yeah," I say simply. I go to leave again, but he keeps going.

"How are you doing with everything?"

We hadn't gotten very far with our conversation with him in our house last night. It mainly was just him and my mom arguing while I sat there in silence staring at that stupid text message Lyla had sent me. When Dean left, he told me he would see me at school, and that was that.

"Fine," I say with a shrug and a look on my face that says "Why wouldn't I be?"

He shrugs in return. "I'm just checking in. I know last night didn't go exactly the way I would've liked it to..."

"No? What conclusion were you trying to get to?" I ask, suddenly more interested.

"I don't know," he says. "I was just sort of hoping we would all get on the same page."

"Were you hoping that Mom and I would forgive you?"

"I mean, it would've been nice, but I wasn't expecting it."

I'm silent for a second because I don't know if I really want to ask this question. But eventually, I decide that I do want to. "Why now?"

I know I don't have to add context to the question. He knows exactly what I'm referring to.

His answer comes with him rubbing the stubble on his face and sighing. "I was a coward, Warner. I won't lie to you. I was scared at first. So, so scared. But it didn't take me long to realize how stupid I was. For years I wanted to be in your life. Just, Maddy—your mom—she would never let me. No matter what I tried. I even stayed out of Toxey to try to distance myself. To get my mind off of it. But it didn't work."

"So you came back."

"I came back. And I'll be honest with you, Warner. My only intention for coming back was to make myself a part of your life, whether your mom wanted me to be or not."

"Wait..."

"Yeah. I became a teacher and a football coach just to get closer to you."

I don't know what to say to that. All that comes out is, "Oh."

"You two done having your little father-son talk yet?" Chance Hobbs calls to us as the rest of the team gathers back on the field, ready to keep going with the practice.

I shake my head, and Coach blows his whistle and calls out another drill for us to work on.

"You can head back out there," he says to me.

"All right." I make it about three steps before I turn around and go back over to him. "Just curious—what was my mom like in high school?"

"Your mom?" He smirks a little. "Almost exactly like she is now."

"How so?"

"Well... she was a bit of an outsider, having come from Seattle. She had this grunginess about her that was different than the other girls at school. And she wasn't afraid to speak her mind. Or get in trouble. And she got in trouble a lot. I'm surprised you're not more rebellious. But I was always a pretty good kid, so I'm guessing you get that from me."

I smirk a little. I can't help it.

"She had all this money from her parents, but she didn't want it," he continues. "That Jeep you drive now, it was like the coolest car in the parking lot when she went here. But she didn't even like it."

I nod. "She doesn't talk to her parents," I say. I don't know anything about my grandparents. She won't even talk to me about them.

"Yeah. Part of it is probably because they spoiled her instead of giving her an ounce of attention."

My mom never spoils me and sometimes I feel like I don't get any attention from her, either. But I don't tell Dean this.

"Was she super secretive?" I ask.

Dean shrugs. "Maybe a little. But any secret she kept was usually just because she didn't want to hurt the people around her."

I roll my eyes at that. "That's lame."

"How so?"

"Secrets destroy people."

I find that I'm done talking about this, so I jog back out onto the field and join the drill.

CHAPTER 9

Audrey

I am already annoyed on the way to cheer practice because in the family group chat I have with my siblings and my parents, Mom has said that we are to go to Dad's new rental after school. Apparently, the two of them talked earlier and decided that it would be good for us to stay with him first so that we can help him get used to his new place and help him unpack and get settled in.

Then when I go into the locker room, Sophia and Olive look at me as if they're curious whether or not I'm going to go up to talk to them. The second I see their eyes on me I look the other way and go to my locker in silence. I get changed quickly and go into the gym practically before anyone else.

When Danielle enters, she walks over directly to me.

"Hey, can I stretch with you?" she asks. Her short hair is pulled up into two high pigtails, making her look like some sort of anime character, but I don't hate the style on her. Her hazel eyes are hopeful as she stands above me while I am getting into my splits on the floor.

"Sure," I say, feeling slightly awkward about it. Not long ago, I confronted her and Sophia and Olive—my former besties—and told them that they were all horrible friends. That they were fake. That they just liked to gossip. That they were not there for me just because they wanted to be—it came with a price. Not to mention there was this ridiculous drama about Madeleine Carpenter somehow convincing Sophia that I was talking to her crush in order to get revenge since she thought I tried to tell Warner about his dad. And to hurt me back, Sophia tried to snag my crush, Ryan Copeland.

Then a short while later, during a search party for Lyla, Danielle came up to me and told me that she was done with Sophia. And that she had talked to Ryan for me and cleared up the whole situation.

So I guess maybe I can continue being friends with her.

But things are still a little weird.

She sits down next to me and we stretch together. When Sophia and Olive enter the gym, they have disgruntled looks on their faces and they go and stand as far away as possible from us.

"So, you're still really not talking to them?" I ask.

Danielle shrugs. "If Sophia would apologize and if Olive would stand up for herself like I did, maybe I would. I don't know. I think you're right about them just wanting to be involved in all of the drama and gossip. They're egocentric and don't care about anyone but themselves. They're way too into their statuses."

"I agree," I say.

As practice continues, I get more warmed up to the idea of Danielle and I being friends again. It's nice to have somebody on my side. Somebody I can giggle with and talk to while trying to avoid Sophia and her wrath. And Danielle is easy to get along with. She has a huge heart and is always so friendly and open to everyone, and some people think she's fake because of it. But I know the truth. Danielle has just always genuinely been a good person.

By the time practice ends, I am overwhelmed with how grateful I am that we resolved things, and I hug her tightly.

"What was that for?" she asks when we pull away before heading into the lockers.

"I'm just... I'm really glad we're friends again."

She smiles back at me. "I am, too."

Dad's new place is weird. It's nice enough and in a good part of Toxey, but it's smaller than our house. It only has three bedrooms, and there's no pool in the backyard. In fact, there's hardly any landscaping in the back at all. The front is done up well to add to the curb appeal, but the backyard is just a large lawn and a few old trees.

It has a very basic layout: when you walk through the front door and turn right, you can either take the stairs up to the two bedrooms up there, or you can go downstairs to where Dad's bedroom is. Then if you go straight, you're in the dining area. If you go to the left, you're in the kitchen. The living room is small on the left of the dining area, but there is a large sunroom that leads to the backyard.

"So, what do you guys think?" Dad asks Lyla and me as we slowly walk through the house, looking at everything and trying not to trip over the boxes Dad has placed everywhere.

"It's nice, Dad," Lyla says, nodding her head reassuringly.

"Sure," I half-heartedly agree, "it's... nice."

"I'm glad you guys are here," he says.

"It's definitely weird," I admit. I can't help myself.

"I know," Dad says. "It's going to take some getting used to. But the quicker we unpack this place and start living in it, it'll get less weird. I was thinking I'll order some pizza for dinner tonight. We'll have an unpacking party and then maybe we can all play a board game?"

"Sounds good to me!" Lyla says, clapping her hands together and then rubbing them like she's ready to get started.

I give her a look. She pretends not to notice it as she opens up one of the boxes.

"And, uh..." Dad trails off. I turn back to him and notice he looks a little nervous.

"Yeah?" I ask. Lyla is still busying herself getting stuff out of one of the boxes.

"Well, I know that you are both aware that I have started seeing somebody else," he begins. This gets Lyla's attention. She drops what she's doing and turns to us. Dad continues. "And it may be hard to grasp because, in your minds, your mom and I haven't been separated that long. But the truth of the matter is that we started seeing other people a long time ago. Or at least... I did. And my girlfriend? I'm going to want you to meet her soon."

"What?" I ask loudly.

"What's wrong?" he asks, standing up a little straighter.

"Are you crazy?" I demand, balling my fists. "I do not want to meet your... lady."

"She's my girlfriend, Audrey," he says.

"I'll meet her," Lyla says like she's completely on board with it.

I growl at her. "Are you serious?" I ask her, sneering. "How could you even want to do that?"

She shrugs. "Dad wants us to," she says simply.

She can't seriously think this is fine. She can't really have accepted that this change is happening. That Mom and Dad are getting a divorce and that they're moving on to be with other people. I refuse to believe her act. She's just pretending. She has to be.

"I'm going to go get started in the sunroom," I say, shaking my head before I walk past the both of them.

I thought I was getting pretty good at faking things.

Apparently, it's just another thing Lyla is better at than me.

CHAPTER 10

MADDY

It happened.

I can't believe it finally happened!

Steven Hall gave me a call while I was at work earlier today and asked me to meet him for an early dinner tonight—he said "early" because he has to pack for his flight in the morning. He's finally ready to talk to me again.

I am a nervous wreck as I get ready for the date. He picked out the restaurant—some cozy Italian joint just outside of town—and I told him I would meet him there.

I want as much time as possible to be alone so I can prepare what I am going to say and figure out just how I can make sure I win him back for good.

I decide on a simple, slightly tight, black dress with strappy black heels. I wear dark purple lipstick that contrasts well against my deeply tanned skin. I put on a dab of my favorite perfume—Gucci Bloom, which I won in a raffle at work forever ago—that I only wear on special occasions.

Special ones such as tonight.

"Um, where are you off to?" Warner asks when he sees me in the hallway, the both of us leaving our bedrooms at the same time. He looks like he just got out of the shower, his hair is stringy and damp.

"Uh, to go see Steven," I admit sheepishly, smoothing out my dress and then my hair. "Do I look okay? Is this too much, you think?"

His forehead creases. "You're seeing Steven? I thought that was over."

My stomach twists. I had mentioned that to him—but only in a moment of weakness when he had asked me about him yesterday and I had been miserable because I hadn't heard from him yet. "Uh, well... I guess it's not."

He shakes his head. "You look good. Have fun."

I can't tell if he means it or not. Maybe he's upset that I am leaving once again in the evening. I know I go out a lot—I do. But I can't stand to be home for too long. I like being around Warner, of course, but he's hardly ever home either, or he just stays holed up in his room, so what's a girl supposed to do? Sit around and mope in her lame house when she could be out spreading her extroverted wings and socializing?

I say goodbye—after making sure it's okay to borrow his car—then I drive to the address Steven sent me.

I look at myself in the rearview mirror as I drive. "Just be sweet, charming, and honest," I say, giving myself a little pep talk before the date. I want to tell Steven the truth about who probably robbed him and why. I really do. I don't want to be in another relationship full of secrets and lies. I care about Steven and I want things to work between us. More than I ever wanted in any of my other previous relationships.

And there had been a lot of those.

When I park, I can see Steven's silver Mercedes G-Wagon is already here, and my nerves deepen at the sight of it. Still, I manage to get out of the old Jeep and go inside anyway, where I am escorted to the white cloth-covered table by a maître d' in all black.

Steven stands from the table, looking hunky and delicious, and offers me a hug and a smile. I inhale the citrusy scent of his cologne as we embrace, and I notice that he's the first one to pull away.

So he's still a little unsure, I see.

We take our seats across from each other, a small lit candlestick between us.

"This place is adorable," I say, looking around with a small smile on my face. The walls are brick but have a black wooden paneled border around them. Pendants with three white glass globes hang throughout the ceiling. The booths along the wall have shiny dark red leather seats. Wooden framed artwork shows places around Italy. The ground is cement painted charcoal black. It looks both traditional and sophisticated in here.

"Wait until you try the food," he tells me. "Do you like seafood? Because I highly recommend the cioppino."

I've never even heard of the term he just told me, but I nod and smile big anyway. "Sounds great," I say.

There's a slightly awkward long moment where neither of us knows what to say to each other—where to begin—but our eyes are locked.

"Thank you for asking me to meet you," I finally say. "And I totally get why you preferred a spot outside of town, given that message you received and all…"

He waves a dismissive hand, and we're temporarily interrupted by the waiter who has come to take our drink order. We both agree to share a bottle of red wine he's recommended. Then we're left alone again. "I really just wanted you to try this place," he says. "Honestly. They don't have restaurants like this in Toxey."

I chuckle. "Just your average chains and dumps," I agree. "Except for where *your* restaurant is, of course."

On the other side of the train tracks, where Toxey looks newer and more desirable, Steven's restaurant is located, along with some fancier bars and cafés and shopping boutiques.

And Mia's interior design office is over there, too.

"Yeah," he says, "But what I mean is that I don't feel a need to see you in secret or anything, Mads. I was a little… freaked out at first, but that was mainly because I was worrying about Wrigley. I've had some time to think it over and—"

The waiter sets our glasses down, pours the wine, and then leaves again, clearly able to tell we aren't ready to order yet. We haven't even opened our menus.

Then Steven continues. "I'm not going to let some punk ex of yours scare me into staying away from you."

When I get home, my cheeks literally hurt from smiling so much. I walk through the front door in a daze, not even realizing Warner is sitting at our small, rickety dining table having a late dinner consisting of instant noodles he heated up on the stove.

"Warner!" I cry in surprise, immediately removing the love-struck look from my face.

How embarrassing.

"Hey, Ma," he says with a snicker. "I take it the date went well."

"It was fine," I say quickly, setting my purse down on the table by the door and going over to join him. "I should have ordered you something to bring home." His meal looks pitiful compared the filet mignon I just devoured.

He shrugs. "The secret to making it taste better is to add butter and hot sauce."

"Mmm," I say sarcastically. He keeps eating while I stare at him.

"What?" he finally says, his mouth full of noodles.

"Don't chew with your mouth full," I say.

"Why are you staring at me?" he asks, ignoring my request.

"I just wanted to check in with you."

"What do you mean?"

"Like..." I trail off, unsure where exactly to start. I know things still aren't exactly great between Warner and me, but I am trying my best to get back on track with him. I don't ever want to feel like I don't know what's going on in his life again. I want us to be close like we used to be once upon a time. "How was it seeing Dean today?"

"Uh... I don't know. Fine, I guess. Weird. He told me I'm the only reason he got a teaching job at Blackfell in the first place."

I groan. "Of course you are."

"He's really trying to be a part of my life, Ma."

"You know what?" I shake my head quickly. "Let's change the subject. Um, how is Lyla doing? Was she at school today? Did anything else happen with you and Jackson? Glad you don't appear to have any new bruises on your face."

He pushes his empty bowl away and takes a deep breath to prepare for his answer. "Lyla was there, but I didn't talk to her. Jackson was there, too, but I didn't talk to him either."

"Oh," I say. "Well, how was your day otherwise?"

"I don't know. People still think I'm a murderer. And whoever—*Carson*—is still out there, so that sucks."

I hate hearing his name. I hate that something I did forever ago is causing my son harm and stress now. If I had known things would be this way, I would have made much different choices the night I thought Mia and I were responsible for the death of Carson Price.

"It does suck," I agree. then I reach out and grasp his forearm firmly on top of the table. "But I promise you, Warner. He's not going to get away with what he's done."

CHAPTER 11

Amelia

The girls and Joey swung by not long ago to grab stuff for their week at their dad's new place. But they left practically just as quickly as they arrived, and now I am sitting alone in my house for what I think might be the first time ever.

I can't get over how strange it feels. And I don't think I've ever quite realized before just how large my house is. I feel like I don't need all of this room if it's just going to be me. But then I remind myself that my kids are going to be back next week and that I won't be alone anymore.

I think I almost preferred it when Nora was staying here, hiding away in the guestroom upstairs and hardly making herself known. At least there was somebody else here.

Now it's just me, and I don't think I like it a whole lot.

I've already checked that all the doors and windows are locked. Then I got myself a glass of wine and curled up on the sofa in front of the TV that I didn't bother turning on. I don't feel like watching TV. I guess I don't really feel like doing anything other than listening to the creaking noises of the house settling.

That is what the creaking noise is, right?

I get restless sitting on the sofa after I finish my wine, so I get up and start wandering aimlessly through the house. I don't know what to do with myself. I purposely left my phone in the kitchen on the charger so that I'm not checking it every twenty seconds like I have been doing all day.

But it's inevitable as I circle through the house and enter the kitchen again. My phone is calling to me. I have to be on it.

I pick it up, and I frown when I see that I have no new messages or missed calls.

I text my kids—without Gentry in the group chat—and see how they're doing. Joey is the only one who replies.

Joey: I get my own room and Audrey and Lyla have to share!

Me: Aren't you lucky? I hope you're having a good time. I miss you all.

To that, I don't get any response.

What I do get, however, is my phone suddenly ringing. Only, the person calling me is not the one I want to hear from.

It's Mom.

"Hello?" I ask uneasily. I feel that whenever my mother calls me, it's not for a good reason.

"Mia, it's your mother," she says.

"I know," I say, "I have a cell phone."

Does she think I wouldn't have her number saved or something?

"How are you?" she asks. "How are things going over there? What's the latest?"

I sigh and scratch my head.

When is the last time I washed my hair?

Then I walk back over to the couch and flop into it. "Everything's fine over here."

"It sounds quiet."

"That would be because everybody is over at Gentry's new place."

"Wow. So... it's really happening then?"

"What is?"

"You and Gentry are divorcing?"

The word still makes me cringe. I never thought in a million years that I would be a divorced woman. I thought I would marry one man and be with him for the rest of my life. I thought I would have a stable relationship for my kids to be proud of. For my kids to want to emulate in their own lives.

"Yes," I say through my teeth. "Listen, Mom, I'm sort of in the middle of something..."

"What could you possibly be in the middle of right now?"

It irks me how well she knows me. It's like she's watching me right now.

I look out the window to the backyard. I don't see anyone, but now I can't seem to shake the feeling. What if I am being watched?

"I'm just... trying to get some housework done and I need two hands," I explain.

"Housework," she says, sounding impressed. "I guess you are doing better."

Too bad I'm lying.

"Yeah. Thanks for checking in and all, but I'm trying to soak up this alone time while I can. Can I talk to you later?"

"All right... Have you heard from your sister?"

"No," I say quickly. "Good night, Mom."

"Fine. Good night, Amelia."

I let out a guttural noise when I hang up. Now I'm irritated. Irritated and anxious.

And afraid to look out the window again.

Carson Price is still out there.

It makes me realize there is something I can do with my alone time.

I make another call. This time, to Detective Craig Fritz.

"How can I help you this evening, Amelia Flynn-Bailey?" he says when he answers. His voice sounds dull and bored already even though I haven't even started talking yet.

"Craig. Have you found him yet?"

"Found who?"

"Don't play dumb with me," I snap. "Have you found Carson Price yet?"

"No. I haven't. Because he's been missing for over twenty years. Presumed dead."

"He kidnapped my daughter."

"Yeah. So you say. No. Whoever did that, no, we haven't found them. But we are still looking, okay? You don't have to call and check-in. We will reach out to you once we find something."

"Sorry that I feel the need to check in and make sure you guys are actually doing your jobs."

"Good night, Mia."

"No, wait—"

But it's too late. Fritz has already hung up on me.

CHAPTER 12

LYLA

D ad has just returned from purchasing all kinds of furniture at some store not too far away. It's the kind of furniture that's in boxes that we have to assemble on our own. So I'm currently in my and Audrey's shared bedroom, working on putting together one of the twin bed frames.

I am alone. I don't know what Dad and Joey and Audrey are up to throughout the rest of the house. But I'm glad to have some alone time. It's hard to put on this act all day long in front of everyone.

No, I don't want to meet Dad's new girlfriend. I'm not even sure I'm comfortable being here in his rental house. I'm not sure I'm comfortable with the fact that my parents aren't together anymore. That my father has started seeing somebody else at all. I keep thinking about Mom alone at home. She hasn't seemed like she's been doing well lately and I don't like the thought of her worrying and being lonely. But I also don't want to hurt Dad's feelings by telling him I'd rather go back home—or back to Mom's.

When I'm alone, I can finally be myself.

But I think I've started to lose who I am. I feel that I don't know anymore.

In fact, it doesn't take long at all for my alone time to start stressing me out. For it to become too overwhelming. I actually begin to look forward to putting my act back on. Because acting has suddenly become easier than living in the reality of what I've been through.

I get out my phone and go to my texts. My first instinct is to find Warner's name and reach out to him. But then I think about how I rejected him yesterday and how he hasn't talked to me since. In all honesty, it sucked rejecting him. But the way Jackson had behaved when he saw us together... I can't get the image of the two of them fighting out of my head. I can't get the image of how angry Jackson looked out of my head. Warner and I are not a good idea.

Besides. As I have to keep reminding myself, I also like Wrigley. And it makes more sense to be with him.

I send him a text instead.

Me: So about that date.

Instead of texting me back, a couple of seconds later, I get a phone call from him.

"Oh," I say when I answer. "Hi."

He chuckles. I like the sound of it—deep and hearty and genuine. "About that date," he says in return.

I smile and stop working on the bed. "I was just thinking about you," I say, "and I was wondering when the date is going to happen."

"Oh yeah?" He sounds intrigued. I know it's probably strange for him to be hearing about me being excited to go on a date with him. This is sort of new territory for us.

"Yeah," I reply. "I hadn't really thought about it with everything going on, but the homecoming dance is coming up quickly..." I recall seeing the posters hung up all over the hallways at school today.

"You mean the dance that's coming up in, like, three days?"

"That would be the one."

He is silent for a moment and it makes me worry.

"Lyla, have you ever seen me at one of the school dances before?"

"I don't know," I say. "What makes you think I'd be looking for you?"

"Touché," he replies. "They're not really my scene. That's why I didn't ask you..."

"I get it," I say, feeling heat creeping into my cheeks. "It's not really my scene, either. I just thought... I think I should go."

Because that's what Old Lyla would do.

"You think you should?"

"Yeah. Just as part of moving on. Of being a regular teenager. All that nonsense. And Audrey is likely going to beg and beg and beg that I go anyway. So I figured if I am going... it would be nice to have a date."

"I get it," he says. "Hmm... you don't make this easy."

"Make what easy?"

"Make it easy for me to say no to you."

I smile. "So, we're going?"

"Looks like it, Lyla Bailey. We are going to homecoming."

CHAPTER 13

Audrey

"Um, hey, Dad?" I ask as I stare down at my phone screen as I yawn, my vision blurring for a moment. "I forgot something at Mom's. Is it okay if I run back over there really fast?"

We've just finished having dinner, and it's close to my bedtime, and it feels like we still haven't even made a dent in unpacking and setting up the new furniture.

So much for game night—not that I really care. I;m exhausted anyway.

Just not exhausted enough for this.

"Can it wait?" Dad asks as he puts the leftover pizza in some foil to toss in his practically empty fridge.

"Not really. I'll need it for school tomorrow."

Lyla and Joey aren't paying us any attention because they're too busy arguing over who gets the cool cloud-like lamp in their bedroom.

"All right, I guess," Dad says. "Just make it quick, okay?"

I smile big, but not because I am happy with him. I'm smiling because I am actually about to go meet Warner at our spot.

I am nervous but also excited. I had texted him and asked him to meet me. He had replied super-fast and told me he was down. I guess Maddy doesn't care as much if he leaves the house whenever he feels like even though there's still a kidnapper out there. I have to be sneakier about it.

"I'll be right back!" I call to Lyla and Joey before I grab my keys and drive to meet Warner.

My fingers drum on the steering wheel the entire way there. My eyes are heavy, but the last thing I feel like doing is sleeping. Not when I have so much running through my mind. I try to distract myself by singing along to some pop music, but it hardly helps.

I'm finally going to do it. I'm going to tell Warner that I like him. I've been wanting to say it for a while now.

I have all these ideas in my head of what could happen if it goes well. Like how he might tell me he likes me back, and that he's liked me for a while. Or he might even kiss me. And maybe he'll ask me to homecoming, which is only days away. I haven't given it a single thought with everything going on, but now that things are calming down, it might be fun to go. Especially if Warner goes as my date.

I pull into the abandoned overgrown parking lot of the unused train station and see that I am the first one here. I wait in my car—with the doors locked—until the headlights from his Jeep appear and he rolls up beside me. Then I get out and greet him.

"Everything okay?" he asks with his eyebrows raised and his eyes worried.

"Oh... yeah," I say, shaking my head. "Totally. I just wanted to hang out."

"Oh," he says awkwardly. "Cool. I was worried something was wrong."

"Sorry," I say just as awkwardly. Thankfully, he smiles.

"No biggie. I'm relieved. Want to go sit by the tracks?"

"Yeah," I say, returning the smile and feeling a little better. I'm still incredibly nervous, though. I wonder if he can sense it. "Sounds perfect."

We walk over to one of the only remaining benches left and sit down beside each other.

"I can't believe more people don't come here. It'd be the perfect spot for someone from school to throw a party," I point out.

"Well, don't go spoiling it for us," he says.

"I wouldn't ever," I say quickly.

"You're the only person that knows about this place—besides your aunt and Detective Fritz, apparently."

"Ugh." That's my instant reaction whenever someone even so much as brings up the aunt that hates me and the police officer that sucks at his job and would love nothing more than to see us all tossed in jail.

"How is Lyla doing?" Warner asks after we watch an entire train go by. It's fun to catch glimpses of all the different graffiti along the sides of the cars.

"She's doing really good, actually," I say, thinking again about how strange it's been to see her be so normal—even more normal than she was before she was kidnapped.

But I'm not here to talk about Lyla with Warner. I need to do what I came here to do.

"I saw that your dad got his own place," Warner says.

"Wait a second—how did you know that?" I ask, caught off guard.

For some reason, he looks slightly guilty. "I saw it on that TikTok page."

"Are you serious?" I quickly pull out my phone and go to Toxeydramaenthusiast's page. At school today, I overheard multiple people talking about it, and so I went and checked for myself. I don't know if Lyla knows about the account yet, and I've been trying to keep her in the dark because I don't want to stress her out.

I go to the most recent video.

Somebody went and filmed the outside of my dad's new place.

"Looks like all of this drama has caused the Bailey family to split up," someone's voice says, sounding like nobody I would know because of the filter they're using on it. "For now, Lyla and her sister have somewhere they can be away from the press. At least, until the press gets a hold of this video and finds out where they're hiding."

Then the video pans over to the street sign, Sycamore Street. And then the video ends.

I click my phone off and shake my head. "Who is this person?" Part of me thinks it's just somebody that has nothing better to do. But then another part of me is extremely worried that it's Carson. Why else would they need such a disguise? Wouldn't anybody else love to do a face reveal to gain recognition for their quickly growing account?

"I don't know," Warner says. "It's like all of a sudden their videos got popular overnight."

"And they're only getting more popular," I say. "I read through some of the comments earlier and a person that doesn't even live in the US was commenting about how this was so interesting and that they lived in England."

"It's messed up," he says. "I've tried reporting the account."

"Good idea," I say. I pull my phone out again and try to do the same.

"I sort of just want to block the page, but I feel like it's better to know what they're posting since everybody else at school is seeing it, you know?"

"Do you think Lyla has seen it?" I ask.

Crap.

I'm talking about Lyla again. I need to get back on track.

"I don't know," he says quickly. "I haven't talked to her."

"Oh," I say. Then we're silent again, listening for train horns.

"So, there's actually something I wanted to talk to you about," I finally say, not looking at him. I can feel his eyes burning a hole into my cheek, but I'm too afraid to make eye contact.

"What's up?" he asks casually. I wonder if he has any idea what's coming.

"Um, when we were here Friday... and you told me that you were really glad we were friends..." I start.

"Yeah?"

You can do this, Audrey. It's Warner. And with all the time you spent together, and the way he's looked at you. The things he's said. There's more a chance than not that he has feelings for you, too.

I finally look at him, my heart beating so hard I can hear it in my ears. "I sort of...um..."

Oh my God, I am butchering this.

"Are you okay?" he asks.

"Yeah," I say quickly. "It's just that..." I take a deep breath. "I like you, Warner. Like... as more than a friend."

I feel this whooshing sensation throughout my body. Like all of the weight is being lifted out of me from carrying these feelings secretly for so long. They're out there in the open. Warner knows now. And what he does about it is in his hands.

"Oh..." he trails off, and immediately, I know it's not a good sign. "Audrey, I... I didn't know. I think you're great. It's just that..."

"Right," I say, looking down onto my lap and fiddling with my fingers. "It's totally fine. If you don't... feel the same way. I get it."

I can't believe how mortified I feel right now.

"It's just that... I think we make better friends. We've been through a lot together, you know? If we try to be anything more, things could get messy down the road. I just... I don't want to jeopardize this."

"Right." I itch my ear just for something to do. "Yeah. Totally."

"I'm sorry," he says. "Come on, dude. Can you look at me?"

I do, and he nudges my knee with his. "Don't tell me that things are going to be weird now."

"They're not," I say, smiling. "We can be friends. Friends is good."

I want Warner in my life. So if I have to settle for this, then so be it.

CHAPTER 14

WARNER

I feel like crap. I am a total jerk. A total complete jerk.

I can't believe I just turned down Audrey Bailey. She's one of the most unattainable, hottest chicks at Blackfell High.

And I just turned her down.

And I didn't even tell her the honest reason for why I did.

Because I'm crazy about her sister.

Why can't I just like Audrey instead? Why is it so hard? They look alike, but they're so different.

I used to think a girl like Audrey was my type. Bubbly. Tons of friends. Always smiling. Always positive. I have since learned my type is Lyla. Brooding. Quiet. Genuine. Blunt.

As I sit there at the train station with Audrey, I want so badly for things to go back to how they were before she even told me that she liked me.

"So..." I trail off, trying to think of anything else we can talk about. "I can't believe that it still hasn't been released that it was Carson Price who kidnapped Lyla." It's the only thing I can think of. The Carson situation is what brought us together in the first place. Besides, it's probably good for us to talk about it.

"Yeah, totally," Audrey says, still sounding stiff and awkward. "Nobody believes my mom."

"And what do you believe?"

She clenches her jaw. "I... I think it was Carson. My mom wouldn't have any reason to make that up."

"Yeah. I don't think she would be making it up. But what if she just thought she saw him, and it wasn't really him?"

"So, you're not even sure you believe it?"

"I believe it, like... ninety-five percent. I'm just saying there's maybe still a chance that it wasn't him."

"Who else would it be?"

"That, I am one-hundred-percent uncertain about."

"Same. That's why I'm leaning toward it definitely being Carson."

"Oh! Uh, kind of related to that... Lyla told me about Megan Young."

"She did?"

I nod. "I think we need to talk to her. I think the three of us need to get together again ASAP and try to get to the bottom of who she was. Why was some random girl named Megan Young attending Blackfell High as Sydney Hutton? Why was she pretending to be somebody else and how did she end up dead?"

"Do you think it's all related or just a coincidence?"

"I'm not sure I believe in coincidences."

She nods her head slowly, thinking it all over. Then in the distance, the bushes rustle. It makes me nearly jump out of my skin and I get to my feet quickly.

"Are you okay?" she asks.

"Did you hear that?"

She looks around us. "Hear what?"

I stare at the spot where I heard the rustling. I'm waiting for something to move. For something to pop out at us. For it to be Carson, ready to attack again.

Then I feel stupid.

"Audrey, we should go," I say sternly.

"Right now?"

"What was I even thinking being out here with you like this? It's completely reckless and unsafe."

She rolls her eyes and slowly gets to her feet. "I'm fine, Warner."

"Yeah. You are for now. But we can't be doing this stuff, Audrey. You need to be thinking smarter. You need to be safer. Whoever kidnapped Lyla, there's a good chance they were trying to kidnap you. And there's a good chance that they want to hurt all of us. Let's go."

I make sure she walks ahead of me over to her car so I have my eyes on her at all times. As we go, I keep looking behind me back at the bushes, but I see nothing. Still, I can't shake the feeling that somebody was there.

CHAPTER 15

LYLA

I am back at Mom's house. There is a knock on the front door. Three loud raps. So loud they echo through the apparently empty house that I'm inside of.

I creep slowly toward the door, no idea who is waiting on the other side. But for some reason, there is fear inside of me. It's like I can sense that it's someone dangerous.

Still, I make my way to the door anyway.

My hand grasps the cold brass handle. There's a peephole, but when I try to look through it, all I see is black, like somebody has covered it.

I even think in my head that it's probably not a good sign that somebody has covered the peephole, but still, I unlock the door and turn the handle.

It creaks open, and I find myself wondering when our door even started creaking in the first place. The sound of it is eerie and slow and it distracts me for a moment until I realize who it is standing out on the front porch.

Jackson Mullens stares at me with his hands in his pockets.

"Hey, Jackson," I say casually even though my heart is thumping. There's something about him that is sinister and dark. Like his hair, which is already pitch black, is overgrown and almost shading his eyes. His jaw is clenched tightly. His overall aura is negative.

"Jackson?" I ask.

But he just stares at me. Stares at me with brown eyes that I can hardly see through his long hair.

"Are you going to say something?" I ask. I am too close to him and I'm very hyper-aware of it. If he just takes one step, he will be touching me. I could just back away. But for some reason, I don't.

"Why did you do it, Lyla?" he asks, his voice dark and ominous. It's nighttime outside, but I have no concept of what the time is exactly. It's funny because there are street lights on down the road from what I can see, but the ones right outside of my house have been turned off as if there's been an electricity outage somehow. What are the chances of an outage happening right out front of my house?

"Do what?" I ask, swallowing audibly.

Out of nowhere, he takes a fist out of his pocket and punches the front door. "You know exactly what I'm talking about!"

I cry out and jump backward. He shoves the door open and steps inside. I scramble to get away from him, falling on my butt, and he quickly grabs my forearm and yanks me back to my feet.

"Let go of me!" I shout.

Jackson struggles with me. He grips me with both of his hands and doesn't let me go. He's pulling me back toward the front door.

"JACKSON! STOP!" I'm screaming at the top of my lungs. So loud because I want anybody to hear me. Where is Mom? Where is Audrey? Where is anybody?

"You're going to pay for what you did!" Jackson hisses at me, spit flying out of his mouth.

"I'm sorry!" I try.

"I don't wanna hear it! You're coming with me."

"NO!"

Jackson is trying to kidnap me. It's going to be just like being in that shed all over again.

I become even more acutely aware of this as he pulls a white cloth out of his back pocket.

"No! Get away from me!"

I keep shouting, but he keeps bringing the rag closer and closer to my mouth. I can't think of anything else to do but just scream.

Then, somebody shakes my body roughly, and my eyes snap open.

"Lyla!" Dad is shouting at me, his hair dangling from his head as he hovers above my face. "Snap out of it, Lyla!"

I gasp for air and realize that I am screaming out loud. I stop and sit up, feeling out of breath.

Dad sits on the bed beside me and brushes his hair back, sweat visible on his forehead.

"You scared the crap out of me," he says.

I try to calm my breathing. I'm still vividly remembering what just happened in my nightmare. Jackson had tried to kidnap me. He had gripped me so tightly he was hurting me.

"I am sorry," I manage to get out. I rest my feet on the ground as if it will help bring me back to reality some more. I just want to forget that the dream ever happened.

"It's okay," Dad says, rubbing my back in big circles. "You just had a nightmare."

"I'm sorry," I say again.

The old Lyla didn't have nightmares that made her scream in her sleep. The old Lyla didn't make her parents worry about her like this.

Dad eventually clears his throat and talks in his usual calm voice again. "I think we need to book you another appointment with your therapist. Now that you're back."

I suck in some more air and nod my head. Whatever Dad wants Dad gets. Anything to make him feel more certain that I'm going to be okay and that he has nothing to worry about.

I have to get through this.

CHAPTER 16

MADDY

I'm still thinking about the amazing time I had with Steven on our date yesterday as I get ready in front of my mirror the next morning. After we had gotten past the first initial awkward part of getting over our recent fight, we talked and laughed as if nothing had ever happened in the first place. We even ordered a second bottle of wine, and we ended up being the last people in the restaurant when it closed around nine.

Then, when Steven walked me to my car, I had totally been expecting us to finally share our first kiss. Instead, Steven held my car door open and gave me a tight hug, where he whispered in my ear, "I so want to kiss you, Maddy. But I've had a lot of wine and I want to have a completely clear head when I finally do it." His breath had sent shivers down my back, and I smiled at him flirtatiously when he pulled away. I instead kissed him on his slightly scratchy, stubbly cheek. Then we went our separate ways.

The kiss hadn't happened, but it had still been an incredible night. Mainly because I had succeeded in getting him back into my life.

The only thing I still had to feel a little guilty over was the fact that I ended up not telling him the truth about why he was robbed and by whom it was who most likely robbed him. We had just changed the subject so quickly and started having such a good time that there never felt a right moment to circle back to it and bring it up again. But I know I have to tell him sooner or later.

Maybe I'll wait until I secure that first kiss at least.

"Ma, you almost ready to go?" Warner asks from out in the hall as he bangs on my bedroom door.

"I'm coming, I'm coming," I call. I put on my scarlet red lipstick, which matches the color of the Jeep I'm about to drive Warner to school in so I can take it to work.

I really need to get a new car.

When I unlock and open my bedroom door, Warner steps back and looks at me curiously.

"What?' I ask.

"You look different."

"It's probably the lipstick," I say with a shrug, moving past him because I don't like how he looks so suspicious. It's not the first time I've worn this color, so I don't know what the big deal is.

"I don't think that's it," he says, following me into the kitchen. When I pick up my purse from the table by the door and turn back to him, he has a contemplative finger on his chin. "You look... happy."

"What are you talking about?" I ask with an eye roll. How can he see right through me all the time when I usually find him nearly impossible to read?!

"You don't have to sound so offended," he says as we walk out the front door together and I turn to lock up. "It's not a bad thing."

"I'll be happy when Carson is caught and thrown in prison where he belongs." We go down the steps together, and I immediately freeze when I see an unfamiliar car parked on the street outside of the house.

"Whose car is that?" Warner asks, bumping into me because he had been checking out the car and hadn't seen me stop walking.

I don't see anyone in the car—which is a super shiny black Audi A7, but what I do see is a note taped to the windshield. Immediately, Warner goes toward it. I grab his wrist and pull him back.

"What's wrong?" he asks, yanking his arm free.

"It could be dangerous," I say, thinking about how one of the times he stood near a car, it exploded.

"It's fine," he groans, continuing his way to it. I hesitantly follow him. We go to the curb and he yanks the note off of it. "It's for you."

"What?"

I take the note out of his hand and read it:

I want you to have this. Even if it's just temporarily. I dropped it off because I had a feeling it wouldn't go over well if I tried to give it to you in person. But you need something safe to drive in. Keys are on the seat. I'll see you when I get home. I don't plan on letting anyone stop that from happening.
-Steven

CHAPTER 17

WARNER

I t puts me in a good mood that I officially have my Jeep back to myself as I drive it to school. I haven't met Steven Hall yet, but from all of the parties I know Wrigley has thrown, my personal opinion is that he's an absent father, but the fact that he lent my mom a car—an Audi—makes me like him just the tiniest bit more. And I suppose she could have picked worse.

She could still be with Freaky Fritz.

The thought makes me shudder as I get out of my Jeep in the parking lot at school. I decide to hold my head high as I walk inside today. I'm going to let everyone think whatever they want to think. I know I didn't kill Sydney—Megan—and I know I never did anything to harm Lyla. I just have to be okay with the fact that not everyone is going to be on my side.

Especially when they're following that TikTok account.

As I shovel books in my locker and take out what I'll need for Physics, I glance over my shoulder and see Lyla about to walk right past me.

"Hey!" I call, slamming my locker door shut and deciding I'm done avoiding her. But now I am wondering if she is trying to avoid me.

"Hey, Warner," she says with a happy, bright smile as I walk alongside her. The bell hasn't rung yet and she seems like she already has all her stuff for first hour, so I'm not sure where we're going, but I walk with her regardless.

"How's it been being back?" I ask. "I didn't get to see you yesterday to welcome you." I only feel the tiniest bit of guilt for lying.

"It's been...weird," she says. "But okay."

"Well, I think you're really brave."

"More like I am just incredibly determined to move past what happened to me," she corrects.

I shrug. "Either way."

"What's your first class?" she asks as we start taking the stairs to the second level, passing a couple showing too much PDA as we go. Lyla giggles awkwardly and sneaks a look at me, and for some reason, I feel my face heat up a little. Just the other day, it had almost been us who had been kissing on some stairs.

"Uh, Physics," I say, trying to focus. "Mr. Palmer."

"Isn't that downstairs?"

"Yeah, it is," I reply, shrugging, "But I wanted to walk with you. Is that okay? Or are you being all weird and avoiding me now because of what happened the other day?" I find it slightly amusing that she turned me down and I, in turn, turned down her sister.

Rejections everywhere.

"No, of course not!" she says, a little loudly at that.

I scoff. "Yeah. Okay."

"I'm serious." She stops walking at the top of the stairs. Kids behind us have to move around us. "I'm not avoiding you."

"Well, good," I say, looking into her mesmerizing, dark blue eyes. "Because I want us to still be friends. All of us."

"We are," she says, seeming to know I'm referring to Audrey when I say, *All of us.*

More kids walk by, and they say hi to Lyla as they pass.

"Hey!" she says back, smiling just as big at them as she had at me moments ago while she waves at them. It strikes me as slightly odd. She seems very happy today. Too happy for someone who just spent nearly a week locked in some shed by a psychopath.

I clear my throat when she turns back to me. "Uh, anyway. When are you free after school, do you know?"

"Practically every day—except we're still sort of helping my dad get settled into his new place. He moved out. Long story. Don't care to get into it."

Did Audrey not tell her we hung out yesterday? It probably just slipped her mind, right? It would be weird for her to keep it a secret on purpose.

"I'm sorry," I say. "Well, if you need to get your mind off of that, I was thinking me, you, and Auds need to meet up anyway so we can start trying to get to the bottom of who Megan Young was. I think figuring that out will be a good starting point when it comes to figuring out why all of this...nonsense has been happening to us."

She shifts weight onto her other hip and tucks some hair behind her ear. I find myself trying to ignore the fact that I wish it had been me to tuck that hair back for her.

Because friends don't do that kind of stuff.

"Oh, um, I'm sorry, Warner, but count me out," she says, thoroughly surprising me.

"Wait, what?" I ask as I tilt my head to the side like a confused dog.

She looks over her shoulder before looking back at me. "Yeah. I just... I don't want to get involved anymore. I don't want to have anything to do with any of it. Like I said, I just want to move forward."

"But, Lyla..."

"I gotta get to class early. I'll talk to you later, okay?"

I don't want her to go, but she turns and leaves me standing there dumbfounded anyway.

"Dude!" someone shouts behind me, making me jump and turn around as three guys from the football team make it to the top of the stairs. Chance Hobbs, Darius Heyworth, and Kaleb Frey. And it appears as if Kaleb, a senior who I'm not particularly fond of just because he's always so annoying, is addressing me. "Did you see the latest?" He and his buddies are snickering.

"What latest?" I ask.

"Oh man, you haven't?" he asks.

"From Toxeydramaenthusiest?" Chance adds, shaking his head like he can't believe I am not more on top of it. Around us, the bell rings.

"Here, man, I'll send it to you." Kaleb pulls out his phone, and seconds later, mine dings.

"Crazy, dude!" Chance calls to me as they walk away, the three of them still snickering together.

My stomach dipping, I pull out my phone and watch the latest TikTok. The caption itself makes me sick to my stomach: Is Warner Carpenter a Murderer?

The video, at first, is of the usual poster wearing their disguise and using their voice changer against the green screen. They're talking about what everyone else has been talking about for forever now. How I might be responsible for Sydney's death.

But they know more than the average person.

They know that my phone and laptop were taken during a search by the police, who had a warrant.

And then the video changes and a camera zooms in on me walking into school this morning from my Jeep.

The anonymous poster continues talking. "I don't know about you guys, but something about the way he's behaving this morning makes me think there's something we all still don't know yet."

And then the video ends.

And as I stand in the quickly emptying hallway, I am thoroughly creeped out.

CHAPTER 18

AUDREY

It feels so off and isolating to be ignoring Sophia and Olive in my second period class. So isolating that I almost want to cave and tell them I am done being mad at them. Instead, I remind myself to be strong—even though I look like a loser with no friends.

It goes okay being all alone in second hour because Mr. Gillens lectures us the whole time about Public Policy and I focus on diligently taking notes and trying to ignore the fact that Sophia and Olive keep whispering at their desks as Mr. Gillens speaks in his loud booming voice. But it's much harder to be alone in my third period class, Fashion and Retail Merchandising. There are only girls in my hour and I can feel their eyes on me as I take a seat at an empty table in the back, my body feeling heavier than usual from my lack of sleep. We do a lot of group work in this class, so I usually sit with Sophia and Olive and work with them. I don't really know the other girls in this class well and I feel that none of them are particularly interested in becoming friends because there is so much drama circulating about me.

Sophia and Olive walk into the classroom at the same time and don't look at me at all as they go and sit at the table right in front of mine, their backs to me.

"Did you hear the latest about Lyla?" Sophia asks Olive, not even trying to be quiet about the fact that she is gossiping when Lyla's sister is right behind them.

"What now?" Olive asks, almost sounding bored.

Shut up, Olive—you'd kill *to be Lyla's friend again.*

"She and Wrigley Hall are going to homecoming together."

Olive gasps.

"I know," Sophia continues. "Wrigley Hall at a school dance? That's, like, unheard of."

I can see the profile of Olive's face as she looks at Sophia, so I notice when her brow lowers over her eyes questioningly. "Yeah. Not to mention... I don't know. I sort of was always under the impression that maybe she and Warner were going to get together. After all that drama with Jackson and all that."

My stomach tumbles. *Warner and Lyla?*

"I know, I thought so, too," Sophia says. Then the bell rings and it's time for class to start.

Doesn't anyone think it seems like Warner and *I* might get together? We hang out all the time, after all. I know that he turned me down, and I still hate to think about that fact, but I am also finding that I am excruciatingly bothered that people think he'd like Lyla over me.

I try to push the thoughts of it from my mind, and instead switch to thinking about how Lyla is apparently going to homecoming now. I don't know why she would want to. The Lyla I was beginning to get used to after the car accident specifically even told me once that she had no desire to go to another school dance as long as she lived.

What changed?

Midway through the class, as we're individually—thankfully—working on answering some questions on a piece of paper by reading our textbooks—which is nearly making me fall asleep and I have to force myself to peel my eyelids away from each other—my phone buzzes in my pocket. I make sure Mrs. Shipp is preoccupied at her desk—she's a huge stickler about phones—before I carefully pull it out to see who has texted me.

Mom: *Lyla's just asked me for some money for a HC dress. Since she's going, r u?*

Me: *I don't think so.*

I haven't even had time to think about homecoming with Lyla's disappearance and with me missing school. Besides, who would I go with? No one has asked me. Warner doesn't like me back. I don't have my usual girlfriends—except for maybe Danielle. But even then, I don't like the idea of having to dodge Sophia and Olive's reproachful looks inside the gym all night or risking seeing Warner there with some other girl.

Mom: *Can u reconsider? I'm freaked out over the idea of her going alone. I'd feel much better about it if u were there 2.*

I groan, and in the deadly quiet classroom, everyone hears it; most of the girls turn to look at me—even Sophia and Olive. I shove my phone back in my pocket before Mrs. Shipp notices, and I hide my face with my hand and get back to the busy work.

I get why Mom would feel better about me going. I don't like the idea of Lyla gone for a whole night, no one entirely sure where she is or what she's up to or who she's with, either. Her kidnapper is still out there, and we need to stick together.

I guess this means I need to find myself a date.

When I wake up, I feel about twenty-five pairs of eyes on me, and the sound of a loud, high-pitched scream somewhere in the room is making my ears hurt.

Then I realize the scream is coming from me.

And all the pairs of eyes on me belong to my classmates.

I'm in my AP Chemistry class—the last period of the day. But I must have fallen asleep at my desk because I don't remember even being in Chemistry. All I remember is being in the woods close to where the swimming hole is and being chased by someone in all black and a scary, cartoonish mask. I had started screaming when I fell into a pile of old brown leaves and the attacker loomed over me, a shiny knife raised in the air, ready to dive into my flesh...

"Are you okay?" Bryson Anthony asks. He's the closest one to me, and one of his hands is on my shoulder. Up at the front of the class, Mrs. Winston is giving me a hard look while the kids around me whisper to each other and stare. Some of them have their phones out. I wonder if they had recorded me.

I long to hide behind my hair, but I can't anymore because it is too short.

"I'm sorry," I whisper, feeling groggy as I try and come back to the present. My heart is still pounding in my chest. The dream had felt so *real*.

But Audrey Bailey never falls asleep in class.

What is happening to me?

"Do you need to be sent to the nurse?" Mrs. Winston asks. "Bryson, it's okay, you can take your seat."

Bryson looks genuinely concerned for me still as he removes his hand from my shoulder and sits back in his desk.

"No, I'm fine," I say to the teacher. This is humiliating.

"Are you sure? You must not be feeling well if you are falling asleep in my classroom, Miss Bailey."

"Come on," my classmate, Allison, says to Mrs. Winston. "She's sort of been through a lot lately. Maybe cut her some slack."

"I'm really sorry," I say. "It won't happen again." I'm too ashamed to even shoot Allison an appreciative look. I don't look anywhere but at the top of my desk, where I think I might have even drooled a little when I was sleeping.

"Okay," Mrs. Winston says with a stern nod, ignoring what Allison told her. "Then everyone settle down and let's get back to learning, shall we?"

I still feel so exhausted. But I don't want to so much as blink my eyes, because I am terrified of the darkness behind my lids when I do.

I'm terrified that in that darkness, I will be forced to face that figure in the mask again.

CHAPTER 19

Amelia

I think about my girls going to homecoming together and I know I should feel a sense of happiness. It's such a normal high school thing for them to do. It makes it seem as if our life is a little bit more average. As if we don't have these demons chasing after us. As if I don't have my *own* demons going after my girls.

But as I drive to Blackfell High school to pick up Lyla for her therapist appointment, I still feel off about it all. I should be thrilled that they are going to homecoming. I should feel confident that they are going to have a good time and that nothing is going to go wrong. Maybe I'm just reflecting back on my own last high school dance I went to. Prom night, April 1998. The night I found my sister with a bloody nose in the bathroom because Carson Price punched her. It was also the night that Maddy and I ended our friendship. One that I thought would last a lifetime. I guess now I can say that it still might; there had just been a slight pause in it.

I guess I just don't want my daughters to have a homecoming night like that. I don't want them to have such a bad experience that they never go to another dance again. But they're only juniors and have plenty of dances ahead of them. Especially prom.

When I pull up to the school, Lyla, who had been sitting on the steps, gets up and gives me a small wave. I wave back and smile, surprised that she doesn't seem more embarrassed to have her parent picking her up. It makes me grateful that she seems to approve of me.

But then a tuft of brown hair catches my eye and I look away from Lyla over at none other than Dean Reeves.

The man who has been avoiding me.

I sink back in my seat a little bit. At first, I don't want him to see me. He clearly doesn't want to talk to me and it's embarrassing.

But then, I straighten up. I get this twitch in my hand. This urge in my brain.

Don't do it, Mia.

I find myself putting the car in park. Then I undo my seatbelt. Lyla hovers with her hand on the door handle outside the passenger seat, looking at me, curious as to what it is I'm doing.

I'm getting out of the car.

"Mom?"

"Hi, honey," I say with a quick smile in her direction. Then I walk around the car and step up on the curb.

"Where are you going?"

"I'll just be one second," I say to my daughter. Then, my heels tapping on the concrete, I make my way toward Dean who, luckily for me, has just finished up a conversation with a man I recognize as one of the assistant principals. He smiles at the other man and turns to leave him, but then he does a double take when he sees me approaching him.

He looks trapped. I watch his eyes dart from right to left, looking for his escape.

You can't escape me this time, Dean.

"Amelia Bailey?"

I turn on my heel and see a woman I don't recognize smiling at me brightly. She has red hair, green eyes, and seventies-looking glasses.

"Yes?" I ask, looking over my shoulder to see that Dean is already turning around and hurrying back inside of the school.

Ugh!

I look back at the woman.

"I was wondering if I could ask you a couple questions about your daughter's kidnapping. I would love to get your thoughts and opinions on some things."

She doesn't look like the press, but I know that she's the press.

"I'm busy," I say quickly, looking over my shoulder again. Dean is gone.

Giving up, I glare at the woman and then get back in my car, where Lyla joins me, giving me a funny look.

"What?" I ask. But then I realize I don't want her to tell me what she's thinking. I am worried she knows that I had been on my way to see Dean and that he dodged me. So instead, I quickly change the subject. "How are you? How was school today?"

"Uh... it was fine," she says, turning to look out the window. "Who is that lady?"

"Probably a journalist for some stupid magazine," I say.

She nods and falls silent. I start driving, side-glancing at her every so often. "Are you sure you are okay to do this? I know it'll help so much."

It's her first session back since her kidnapping. I made her go to therapy after the accident that killed Trinity Cruz, but then she stopped going. She stopped going right up until before her kidnapping, when her father and I suggested she go back because of the way she had been behaving.

And then shortly after, she was taken.

She starts to answer me, but my mind has drifted. Drifted back to Dean. I can't believe he looked directly into my eyes and *still* had the audacity to completely ignore me. What on earth did I do to him?

"Mom?"

Shoot. I completely ignored whatever it is Lyla just said.

"I'm sorry, Ly. What was that?"

"Are you okay?" she asks instead of telling me what it was she had said before.

I smile brightly. "I'm Fine," I say, even though the smile is forced. Then when I catch a glimpse of myself and the review mirror, I can tell how forced it is, so I get the feeling that my daughter can as well.

"Okay..." Lyla says, trailing off like she's unsure if she believes me.

"*You* seem to be doing *more* than fine," I comment. "Going to school. Going to therapy. Going to homecoming with a date? Look at you. It's like you are ready to just move past this whole thing."

She shrugs. "I am more than ready."

I squeeze her arm. She doesn't even seem to be tense like she usually is whenever we get into a car. It's another good sign.

"I have to admit," I say, hoping that my skepticism doesn't offend her. "I'm surprised to see you acting so much like..." *How do I say it?*

"Like Audrey?" she finishes for me.

"Exactly."

I *wanted* to say that she is acting a lot like how she used to act before Trinity died. But back then, she and her sister were a lot more similar. So her answer is also a good one.

"I just don't want to get stuck in another rut," she says. "I'm really doing okay."

"I'm really sorry that this happened to you," I say for the hundredth time. "That you and Audrey are dealing with this. It's all my fault that Carson kidnapped you. For his own, personal revenge. I... I'll never be able to forgive myself. And I'm still working on it, but I promise you that I'm going to fix things. He's going to get locked away and he is never going to be able to lay his hands on you again."

Whatever her reply to this is, I tune it out again because I'm thinking about how I saw Carson's face in the woods. About how, surrounded by flames engulfing the shed and the house and the woods around him, his cartoonish facemask fell off and revealed him. About how our eyes had connected. About how I had been so certain it was *his* face, aged by several years, looking right back at me.

When I feel Lyla staring at me like she's waiting for a response, I cringe. "Sorry," I say, blushing slightly. "What?"

"Are you sure you're all right?"

"Don't worry about me," I decide to say. "We need to focus on you and Audrey and getting that creep locked up for good."

It's all I want.

That, and maybe for Dean to finally talk to me again, too.

LYLA

Gloria Morton.

That is the name of my therapist. She's in her early sixties with short, soft gray hair, piercing blue eyes that often look like they're glowing, and surprisingly amazing skin. Looking at her, I'd guess she was in her late forties, but I only know her age because I asked her once.

After Mom drops me off, I am so busy thinking about how weird she had acted in the car and wondering why she had seemed so determined to talk to Mr. Reeves before that random woman interrupted her, that I don't even have time to feel nervous to see Gloria again. Before I know it, I am being led into her office.

It feels weird being in here again. Gloria's office isn't anything fancy like the psychiatrists' offices I've seen in movies and TV shows are. She doesn't have a wall full of bookcases overflowing with intelligently titled books. She doesn't have a leather daybed or settee for her clients to lay on while they speak.

Gloria Morton's office has commercial gray carpeting, pastel blue painted walls, a basic beige couch with navy blue and red plaid pillows, a dark gray fake leather chair that looks like it belongs in a medical building, a single brown bookcase in the middle of one of the walls with only a total of twelve books on it, and a couple succulents. There's a giant fake tree in the corner of the room and one of those overhanging floor lamps in the other corner. Beside the sofa is an end table with nothing on it except for a box of tissues.

The room is small, too. If Gloria and I were to sit at the very edges of our seats, our knees would nearly touch each other's.

Gloria stands from her gray chair when she sees me. She smiles, but it's not the warmest of smiles. Gloria has never really had the warmest presence about her, which I find strange as a therapist.

The door closes behind me and Gloria motions for me to take a seat on the beige sofa, as if I've never been in here before.

"Hey, Lyla, how are you?" she asks in her smooth voice.

"I'm doing good," I say, even though I know this is just a formality question. We haven't really delved into the hard topics yet.

"I've been really looking forward to meeting with you again," she says. I'm thinking that *of course* she has—I'm probably her most exciting patient, given everything that I've been through recently. "And I'm surprised to see you in here so soon after your... escape."

"Just ready to move on," I say, gripping my knees with my hands and sitting in the seat uncomfortably. It's rather stiff.

"That's very brave."

I nod and say nothing. I stare right at her, wondering something I have not thought about since before I was kidnapped.

The word spread fast that I was the one responsible for the car accident that killed Trinity. But I only told two people the truth. One of them was Sydney, who is dead.

The other one is sitting right in front of me.

"So, is there anything in particular you'd like to talk about?" Gloria asks. "Anything you need to get off of your chest or anything you want to ask me?"

"I don't know," I admit. I hadn't planned any of this out before I came. I just sort of... showed up. Just like I did the first time I came here.

But this time, not knowing what to say is not just because I'm nervous and don't know how this works. This time it's because I don't know what I *can* say to her. Who is she talking to behind my back? Who is she giving information to?

What if she is the owner of the TikTok account?

I know it's crazy to think it, but I have had quite a crazy life as of recently.

"That's fine," she says. "Are you back at school?"

"Yes."

"And how is that going?"

"It was my first day back today. Everyone was really nice. Even if they were faking it."

"What makes you think they would fake it?"

"I don't know."

Maybe because before I was kidnapped everybody hated me for killing Trinity. Because somebody told them that I did...

"Are you concerned that some of them don't believe everything they've heard on the news?"

"What do you believe?" I deadpan.

"I believe you went through a really traumatic ordeal, Lyla. And I want to help you through it. I know you can get past it. I know it must've been terrifying. But you are strong. One of the strongest teenage girls I know."

"Uh huh."

She writes something down on her notepad. This is where it *is* just like the movies; I talk, and she writes. She's in a very formal skirt suite, one knee crossed over the other, her shins incredibly shiny in the overhead lighting from the lotion she uses.

"Do you want to tell me what it was like?" she asks. "Being locked in that shed?"

"It was really boring," I say as I lean back into the cushion. "I had nothing to do. Nothing to pass the time. Nothing except for sleeping on the hard ground and trying not to devour every single one of the snacks I was given. But... I was actually wondering if we could talk about something else."

"Of course, Lyla. What is it?"

"Did you ever tell anybody about how I was responsible for Trinity Cruz's death?"

I look her dead in the eye as I ask her because it's the only way for me to properly gauge whether or not I think she's telling me the truth when she replies.

"Of course not," she says quickly, but sincerely, as she right back at me. "Everything you tell me is confidential, Lyla. Unless I think you are a harm to yourself or others."

"Okay," I say in a careful tone. "I just find it strange because somehow everybody found out, and you and Sydney Hutton—who is dead—are the only ones I told."

This takes her a moment to consider. She writes something down and then looks back at me.

"Are you sure nobody else knew?"

"Positive."

"You went through a trauma. You might have confided in somebody and completely forgotten about it. It happens all of the time.

Or maybe Sydney told people before she passed away. And maybe that person found whatever time was opportunistic enough for them to tell others."

"I guess."

Still, I look around her office, searching for hidden cameras. A voice recorder. But I see nothing. I should probably trust Dr. Morton. After all, if she can't get me through this, who can?

Chapter 21

Audrey

I pick my sister up from her therapy appointment, and when she gets in the car, she gives me a smile. A smile is not what I was expecting from somebody who just got out of a surely tough therapy session.

"How was it?" I ask as I put my car in drive, and she buckles in. "By the way, I know yesterday I said I was going to Mom's because I forgot something, but that was really because I went to go meet Warner. This time, I really *did* forget something, so we have to swing by Mom's really quick."

"It's so strange to call it that."

"What do you mean?"

"To differentiate between Mom's house and Dad's house. Like, it just used to be *our* house. You know? I'm not saying I am super bothered by it or anything. It's just weird."

"Is that what you talked about with the therapist?"

"No. I actually didn't even bring that up at all."

I nod. "Lots of other things to talk about, huh?"

"Something like that."

When we pull into the driveway at Mom's house, I park the car and take my phone out. I can't help myself, but I see that I have no new notifications, and still, I go onto TikTok and go to Toxeydramaenthusiast's page. There are no new videos yet, but I've watched all of the ones on the account.

Multiple times.

I don't even realize that Lyla is looking at my phone over my shoulder until I hear her breathing.

I try to hide my phone from her.

"Are you looking at that stupid TikTok page?" she asks, rolling her eyes.

"So, you've seen it?" I wonder she didn't say anything to me about it when she did.

"Yeah. It's stupid. Just ignore it."

"Ignore it?" I ask as we get out of the car. "I can't just... *ignore* it, Ly. It's about us. Our lives. Warner's life. They say stuff about our moms. About Joey, even. Someone is, like, legit spying on us. It's creepy."

"If you just ignore it, it's not creepy." She walks to the front door.

"I don't think that's entirely true," I disagree. She doesn't say anything, so I consider the conversation dropped for now.

But it does bring up something else I want to ask her about. Something Warner told me.

"Oh, before I forget—Warner told me that you don't want to help us get to the bottom of this whole thing."

"Okay?" We go inside after Lyla unlocks the front door with her key.

"So... why not?" I ask.

"Mom!" Lyla calls. "It's just us! Audrey has to grab something!"

It's quiet in here. I don't know where Mom is.

"Lyla," I continue, wanting to get an answer out of her.

"I just don't want to, okay?" she says, rather snippily. Now *this* sounds more like the new-old Lyla. The one after Trinity's accident and before the kidnapping.

"It's fine..." I tell her, holding my hands up to her in surrender. "We will just handle it without you."

"I think you guys should just let the police handle their business. I think we should all just focus on being safe and moving on with our lives. They will find Carson. They have to eventually."

I can't even make a retort because she saunters away into the kitchen and leaves me in the foyer.

"Mom?" I call. I look down the hallway that has the study and the door to her master bedroom—where I slipped and got a concussion when I was being chased by the masked figure once. But I don't hear any movement.

I jog up the staircase and go to my room. I know it's silly, but I have this outfit idea planned in my head for tomorrow—I want to look irresistible so that maybe I can snag myself a date to homecoming—and it involves my cute, cropped denim jacket.

I pull it out of the closet and throw it over my shoulder, and then I head back down the stairs. In the kitchen, I can hear Lyla rummaging through the cupboard for a snack. But I still want to know where Mom is.

I walk down the hallway leading to her bedroom, where I assume she's napping. But then I stop when I step in front of the door to the study.

I can hear her inside.

"Mom, are you in there?" I ask. For half of a second, I'm worried it's not Mom in there, but an intruder.

Maybe a *masked* one.

"Oh, is that you, Lyla?" Mom asks from inside the study, making me breathe out a sigh of relief.

"Audrey," I correct. "What are you doing in there?" Usually Dad was the one who liked to spend time in the study. Mom hardly ever goes in there.

I move to put my hand on the door handle, but before I can grasp it, the door swings open, and Mom steps out swiftly, making me back up so that she doesn't bump into me. Then she closes the door behind her, and to my utter astonishment, I watch as she turns toward it and sticks the key in the lock.

"Why are you locking the study?" I ask.

"We've been broken into once before. And I don't know if you heard, but Maddy's boyfriend's house was also broken into recently. I have decided to keep all of the valuables in there. So it's just a little bit of an extra precaution."

I give her a look that hopefully shows that I don't quite believe her, but she smiles and flips her hair behind her shoulder. "What are you guys doing here?" she asks, walking down the hall and expecting me to follow her.

"I just forgot something. We're going back to Dad's now."

"Oh," she says, sounding slightly disappointed. "All right. How's it going over there?"

We enter the kitchen where Lyla is snacking on a Nutri-Grain bar.

"How was your appointment?" Mom asks, apparently completely forgetting that she just asked a question right before this.

"Good," Lyla says simply. "*That's* what you forgot?" she then asks me, eying my jacket.

I shrug, not feeling like offering an explanation. Lyla doesn't care about fashion like Mom and I do.

But upon looking at Mom in her sweatpants and baggy T-shirt, I'm wondering if she still cares about it as much as she used to.

"Are you ready to go?" I ask Lyla quickly. I can't wait to get out of this house and go somewhere private so that I can tell my sister about Mom locking the study, and about how I think she's lying to me about why.

CHAPTER 22

MADDY

As much as I would like to ignore Nora for possibly the rest of eternity, when she asks me to meet her for a drink, I feel I cannot say no. It's this invisible hold that Nora has on me. I bend to her every want.

I haven't really talked to her since she came to my house a crying mess over how Amelia told her that Carson Price kidnapped Lyla, and I told her that I was on her side and that I thought Carson Price was dead, too.

When I go inside The Mix, my favorite watering hole that she has agreed to meet me at, she's already seated at a high top and has two cold beers on the table waiting.

I slide onto my stool and hang my purse behind me.

"How are you?" I ask, tilting my head like a concerned friend.

Nora *looks* okay. Her dark hair is brushed back into a sleek ponytail. Her eyebrows look freshly tweezed. She has on the perfect amount of mascara on her upper lashes and doesn't need any on her lower ones. She has simple gold hoops in her ears and a slightly faded body con dress that goes down to the middle of her thigh.

"Can we not start the conversation like that?" she asks, looking insulted. "It makes me feel like some sort of charity case."

It's awkward hearing her say that because I handed over to her the majority of my trust fund years ago when I was being a rebellious teenager. It was my own secret way of trying to ease my guilt over the fact that I thought Amelia and I had killed her boyfriend. I thought we were the reason that Nora was thrown into a mental institution. I do still believe this. If we had never harmed Carson, she wouldn't have gone. And I don't regret giving her the money. Sure, it would be nice to have now, but that was the only way my parents ever paid me any attention. With cash. So, it felt good to rid myself of it.

"You're not a charity case," I say quickly, taking a deep sip of my beer. "Things were just kind of rough the last time I saw you. I just want to make sure you're doing okay with everything."

"Notice how it hasn't been on the news that it was a Carson Price who kidnapped Lyla?" she asks, apparently wanting to dive right into it. "Because it's not true. *God*, I can't believe Amelia tried to tell me that it is. That he's alive. What kind of psychopath *is* she?"

"I don't know that she's a psychopath," I say. I can't be totally bashing on Amelia. She is my friend, after all. "I think she *thinks* she saw him. I think she's just looking for somebody to blame over all of this since she doesn't have any idea who else it could be. She just can't accept the fact that Carson is dead."

Nora pouts. "Why can't *you* be my sister?"

I giggle. "We do look more like than you and Mia do." We both have chocolatey brown hair. We're about the same height—Nora is just a little bit shorter. I think we have similar laughs, too.

Nora nods in agreement and drinks some of her beer. "So, you say you are a regular here?"

I look around the place, and to validate what I told her, the bartender and one of the guys sitting at the bar both wave over at us. I wave back and smile.

"Sure am," I say. "It's where Craig and I would go a lot when we were dating."

She visibly cringes. "I can't believe you dated Craig Fritz."

"Why? He was always the hotter one between him and his brother," I point out. Granted, I have no idea what Parker looks like these days as he doesn't have social media and he lives on the other side of the country. But in high school, everyone always thought Craig was cuter. I agreed.

"He's just... I don't know. He's a cop. Didn't really think cops would be your type, *Mrs. Rebel*."

I roll my eyes. "He was a cool cop. Emphasis on the *was*."

"I think for a second, Mia was into him," Nora tells me. "He kept coming over claiming he had more questions to ask her about the Sydney Hutton case."

I shrug. I'm not about to tell her that that was all something we had planned out to see if we could figure out what he wanted with us. "Well, she has been single for *apparently* a long time."

"How do you know that?" Nora asks.

I make up the lie quickly. "Warner told me. One of the twins told him."

In all truth, Mia called me and told me all about it.

"I don't get her," Nora says. "You know, when she told me that it was Carson who kidnapped Lyla... I sort of... slapped her?"

I put a hand over my mouth and stifle my giggling gasp. "Are you kidding?" This was something Amelia had omitted from me.

Nora looks like she's embarrassed as she slowly shakes her head no. "It wasn't my finest moment. I think I did it more out of shock than anything. Shock that she would say that to me. I don't know."

"I... I don't blame you," I say. But I'm definitely excited to ask Mia to replay the whole scene for me when I talk to her later.

The rest of my meet-up with Nora goes smoothly. It's easier than I thought it would be to keep the lie up that I believe her over Amelia. Maybe it's because I'm getting so used to lying. I know it's not a good thing, but oh well.

When we finish up and pay—I get the bill—we walk outside together. It's chilly in the late October air. Leaves flow on the ground of various fall colors around us, and a little bit to our right, two older men are both smoking cigarettes.

"So, let's hang again soon," Nora says to me. "Maybe later this week even?"

"Where are you staying?" I ask.

"I have a rental right now. I'm still in town for a while."

I tilt my head. "Why?" Why would anyone want to stay in Toxey if they didn't have to be here?

"I'm still hoping to see Joey and Lyla. I got quite close with them when I was staying with Mia. I don't want to leave them again just like that."

"And Audrey, right?"

"It's a cute rental," Nora continues as if she didn't hear me. "We should have a girly movie night. Put on something stupid, eat a bunch of popcorn, and wear pajamas."

"Um, yeah," I say, giving her a smile. "Sounds absolutely perfect."

We hug goodbye, but as I walk to the fancy Audi I've been lent by sweet, sweet Steven, I can't help but think about Audrey. Nora does *not* seem to like her, but I'm very curious as to why that is.

CHAPTER 23

Audrey

I would have thought that with all of this free time I have since I hardly sleep anymore, I would be able to get all of my homework done. That I'd be on top of all of my projects. That I'd be ahead of the game in all of my classes.

But it's not the case.

When I'm not sleeping, I lay in bed, telling myself that I know I need to be sleeping. Then I scroll through Instagram and TikTok, and I creep on the Toxeydramaenthusiast's page religiously. I know Lyla told me to ignore it, but I find it impossible. I'm borderline obsessed. Obsessed with the things they're posting. With whom they could be. With why they're doing it.

The next morning, I wear my cute, cropped denim jacket, a white turtleneck sweater, black flare yoga pants, and my white sneakers. I put my short blonde hair in two cute pigtails behind my head and red lip gloss on my lips.

Cute as a button, I think to myself as I look at my reflection in the mirror. Sure, my concealer didn't quite hide all of those dark circles, and sure, my cheeks look a little puffier than normal, but still, I think I do a good job making myself look presentable.

It's important because I have a job to do.

Get a date to homecoming.

And since it's obvious I'm not going to be going with Warner Carpenter, I need to get somebody else to ask me.

And that someone else is Ryan Copeland.

"It's not that I *want* to abandon you this morning," I say to Lyla as we walk up the school steps together, "but if I see Ryan Copeland and have an opportunity to get him alone, I have to take it."

Lyla rolls her eyes but smiles. She also looks cute today. Her hair is half-up, half-down with a simple beige beanie over it. She's wearing a cutesy, cream-colored tank top dress with black long sleeves underneath it and Doc Martens on her feet.

I'm worried she looks cuter than me. It's weird because I haven't felt this way in a while.

"I didn't know you and Ryan were still a thing," Lyla says.

"I don't know *what* we are," I say. "We were nonexistent for a while, but he's apologized profusely about the whole Sophia thing, so I think I've decided to give him another chance."

"Well," she says as we walk in the school together. "Today's your lucky day." She nods her head in the direction of Ryan's locker, and I look and see that he is, indeed, standing alone at it, pulling a couple of books out.

My stomach dips. If I can tell Warner I like him and get rejected, then I can flirt with Ryan and risk getting rejected, too. I've had experience.

I squeeze her forearm tightly and let out a little squeal, then I ditch her.

"Hey, you," I say when I walk up next to Ryan and lean my arm against the locker next to his. I am very aware that I have homework I need to get done before first period and I should be scrambling to finish it right now instead of talking to him, but I think my priorities are allowed to be a little out of whack right now.

Ryan smiles at me widely. The hottest senior at Blackfell High is standing in front of me and giving me a huge smile. One that reveals the premature crow's feet at the corners of his eyes. It's the most heart-melting thing about him.

"Audrey, don't you look gorgeous," he says, scanning me up and down approvingly.

"Oh my God, stop," I say, pretending to be bashful. "I had fun Snapchatting you last night."

I had initiated our Snapchat conversation. It was also another thing I stayed up late doing when I should have been sleeping. But it's all part of my plan.

"Yeah, I'm glad we're talking again," he says.

"Yeah..." I trail off, looking up toward the ceiling underneath my lashes in what I hope is a cute way. "*Talking* is nice and all..."

I'm trying to hint at wanting to do more than talk. I'm trying to hint that I want to flirt. That I want to dance with him. At homecoming.

He closes his locker and leans against it like I'm leaning against the one next to his. We are closer together than two casual peers usually stand.

"You know..." he trails off, mimicking my tone. "The last time I think I really talked to you in person was at your house when you turned me down after I asked you on a date."

Heat seeps into my face. "Sorry about that," I say. But in all fairness, it would have been impossible to date a guy while my sister was locked in a shed in the middle of the woods and I had no idea if I'd ever see her again.

"Don't apologize," he says sincerely. "I get it. You were having a rough time."

"I was," I say truthfully. "But... Lyla is back now."

He gives me a half-smirk. "That she is."

"And she's going to the dance. With Wrigley Hall."

"Good for her. I don't really know Wrigley much. But he throws awesome parties."

"Agreed," I say with a smile. "I don't have a date yet."

"No?"

I bite my bottom lip as I smile at him. "Nope. Anyway. Snapchat me later?"

I lean away from the locker and step to the side.

"You're just gonna take off on me like that?" he asks, still smiling.

"Sorry," I say flirtatiously. "I just have some guy I have to meet up with. I think he wants to ask me something. But I *hope* it's not what I think it is." Then I give him a very hard stare, trying to tell him as much as possible without words that I want *him* to be the one to ask me to the dance. Then I giggle, wave at him, and practically skip away.

* * *

Not turning in my assignment First Hour threw off my entire day. In every single class so far, I have felt behind. The stress grows more and more each time the bell rings. I know I'm falling behind on all of my classwork. When I walk to the cafeteria for lunch, I'm thinking about how maybe I should just go to the library after school to sit down and try to get some homework done. But then I think about how quiet the library is. How warm it is with the fireplace lit. How I'd probably doze off the second I sat down in one of those old cushioned chairs.

"Audrey Bailey, please report to the varsity football team lunch table."

I look around, confused as to why I'm hearing this announcement so loudly throughout the already bustling cafeteria. When my eyes fall on the football team's lunch table, I raise my eyebrows. Ryan Copeland has a megaphone in his hand. It's what he made the announcement on.

But what's cuter than that is that all of his teammates are holding and shaking pom-poms. Or, *most* of them are, I should say.

Warner is nowhere to be seen.

Not that I'm looking for him right now.

My stomach dips. I giggle as warmth rushes to my face and I make my way over to their table. They're all standing in a straight line on one side of it, Ryan in the middle of them. The boys keep shaking the pom-poms.

"All right, boys," Ryan says on the megaphone to his teammates when I get close enough. "Take it away."

They all shout, as loudly as possible, in perfect unison while they shake their pom-poms, "Two, four, six, eight!"

I giggle at how ridiculous this all is.

They continue the cheer. "Will you be Copeland's hoco date?!"

Around me, I think the entire school is watching.

Ryan smiles at me and speaks into the megaphone again. "What do you say, Audrey?"

I shake my head at how lame and cheesy this is, but then I realize he might think I'm saying no, so I laugh and playfully call out, "Yes!"

Then the cafeteria applauds.

So, I have finally landed my date. With literally *days* to spare. I hadn't expected Ryan to be so public about asking me, but I am incredibly flattered and finding that in this moment, I am actually really happy.

This is the kind of thing normal high school girls dream about. And it's happening to me.

CHAPTER 24

AMELIA

Maddy has the day off today, so we texted a little bit and I decided to invite her over. *I* don't exactly have the day off today, but I guess maybe I'm giving myself a little bit of a mental health day.

And I suppose I sort of maybe gave myself another mental health day yesterday as well. I made it to work for a little bit, but only after I took care of a couple of things first.

I spend the time in locked up in my study before Maddy finally arrives, and then I leave it and lock it up behind me. I go and answer the front door and see her holding a bottle of white wine in one hand and a loaf of French bread in the other.

"Oh, it's *that* kind of hang out?" I ask, raising my eyebrows excitedly.

"Always." She comes inside and I close the door behind her. Even though she's been here before, she looks around like this whole place is new to her.

"We can hang out in here. You can take your shoes off if you want," I say, motioning to my precious front room with its cream colored décor—and *extremely* white rug. I am really wanting to say that I *need* her to take her shoes off if she's even *thinking* about stepping foot in this room, but I don't want to be one of those needy, nagging hosts. So I pretend like it's a casual choice. But I hope that she sees that I don't have any shoes on and decides to follow suit.

"Let's go into the kitchen and break this open first," Maddy says.

I follow her.

She sets the wine and the bread on the counter and I get out a cutting board and some cheese slices for the bread. I get her a knife and she begins cutting it up for us. I grab wine glasses and uncork the bottle.

"So..." she says slowly. "How have things been?"

"Fine, I guess," I say.

"Right," she says. Then she nods. "It's just that, we haven't really gotten a chance to talk much since... you know, that night."

"I know," I say. "I agree. Things have been a little crazy. I'm sure they have been for you, too."

"Yeah. Crazy."

We bring the items into the front room, and thankfully, she takes off her shoes before stepping onto the white rug.

"I'm surprised you're able to hang out," she says to me. "Do you always get to make your own work schedule and go in whenever you want?"

"I try to keep it the same every day," I say. "I've just been having an off week."

"Are you sure everything is okay?"

I shrug. "I don't know. The kids are at Gentry's new place this week. So I'm here all alone. It's just weird how official it is. Gentry and I have been putting this act on for so long, I don't even know if you realize. And now it's weird that we don't have to put on the act anymore. I had started to get really used to it. But this? Being here alone in this house that's too big for me? I don't know how I feel about it yet. I should be soaking up the time I have by myself. But it just feels all wrong. I'm thinking about the girls constantly. Joey, too. He's a *whole* other story. I don't even wanna get into it."

Besides, I don't even know if it is my problems that Maddy and I should be discussing right now. The last time we saw each other in person was the night we found Lyla locked in that pool shed. The night of the fire. The night that I saw Carson. And while that in itself is a lot to discuss, too, there's more I think we need to hash out.

For one, I found out through Nora that even though Maddy told me she and Nora lost touch years ago, they actually had *remained* in touch this entire time. They've stayed friends, and Maddy kept it a secret from me. And I admitted to her that I knew the truth.

And two, Maddy also found out that Dean Reeves and I had a fling years ago. So, I am expecting that she's going to want to talk about that, too. Dean was an ex of hers. And he's also the father of her son.

We both confronted each other, but we were so busy dealing with our kids and the situation with Carson that we didn't really talk about it again. So it kind of hovers in the air between us now. We both know it needs to be talked about. Us rekindling our friendship again is new, and if we're going to make it work, we need to be honest with each other. But honesty is something we had a hard time doing even when we were friends back in high school.

"You don't have to get into it," Maddy says as she sips her wine. I grab a piece of bread and cheese. "Besides, there is something else I sort of wanted to talk to you about."

I get a lurching feeling in my stomach because I already have an idea about what it is she's going to say.

"What's up?" I decide to ask anyway.

"It's about Nora."

I chew my bread slowly and cautiously as I nod and stare at Maddy.

"I'm sorry that I didn't tell you the truth about how I stayed in touch with her. I don't even know why it needed to be a secret. It really didn't. I just... I didn't want to cause any more drama. I didn't want you to worry that I was going to say something to her about what we did to Carson or anything like that."

It hurts that she lied to me. It does make me nervous knowing that Nora and Maddy have had all of these conversations over the years while I've stayed far, far away from the both of them. I feel like an outsider in their little "dynamic duo." I feel that Maddy and Nora must be closer than Nora and I or Maddy and I are. And I don't think I like it very much. I'm the one that introduced them. Nora is *my* sister. Maddy was *my* friend first.

"Honestly, I was a little upset at first, I admit," I say. "But I'm over it. We have so much other stuff going on, Mads. That was in the past. And Nora clearly still doesn't know what went down that night, so I don't think that you told her anything I wouldn't have wanted you to."

"Okay, good." Maddy reaches out and gives my knee a squeeze, a smile on her lips.

"I guess I have something to apologize for, too," I say, feeling rather embarrassed about it. I know I should have never gotten together with Dean. But the thing is, Dean and I started having a fling before I knew Maddy was pregnant with his son. I knew that Maddy and Dean were exes of each other, but I figured it was okay to go for him—even though he was also my sister's first love—because Maddy and I no longer spoke, and Nora didn't seem the least bit interested in Dean anymore. When I found out that Dean was expecting Maddy's kid, the fling ended abruptly.

"Oh, you mean that thing about Dean?" Maddy asks, waving a dismissive hand. "It's okay."

"No, it's really not okay," I say. "We had a quick fling while I was a sophomore in college. It was over before it even began, Maddy. I mean it. I didn't know you were pregnant with his kid. Not until he told me. And... I don't know. It was stupid. I don't know what I was thinking."

"It sucked to find out the way I did," she says. "And I want to know who exactly mailed me that photo of you two and how they got their hands on it. Do you think it was Carson?"

"Who knows what Carson is capable of? He's been missing for years, but he could have been sneaking around our backyards and our homes this entire time. We really know nothing. We all stopped looking for him so long ago, so it made things easier for him. I'm sure of it."

Maddy nibbles on some bread and looks away from me.

"What?" I ask, not liking the look on her face.

She swallows and bites her bottom lip. "So, you're absolutely *sure* it was Carson in the woods, right?"

I'm offended that she's even double-checking with me.

"Yes, I'm positive," I say. "His mask fell off and he looked right at me. And the recognition of me was plain on his face. I know he aged a bit, but it was still him, Maddy."

"Don't worry, I believe you," she says quickly. "Just... since I haven't talk to you in a couple of days and it hasn't been released on the news or any of that, I wasn't sure if you had changed your mind or not."

"No," I say sternly. "I definitely haven't. It was him."

"Well, it seems that Carson knows everything. He knows all of our secrets. He knows how to mess with us. So... I really don't think you and I can even keep secrets from each other anymore, Mia. What do you think?"

"Definitely not."

She smiles at me lovingly. It reminds me so much of the look she would give me in high school. When we were the closest we had ever been.

I return the look.

"Oh," she says after sipping some more wine. She sets her glass on the coaster on the table and then leans back into the sofa. "Speaking of Dean, though. Did you know that he won't stop bugging me? He wants me and him and Warner to be some sort of 'family.'"

"He—he does?" The news takes me by surprise. But why does it? Of course, Dean would be done with me. Of course, time and time again, he would choose her.

I wonder if I even really ever stood a chance.

CHAPTER 25

WARNER

After school, Audrey and I decide to meet up at my Jeep, and I drive us to the public library, where we think we'll be able to dig up more information on websites from their computers than we would have been able to on the ones at school—those ones have strict monitoring and restricted access.

"Megan Young," Audrey says in my passenger seat as I pull into a parking spot and turn the car off. "Who the heck is Megan young?"

I shake my head disappointedly. "I don't know. And I'm worried we won't ever figure it out, either."

"She was a missing person. We should at least be able to get *some* info on her. The reason we could never find dirt on her before is because we were researching Sydney Hutton. Who doesn't exist."

It's a breezy October day as we walk inside together. Immediately I want to take my jacket off when we get inside because they appear to have turned the thermostat up to a million degrees in here.

We go over to the computers and take a seat at two next to each other.

"Do you think we will find anything that correlates to Carson Price?" I ask her curiously.

She looks doubtful. "Wouldn't that be nice."

"It would," I say. "Hey, thank you for doing this with me."

"You mean since Lyla won't?" she asks, but she has a playful look on her face so I know she's just joking around.

"*Why* won't she, though?" I wonder out loud. I don't expect Audrey to have the answer, even though they are twins.

"Weird, right?" Audrey asks. "I don't know what's gotten into her. I mean, I know she just went through a lot with the kidnapping and what not, but you'd think she'd be more determined now to figure out who her kidnapper was then ever. To figure out who has been doing this to us and how we can stop him."

"Stop Carson, you mean."

"Right. Stop Carson."

"Is she doing okay? Like, how has she been at home?"

"Nothing different than since I told you about her last time. She seems fine. Which is freaky."

"Yeah."

I try to start googling Megan Young. But I'm still stuck on Lyla. When am I *not* stuck on her?

"I just... I've also noticed that I haven't seen her at lunch lately," I say.

Audrey rolls her eyes and types away on the keyboard. "Yeah, well, that would be because she's spending every waking moment of her existence with Wrigley now."

"Wrigley *Hall?*" I don't know why I even ask, because there is no other Wrigley, probably in the entire world.

"That would be the one," she says.

I'm not going to lie. To hear her say it, it hurts. Bad. Like, in a crushing sort of way. Lyla and Wrigley Hall? I had a feeling he was into her, but I didn't know the extent of it. I didn't know they were hanging out.

"Oh." I don't know what else to say about it. It's not like I can exactly confide in Audrey about how bummed out I am to hear her say it. I am sure she is still recovering from me telling her I want to stay just friends with her. So, instead of saying anything else about it, even though it's all I can think about, I get started on researching Megan Young.

CHAPTER 26

LYLA

"I had fun hanging out with you in the library today," Wrigley says to me as we stand in the student parking lot after school.

I giggle. I don't know why. Something about being around Wrigley has me in this giggly mood. "I had fun, too."

Although, I didn't get as much work done as I had wanted to. I should have known that going into it with Wrigley. I still have a bunch of makeup work to do from my lovely week spent away on that awesome vacation of mine.

"We should do it more often," Wrigley says.

"I don't know about that," I tell him. "You're too distracting."

"But that's what's so fun about it."

I roll my eyes and giggle some more.

"Where is Audrey?" Wrigley asks, looking around the student parking lot.

"She's hanging out with Warner today. I was just going to walk home."

"Walk home?" Immediately, his attitude changes. "Alone?"

I shrug. "It's the middle of the day. It's sunny out. Other students are walking home. I don't feel like I would be totally alone."

He shakes his head. "Nuh uh. Not okay with me."

"Wrigley."

"I'm not kidding, Lyla. You can't just walk home *alone*."

I am honestly a little bit surprised by his reaction. I've never seen him sound so serious before. Wrigley is one of the most laid-back, carefree guys I know.

"Oh... okay," I say, caving and feeling slightly awkward.

"I'm sorry," he says, running a hand through his curls. "I just—Lyla, I don't know if I can tell you this enough. But you don't understand how your being gone affected me. And I'm not trying to get you to feel pity for me because obviously what you went through was way more traumatic. I'm just—I don't know. I worry about you. Like all the time. I want whoever did this to you caught. It sucks that they're still out there."

"We don't have to talk about this," I say, feeling myself shut down.

"Yeah, you've said that before," he says.

"I mean... there's nothing to talk about. What happened and I can't go back and change anything. So why not just move forward instead?"

"Because I think..." He trails off and just stares at me instead of finishing his sentence.

"What?" I ask.

He is silent for a moment longer, then eventually, he just shakes his head and sags his shoulders. "You know what? Never mind."

You don't have to tell me twice.

"Okay. So, what, then? Are you walking me home?"

"Do you have any plans right now?"

"None other than more catch-up work. Why?"

"I still need an outfit for homecoming. Maybe you want to hit up some stores together?"

"You want to shop for outfits together?"

It feels strange. I had never gone homecoming—or any type of dance shopping—with Jackson. I always went with Audrey and usually the other girls, Sophia, Danielle, and Olive.

And Trinity.

But that feels like a lifetime ago.

"I don't know," he says, stuffing his hands in his pockets. "It was just a thought. Is that too strange? Is it, like, supposed to be a surprise with what you decide to wear?"

"I don't think so," I say, wondering if this is allowed or not. "You know what? I say we do it."

He grins at me, and my stomach flutters. We walk over to his car and get in. I rode in his car the entire way to the Boldosa Redwoods once before, and he had made me feel safe. I hadn't felt nervous while in his vehicle with him. So remembering that, I lower my shoulders from my ear and enjoy the ride to downtown Toxey, where even though it's a rather rundown area, there's still some great shops where usually the kids from school get their dresses and suits.

"I still can't believe I'm doing this," Wrigley says to me as he drives. He flashes me another quick grin. "I, Wrigley Hall, I am going to a high school dance."

"And I, Lyla Bailey, I am going as your date."

"I guess that's sort of unheard of, too. We're breaking all kinds of records together."

"And you know how I feel about that?" I decide to ask, smiling again. I've smiled so much today that my cheeks physically hurt. I think it's because I've spent most of the day with Wrigley. Before school, in the halls, during lunch at the library, and now.

"What?" he asks.

"I think I like it."

He reaches over and rests one of his hands on my thigh. "You know what, Lyla Bailey?" he asks. "I like it, too. I think I could really get used to this."

CHAPTER 27

WARNER

Audrey and I are both nervous as heck when we get back in my Jeep and make our way over to the address I printed out on a piece of paper.

While in the library together, we managed to find the missing person poster for Megan Young, but not much else was said about her. We couldn't even find any press releases of her parents saying how worried they were about her. No one really seemed to care that she had gone missing. Women go missing all the time, apparently. It's not a fact that makes me feel any better.

But what Audrey *did* manage to find, via a lot of internet research and stalking people's social media, was info—surprisingly—on Sydney Hutton. And that info she found was who her foster parents were. Not only who they were, but where they resided, as well.

And that's where we are headed now.

"Do you think they'll even want to talk to us?" I ask, clenching my jaw as we drive.

"I hope so," Audrey replies. She seems a lot more confident than I do, even if she still looks tense.

"Should we, like, plan out what we're going to ask? What we're going to say? Do we need to come up with some lie as to why we're there? Like we're doing some sort of report for school or whatever?"

"I think we just need to go there and be completely honest. We'll say we want to know what happened to her. Just as much as the police do."

I squint, thinking about it. "Honest..."

What a strange concept. It's not something that's done very often around Toxey.

"Yeah. I mean... maybe we embellish a *little* and say that we were really close friends of hers or something. I don't know."

I wince uncomfortably. "Audrey, it spread around the entire school that everyone thinks I'm the one who killed her. I don't think her foster parents are going to believe that we were really close."

"Right." She blushes slightly. "Okay, we will say that we are trying to prove your innocence. You will just have to express how sorry you are that she died and how awful it is and then you'll just have to convince her that it definitely was not your fault."

"Oh. Great. Easy."

I'm beginning to feel worse and worse.

Finally, we pull up to the address I had printed. Sydney's foster parents, a man and woman named Ellen and Rex Sullivan, live in a house not much bigger than mine. And it's in a similar style neighborhood to mine, as well. It looks cleaner over here, however. All the lawns are more manicured and the roads in front of the houses are paved instead of dirt. There's no junk in everyone side yards. No chain-link fences. It seems like a good place for a foster family to live.

"Are we really doing this?" I ask.

"Don't be such a baby, Carpenter." Audrey sticks her tongue out at me and then hops out of the car. "I'm glad we're finally doing something."

I suppose I should be glad, too. This is what we wanted. To get to the bottom of this whole mess. And starting here is our best bet of getting anywhere.

I get out of the car as well and follow Audrey over to the front door through the front yard.

She's the one who rings the doorbell.

"This is crazy," I mutter.

"Shush," she says.

I roll my eyes and we step back as we hear someone unlocking the front door. A woman pops it open. She's middle aged with short black hair and beady hazel eyes. She has a large nose and a slightly crooked smile. But the fact that she's smiling upon seeing us makes me feel a little bit better, at least.

"Well, hello there," she says. "What can I do for you kids?"

I'm trying to think of the correct way to start this conversation, but apparently, it's pointless for me to do so because Audrey is the one who speaks first.

"We were hoping we could ask you some questions about Sydney Hutton."

Blunt much, Audrey?

"You want to know about Sydney?" Ellen gets wrinkles on her forehead like she isn't sure if she wants to help us anymore. Suddenly, she doesn't seem a-s excited to see us.

"It's just that... I was a good friend of Sydney's, and Warner here... Well..." Audrey looks at me and waits for me to say something.

It's time for me to put my game face on.

"I was close with Sydney, too," I lie. "And because of that, people think that I had something to do with her death. But it's not true, Mrs. Sullivan. And I'm trying to do whatever I can to prove that. Which is why we want to talk to you."

"You're Warner Carpenter?" she asks. She doesn't look ready to run away from us. She just looks... curious.

"I am," I say. "And this is Audrey Bailey."

She scans both of us up and down. "I see." Then she opens the door wider. "Why don't you guys come in."

Audrey and I look at each other like we can't believe we've gotten this far. I don't know if we should go into a stranger's house like this, but once Audrey takes that first step inside, I know that I have to go, too. There's no way I'm leaving her alone in there.

We follow Ellen over to the living area where she motions for us to take a seat on her yellow striped sofa. "You guys want anything to drink? I have ice tea and lemonade."

"I'm fine," I say.

"A lemonade sounds fantastic," Audrey says with a bright smile.

I look at her like she's crazy. She just smiles at me and says nothing.

"I'll be right back, then." Ellen says.

"Where is Mr. Sullivan?" Audrey asks.

"He doesn't get off work until very late. He is in retail."

"I see."

Ellen disappears into her kitchen. I turn to Audrey.

"You're crazy," I say as quietly as possible. "She could put something in your drink!"

"Why would she do that?"

"What was she doing being Sydney's foster parent when Sydney wasn't even a real teenager to be adopted?"

"I don't know," she whispers. "That's why we're here."

Ellen returns with two glasses of lemonade even though I said I was fine without one, and Audrey and I fall silent again.

"So," Ellen says as she takes a seat in her leather armchair. I can tell it's her favorite spot in the house because it looks well worn.

"Mrs. Sullivan," Audrey starts. I'm really glad that she's taking control of this whole situation. "How long were you fostering Sydney Hutton?"

"Well... not very long. Only a few months."

"And what was the whole process of becoming her foster parent?"

Ellen immediately shifts in her seat, looking uncomfortable. Already, Audrey is trying to catch her in a lie.

"It's a bit complicated," Ellen says.

Audrey sips her lemonade. "It's delicious, thank you," she says before setting the cup back down. "By 'complicated,' do you mean because it wasn't done in a legal, ethical way?"

"*Audrey*," I scold.

Audrey ignores me and just stares at Ellen, waiting for an answer.

"It seems like you to already know a bit more than you're probably letting on," Ellen says, squinting her beady eyes.

"Not much," Audrey says. "But we do know a little bit."

"That's why we're here," I join in. "Because we want to know everything. We want to know what really happened to her."

"I would like that, too," Ellen says. "But, if you know that I got her in an unethical and illegal way, then you know it was through an under the table deal with somebody."

"Yes," Audrey says.

"Who was that somebody?" I ask.

"I'm afraid it was never disclosed. The person doing the deal remain anonymous."

"Of course," I say, feeling discouraged.

"Were you doing it for the money?" Audrey asks innocently.

"I don't see how that's any of your business," Ellen says. It's clear now that she's starting to get annoyed.

"I'm sorry, Mrs. Sullivan," I say, interjecting what crude thing Audrey was about to say next. I don't want this lady kicking us out of her house before we've even gotten any real answers. "You're right. It's not any of our business. But we are wondering... do you know anything about who Sydney Hutton really was?"

She stares back-and-forth between the two of us for a long while before she finally gives us an answer. "Megan Young."

Audrey and I exchange a quick look.

"So, you know," Audrey says, sounding staggered. She sips her lemonade again. I haven't touched mine. "You know that she is a missing person and that she was actually nineteen years old."

"I didn't know it at the time of fostering her," Ellen says. "I recently had the police come to my door and ask me if I knew anything about it."

"What police?" I ask.

"I don't remember their names," she says, waving it off. "Two men in blue uniforms. That's all I know."

So, the cops know that Sydney Hutton was actually Megan Young, and they're not even releasing that information to the public.

Why?

Suddenly, Ellen looks sad. She puts her hand to her chest and rocks slightly in her chair. "Rex and I have always wanted kids of our own," she says somberly. "We jumped on the chance to be able to help Sydney. Or Megan. Whoever she was. We were eager to finally have a kid around here. And it didn't even last long. It's completely discouraging and makes us never want to do it again. And I'm telling you, if I had *ever* known that she was a missing girl... someone missing from her own parents who were probably worried about her terribly, I would have never gone through with the deal."

"I'm so sorry for what happened to her, Mrs. Sullivan," Audrey says. Her eyes look sincere.

"Me, too," I say, trying to look just as believable.

Now my mind is racing with all of this new information. An anonymous under the table deal to become a foster child in Toxey?

Someone had paid for Megan Young to stay in this house. And the police know about it.

I know this all connects somehow, but now my head is pounding more than ever.

CHAPTER 28

MADDY

I'm sitting on the sofa at home when the door bursts open and in stumbles Warner in a hurry. Behind him, it's none other than one of the Bailey twins.

"Warner?" I ask, looking at the two of them over the back of the sofa.

"Hey, Mom," Warner says hurriedly. "Audrey and I are just gonna go chill in my room, okay?"

"Oh... all right then."

"Hi, Maddy," Audrey says with a bright smile, then she follows Warner down the hall and the two disappear.

I face the TV again, feeling confused. I think it's odd that Audrey and Warner are hanging out together when all this time, I thought he was interested in Lyla, the same twin Wrigley is interested in.

I stop thinking about it as quickly as I started because I'm still digesting everything that happened over at Mia's house while I sit here and text Steven about his day.

It's just that... Mia had seemed... off. Not like her normal self. She was super fidgety. She kept looking around her house, like at the windows and such, as if she were paranoid. She seemed stressed. She kept tugging at her own hair. She talked at a mile a minute. Honestly, the Mia that I've come to know has always been so put together. So sure of herself and confident. It was all off-putting and unsettling to see her acting the way she acted today. And as much as I don't want to think back to what Nora had told me when I saw her, I can't help it. Nora had called Mia a psychopath. That is never a word I would have used to describe Amelia Flynn-Bailey. Not until today.

But I need to not think like that. I shake my head quickly, trying to get the thoughts away from me. Mia is *not* a psychopath. She's just going through a rough time. She and Gentry are divorcing. Her daughter had just been missing. Some guy she thought she killed in high school suddenly came back from the dead. It would make anyone a little... crazy.

I read my most recent text from Steven:

Steven: *I worry about you. I don't like that I am so far away from you. Not when that freak is still out there.*

I know that by "freak" he's referring to my fake psycho ex-boyfriend. But in my head, I see it as Carson. I don't like that Steven is still so far away from me with Carson still out there. With Steven around, I feel so much safer. Although, since Lyla has been found, I *have* noticed that I haven't received any more suspicious notes, and no other dangerous incidents have occurred. But as I think this, I reach out and knock my fist on the wooden coffee table so that I don't jinx myself. Then I send my reply.

Me: *Well, I happen to be glad that you are safe and far away from him.*

Steven: *I'm not going to be gone for long. And I want to see you as soon as possible when I get back.*

My stomach flutters excitedly, but it also comes with the nausea of how untruthful I have been. I know I have to come clean. I say it to myself over and over again. The pit in my stomach will not leave until I do so. I want to have a relationship with Steven, but I can't have a relationship that starts with lies. I know this. So I need to fix it.

When my phone vibrates again, I think I'm getting another reply from Steven. Instead, I see that Dean has sent me a text.

Dean: *When can we all get together again? I was thinking maybe we could go see a ball game or go out to dinner together.*

I read the text over and over and don't even know what to make of it. I let Dean come over one time and he thinks we're suddenly some sort of family that has outings together? Does he seriously think that Warner, Dean and I will all go to a baseball game and act as one happy family, trying to catch foul balls and sharing popcorn from the same bin?

I decide to just leave Dean on "unread".

CHAPTER 29

LYLA

Upon walking up to the gymnasium during First Period for the homecoming pep rally, I send Wrigley a text message.

Me: *Hey :-) we should meet up for the assembly. Find me in the stands.*

I follow the massive crowd of students in through the double doors and then I clamber up some steps and find myself a good seat in the middle of the crowd. Everyone is wearing their school colors, maroon and black. People are chatting excitedly and meeting up with their friends. The sports teams and cheerleaders are missing from the crowd because they will be coming out onto the floor at various times during the rally.

As the gymnasium fills more and more, I look around the place for signs of Wrigley. However, even when it seems as if every student has entered and the doors are closed, Wrigley is still nowhere to be found.

I check my phone, wondering if maybe he's texted me that he's trying to find me. Instead, I see that he hasn't even texted me back at all.

So instead of getting to sit next to anybody that I know, I'm wedged between two groups of freshmen who keep obnoxiously bumping into me as they turn to talk to their friends.

I keep looking around for Wrigley.

Where could he be?

I keep checking my phone still, too. And I get nothing from him.

Eventually, I force myself to stop caring. Mr. Gillens has walked onto the floor with his microphone, and the school has started cheering for him. Everyone loves Mr. Gillens, the junior government teacher. His loud booming voice is perfect to get everyone amped up during these pep assemblies.

I join the cheering crowd and smile. I loved going to pep rallies when I was a cheerleader. I hated them afterward. Until now. If old me liked pep rallies, then the current new me will, too.

Mr. Gillens shouts through his megaphone, cracks some jokes, and gets everybody cheering and laughing. He talks about the big homecoming game we have tonight. And then, the cheerleaders run out through some doors from the locker room. They all shake their pom-poms and they're cheering and smiling and running as they form a line at the doors for the football team to run through. Everyone is going nuts. It's clear that the football team is everyone's favorite out of all the sports teams we have here at Blackfell High.

I watch Audrey among the cheerleaders. She's standing next to Danielle, and they keep looking at each other and giggling and talking behind their pom-poms as they wait for the football team to burst through the doors. She looks beautiful down there in her cute cheerleading outfit. I used to look like that. It makes me wonder if I should try becoming a cheerleader again. Maybe it would make me feel more normal.

And that way, at least I wouldn't be sitting here in the stands with absolutely no friends around me.

Finally, the metal doors slam open, so loudly even over the crowd that I jump in my seat. The football team runs out, led by their football captain, Warner. They are all in their game day uniforms and helmets, and they're yelling and roaring and bumping each other's fists and slamming into each other's chest. They wave at the crowd, which is going nuts over them. I even hear some girls yelling, "We love you, Jackson!" from somewhere far off. I try to figure out who said it, but I can't tell. There are too many people around.

It's madness as I stand there and watch all the cheerleaders chant for them as they keep showing off. Then I look at number 26, Jackson, and watch him throw his helmet off and yell so loudly that veins are popping out of the side of his neck and his face is red. He pumps his chest. He gets an angry look on his face when Mr. Gillens talks about how they're going to destroy the other team tonight.

Watching Jackson, the strangest sensation comes over me. It's as if the entire room falls silent. As if I've lost my hearing completely. And the corners of my vision have blurred everything except for Jackson, who's acting like a complete madman.

I see him, thumping his chest and yelling angrily, pumped full of testosterone.

I see the masked man inside of the shed, pulling that white rag out of his pocket and forcing it over my mouth.

I see the two of their faces switching places. I see Jackson putting the chloroformed rag over me. The mask man standing in Jackson's place, thumping his chest and yelling angrily in front of everybody.

My ability to breathe completely disappears, and I launch out of my seat and race down the steps. I don't care if people are staring, but hopefully they're not anyway because they're too distracted looking at the football players and cheerleaders. Hopefully nobody sees as I run out of there and into the hall. It's empty out here, but I can still hear all the cheering coming from inside. I lean against a white brick wall and slide down to the floor, running a hand through my hair and trying to get myself to take a deep breath.

I just don't understand it. The sight of Jackson out in there like that... it had terrified me. Why am I so scared of him when he's never scared me before? He's never hurt me before. We were together for so long. Jackson used to make me feel so safe.

Now I wonder if maybe I will never feel safe, truly safe, ever again.

CHAPTER 30

WARNER

I have to admit: it's a powerful feeling having the entire school cheering for you and your teammates. It makes me... I don't know... cocky. It makes me smile. It makes me yell louder than I thought I would. It makes me pump my fist in the air and slap my teammates on the back. It makes me smile around at all of the cheerleaders that are waving their pom-poms in our faces. It makes every word Mr. Gillens shouts into his microphone really resonate inside of me.

I'm filled with a sort of adrenaline. It's the only way I can describe it. And with my bout of overconfidence, I see a curly-haired brunette in the crowd, and I make a quick decision. Something that will *really* get the school going. Something that will bode well for me—hopefully—and stick it to somebody else.

Taking my chance and not thinking twice about it, I jump into the stands, where people reach their hands out to try to hi-five me or grab some chunk of my clothing or yell my name. I smile at everyone as I race up the steps to the row I need to get to. Then I find Jessica Vaccari and step over people's legs until I am in front of her.

"Hi, Warner," she says with a bright smile, looking confused as she side-glances at her friends sitting on either side of her.

Jackson told me she was into me. So this has to work. Hopefully.

"Hi," I say awkwardly. It's a million degrees in here, and my breathing is shallow, and my heart is pounding, but I don't care. I'm still going to go through with this. "Look. I know it's tomorrow, and I know there's probably *zero* chance that you don't already have a date, but do you maybe want to go to homecoming with me?"

"Folks, it looks as if Warner Carpenter has just asked a girl to homecoming! Sorry ladies!" Mr. Gillen says into his microphone, updating the entire school about what I have just done. It makes everyone fall silent as they wait for Jessica's answer with me. Jessica puts a hand over her mouth, embarrassed, and her friends beside her giggle and shake her and tell her to say yes.

"I'd love to," she finally says, her face bright red. I'm sure mine is, too, as I smile back at her. She stands up and throws her arms around me and I hug her.

Around us, the school applauds.

I can't believe that worked. I am almost feeling like maybe I dreamt the whole thing as I make my way back down the stairs onto the gym floor to re-join my teammates for the rest of the assembly. My heart is still racing with the adrenaline from what I just did. People can't stop tugging at me and slapping my back and telling me, "Congrats." And I smile and playfully mess around with them and return, but as I'm doing so, I'm looking through the stands again.

Because I'm looking for Lyla.

Hearing yesterday from Audrey that she has been spending all of her time with Wrigley Hall—it sucked. And it made me realize that I have to get over her. And fast.

And I figured may be a good way to do that was to just finally move on to somebody who I know is interested in me.

But as I scan the stands, I don't see Lyla anywhere. I feel like I *never* see Lyla anywhere. In the hallways. In the lunchroom. Before and after school. And now, I'm pretty certain she's not here, either. It bums me out because I wanted her to see that I don't care that she rejected me. That I've happily moved on to somebody else.

But now, I can't help but feel a little worried.

Why is Lyla always missing?

CHAPTER 31

AMELIA

The last thing I want to do is go to the homecoming football game with Gentry beside me, but I want to go to the game in support of Audrey, who is cheerleading during it.

The reason that Gentry and I decide to go together is because we haven't exactly announced our divorce to the public yet, and Gentry understands that I am not ready to do so.

We meet outside of the ticket booth, Gentry nods at me hello, I give a quiet, "Hi," back, and then he goes and buys our tickets and we walk into the stands together. We go up the steps on the bleachers and say hi to some couples that we know who are parents of other kids at school, and when I spot Maddy higher up on the bleachers with her hot date, Steven Hall, who must have just gotten back to town, I wink at her and she waves. Then Gentry and I find a seat close to where Audrey is standing in the cheerleading lineup and we wave over to her. She smiles brightly and waves at us back. I'm glad that I have a daughter who is genuinely happy to see me. The other daughter is at Gentry's house babysitting Joey.

"How has your week with the kids been?" I ask Gentry after a long while of both of us just looking at our phones and not talking to each other. The game has begun, and already, our team is dominating the away team.

"Good," Gentry replies casually, his elbows on his knees as he leans forward in his seat. He has to look back at me to talk and make eye contact. "It seems that they're all settling in very well. I think they like it over there."

I arch one eyebrow. An eyebrow that I need to get threaded. I haven't been to a salon in ages. "You think Audrey and Lyla are enjoying having to share a bedroom?"

I know I sound snobbish, but I don't much care. I am bitter about everything. I know that Gentry and I had to come clean about not being in love anymore eventually, but I just hate how quickly Gentry has seemed to settle down and move on. I'm still stuck hating being alone in my big house and missing my kids and feeling like a failure as a person for not having a successful marriage.

And maybe I'm also bitter because I thought I would be able to move on, but the person I want to move on with doesn't even want to give me the time of day.

"It's not for forever," Gentry reminds me. "This is just a rental. When I finally buy a place, I plan on letting them have their own rooms. But for now, yeah. They're not complaining about it."

"To your face," I mutter. If Gentry heard me, he decides to pretend that he didn't.

I had gotten more ready tonight than I should have. I am over-dressed. My makeup is overdone. I've styled my hair with more hairspray than I needed to. It's just that I really care about my appearance in front of everybody in Toxey. Everybody sees me as one way, and I want them to continue seeing me that way. I want them to think that I am strong and brave and even though I've been through a tragedy, I want them to think that Gentry and I are handling it well.

So what if that's not at all true?

At first, during the game, I do a pretty decent job focusing on Audrey and her cheerleading. She's really is good. She can do backflips and front flips and back handsprings. It's very impressive to watch, and it makes me beam when people cheer her on.

But then, I catch a glimpse of Dean. He is on the sideline of course, a Nike hat on his head and a whistle in his mouth as he's yelling things at his team.

My tunnel vision starts to focus only on him. I stare at his broad, muscular back, trying to will him to turn around and look at me. I want him to notice that I'm even here at all. I want him to acknowl-edge that he's seen me. And sure, I know he has a team that he's coaching, but I'm beginning to feel like he's not turning around on purpose. Like he's not turning around because he knows his eyes will find mine immediately.

You spent years of your life being in love with me, Dean. I'm finally available and ready to possibly have a future with you, and now you clam up?

I shake my head miserably.

"What's wrong?" Gentry asks. I hadn't realized he had been watching me, and I feel the tips of my ears turning red. "Nothing. Just... thinking. It doesn't matter."

Okay."

We fall silent again. But when Gentry removes his elbows from his knees and sits up straighter, the way he's acting outwardly tells me that there's something he wants to talk to me about. I may not be in a relationship with him now—except for legally—but I still know everything about him. I can still read his body language well.

"What?" I ask him.

"Look," he starts. "You should know. I know we've kind of talked about this a little bit already, but I don't think you really grasp the seriousness of the situation. After we can finalize this divorce, Amelia, I'm going to adopt Joey."

Is he serious? Does he really want to do this right here and right now with me?

I smirk at him. "No you're not," I say. My voice is full of confidence.

"What do you mean no I'm not?"

"*I'm* going to adopt him, Gentry."

He shakes his head. "Mia. Think about this logically. I was the one who spent so much of our marriage wanting him in the first place. You can't just take him from me."

"But you can take him from me?"

"Well, it's not exactly ideal, but I want him to be my son, Mia."

"And I want him to be mine."

"Well, that's too bad!" His voice has gotten louder. I look at him in alarm. He realizes what has happened and turns and faces the field, his body stiff. I know he didn't mean to raise his voice at me in public. He knows to never do that. And he's been pretty good about it our whole marriage.

I face the field, too. Neither of us say anything else about it the entire rest of the game.

CHAPTER 32

AUDREY

I can't help but repeatedly stare at stupid Number 4, Warner, as I cheer on the sidelines for Blackfell High's football team. I know I should be happy and thrilled with the fact that I have Number 66 taking me to homecoming. I should have gotten over Warner's rejection of wanting to be with me in a heartbeat after that happened. But still, I am hurt. The reason why Warner doesn't want to be with me is because he wants to be with Jessica Vaccari, the pretty, exotic brunette who is older and more mature than I am. Stupid Jessica and her long hair. Maybe Warner would have liked me if I never chopped mine off.

That's stupid, Audrey.

Besides, Warner was the one who suggested I cut it, anyway.

There are a few times when Ryan thinks that I'm looking at him and waves at me, and I wave and smile back like a dutiful potential girlfriend would do. But the smile doesn't feel real. And after finishing waving to him, I look back at Warner again anyway. I hate that I can't stop staring at him. And when I turn to face the crowd, I'm also looking for Jessica. I assume she'll be sitting there somewhere, wearing a plain white T-shirt with a number 4 painted on it and holding a poster for him. Thankfully, I don't see her. I see my mom with my dad, in what is surely an awkward fake date that they're having. I see Maddy Carpenter and Steven Hall, Wrigley's father, sitting together a few rows above my parents, Maddy giggling and sitting closely as Steven whispers something in her ear.

"God, Audrey, you are *so* lucky," a senior girl named Cami says to me when we take a break from cheering to get water.

"What do you mean?" I ask, completely forgetting about the scene in the cafeteria and the fact that I had a really big reason to feel lucky. I just didn't feel so lucky after watching Warner go up to Jessica in the crowd today during the pep rally.

"You snagged a date with a Ryan Copeland to the dance!"

Another senior girl, Kiley, walks over and joins us. "I hate you," she says, but she has a smile on her face that tells me she's joking. Or at least, half-joking. "I sent him *so* many hints. I made myself *so* available for him and he never asked."

"I honestly didn't think he was going to," I say, as if that will make her feel a little bit better. I'm surprised the senior girls are talking to me at all. Even though there are a few juniors on the team, the juniors tend to stick together, apart from the seniors.

"He did kind of wait a little long to ask you," Cami agrees. "Granted, I know that you and your family were going through a lot, so that's probably why."

"I like to think that he was really torn between asking you or me, and it took him this long to finally make up his mind," Kiley says. Then she shrugs. "But that's just to make myself feel better."

The three of us giggle. Then Cami swipes at me. "Shh, he's coming!"

I look where she's looking, and see that while Ryan isn't walking directly over to us, he is walking over to his coach, who is only a couple steps away from us. I watch his eyes find mine as he goes. Then I blush and turn away from him. Cami, Kiley, and I giggle some more.

Then, to my left, a snarky-sounding voice catches my attention. It's Sophia, and she's talking to Olive not far away from me, her voice loud enough for me to easily overhear her. In fact, it makes me think she's talking that loud on purpose.

"I sort of have some news," Sophia says to Olive.

"What do you mean?" Olive asks.

"As it turns out, I *do* have a date to homecoming after all."

"But... I thought we were going to go together."

"You'll find someone."

"By *tomorrow*?" Olive sounds panicked.

When I glance over at Sophia, she just shrugs at Olive like she doesn't care about her predicament.

Biting the inside of her cheek, Olive continues. "Well... who are you going with, then?"

I drink my water and pretend to be fixing my super high ponytail.

"You know what, Olive?" Sophia says, mischievousness in her voice. "You're actually going to just have to wait and see like everybody else."

I'm about to turn and give Sophia a look that says, "Why are you keeping it a secret from your own best friend?" when something catches my eyes from under the bleachers.

It's a face. Staring right at me. The person has sandy blond hair. Hard, piercing eyes. A larger build. They're wearing all black. A hood is covering some of their hair.

I nearly cough up the water I just drank as my stomach threatens to fly out of my butt. The world around me freezes. My body grows cold.

Staring at me, under the bleachers, I think it's Carson Price.

"Audrey!"

I snap my head around to see who called my name and find that it is Cami again. "So, what are your plans before and after homecoming?"

"Oh," I say, trying to think of an answer. I look back over at the bleachers to where I saw the person watching me. But as I scan underneath everyone's feet, no one is there anymore.

"You good?" Cami asks.

I'm forced to bring my attention back to her. But I can feel my body trembling slightly. I can feel how clammy my palms are.

Maybe nobody is underneath the bleachers, staring at me.

But it had certainly seemed like there was.

CHAPTER 33

AMELIA

I end up doing the most ridiculous thing The next day—parking my car outside of Dean's house and waiting for him to get home.

What on earth is wrong with me? Why can't I stop acting like this?

I tossed another pill back not too long ago, but my pills don't seem to be working as well as they used to. I'm still full of so much anxiety. I still have so many questions. So many concerns. I am completely plagued by thoughts of Carson Price and Dean Reeves. Carson Price, I don't have much control over. But Dean Reeves is the only one I can do something about. So I just need to get him to talk to me. And with his constant dodging me, I feel that I've been left with no other option.

I sit outside his house, wondering where he is and what's taking him so long to get home, but then I actually realize that it's Friday and not Saturday.

My days are blurring together.

But of *course* it's only Friday. I was thinking homecoming was on a Saturday, but it's today. My girls are going to homecoming today.

I palm my forehead rather hard, feeling stupid, and then I put my car in drive and speed over to the high school. When I get another call from work, probably from Ivory, my assistant, I ignore it yet again. I have other things I need to do. People wanting their home to look nice may be a priority for *them*, but it's not for me. Not right now.

I squeeze my eyes shut tightly, trying to regain some focus on what I'm doing and to ease some of my stress. But then I remember that I'm driving and that I can't just close my eyes when I feel like it, and when I pop them back open, I see that I have swerved into the other lane.

I gasp, my heart skips a beat, and I correct myself. Luckily, the streets are rather empty over here and no one was around to see it.

Should I take another pill? Maybe I need to see my doctor again and have her up my dose. Would that help?

I drive to Blackfell High School. Classes have been out for a little while now, but I'm sure the teachers are still lingering in their classrooms grading and cleaning and doing whatever they do once all of their students go home.

Which means that is exactly where Dean must be. In his class-room.

I park the car in the guest parking lot by the library and march inside the school. I don't come in here too often, but each time I do, I am reminded of how much—and how little—it's changed since I went to high school here. Mostly everything was kept the same except for some painting and re-tiling. I almost feel like my old teenage self again. Like I'm still living in the nineties. But the phone buzzing in my purse again reminds me that I'm not. I let it keep buzzing this time, not even bothering to pull it out and put it to voicemail. I don't care who it is. There's only one thing on my mind.

When I get to Dean's classroom, I don't bother knocking on the closed door or peeking my head through the skinny window first. I just tug on the handle and open it right up.

Dean is sitting at his desk. But upon seeing me, he jumps to his feet, looking like I've interrupted something. But when I look around the rest of the classroom, he's alone.

I make sure the door is closed behind me and stand in front of it so that he can't run from me.

But he wouldn't seriously do that, would he?

"Geez, Mia. What are you doing here?"

"What am I doing here?" I parrot back coldly. "Is that how you talk to all of your students' parents?"

He runs a hand over his face, exasperated. "No. I... am—I'm sorry. What can I do for you?"

He's probably thinking I'm here in regards to something about Audrey or Lyla.

But it's simply not the case.

"It appears that this is the only way I'm going to get to talk to you," I start off by saying.

"What?" His eyes widen. I stare into them confidently. "What is it that you need to talk to me about?"

"Are you kidding?" I take a single step toward him. "What do you *think*? You've been avoiding me." I take another step toward him. He doesn't move from behind his desk. His hands are on his hips in a way that is very macho.

"I just... I have a lot going on, okay?" he says.

"Then, when I was at your house, and we... we kissed..."

He whispers the words. "It was a mistake."

And the whispers wrap around my heart and suffocate it.

"I don't think it was," I try. I take yet another step. There is plenty of gap between me and the door handle now. Plenty of room for him to run. For him to escape me. But I desperately don't want him to.

"What changed, Dean?" I continue. "I thought you would be happy to know that Gentry and I aren't really together. I'm sorry that I didn't tell you about it sooner. Things have just been really difficult, okay?"

"Mia, I understand, but—"

"Then what is it? Is it Maddy? Why are you suddenly so invested in hanging out with her and Warner? Or is it what I told you the last time I was at your house? That I saw Carson Price in the woods during that fire. Do you... do *you* not believe me either?"

"Does Maddy know about us?" he asks, deflecting all of my questions.

"Yes," I say simply.

"Because you told her? Why? What did you have to gain from that? Did you wanna make sure I never had a chance at being a family with them?"

"Is that what you really want? To be with Maddy? Or do you just want to be closer to Warner, so you're willing to do whatever it takes to make it happen?" I don't even want him to answer the question. In fact, I'm going to answer it for him. "I know you don't want to be with Maddy, Dean."

He sighs heavily. Like I completely exhaust him. Like I deplete every ounce of energy inside of him, even more than his students do every day.

"Is it so wrong for me to want to be in Warner's life? I'm not going to stand here and let you make me feel bad for that. He's my son, Mia."

"I know. That's not what I'm trying to say. I just want to know... why you suddenly hate me."

"Don't do that."

"Don't do what?"

He tilts his head to the side slightly. "You know I could never hate you."

"I'm just confused," I whisper. Again, I take another step. He seems a little more relaxed. His hands fall from his hips. He doesn't appear completely repulsed by the idea of me moving closer to him. I decide to take it as a good sign.

"You... you should've told me about you and Gentry," he says, "a long time ago."

"I know," I say.

"I don't like being lied to."

"I completely understand. I just—I'm sorry."

"Are you sure you two are even getting divorced?"

I stop any approach toward him. "What's that supposed to mean?"

"I mean... I saw you, at the game yesterday, with Gentry."

"So?"

"So? I don't know many couples going through a divorce that still hang out with each other. That still spend time together. Are you guys still sleeping in the same house? The same *room*?"

I just stand there and stare at him. I am appalled that he's asking me these things. It shouldn't matter. He should just take my word for what I've told him. Be on my side. Just accept that things are complicated right now. Accept me anyway.

"What, Mia?" he asks when I shake my head at him.

Then there's a knock at the door. One of the front office ladies pops their head into the room, smiling brightly. "Dean, you got a sec?" Then when the woman sees me, her squinty eyes widen slightly. "My apologies!"

"It's fine," I say as I wave a dismissive hand. "We're done here." I don't even look at Dean again. Instead, I offer the woman a friendly smile and then I walk around her and leave the classroom.

CHAPTER 34

MADDY

I can't stand it how cute Warner looks in his homecoming outfit. He decided to go with a completely all-black look, except for his super clean white sneakers. He has on a black shirt that the first few buttons are undone on. It looks very casual and trendy, and I feel like I could take a picture of him and put it on the cover of a fashion magazine.

Dean and I definitely gave that kid the best of our genes.

"Let me take a few more pictures," I complain. "Before your date gets here and we have to take those cringey ones."

"You know, we don't *have* to take the cringey ones," he tries. But I shake my head.

"Turn to the left a little bit." We're standing outside with the sun perfectly setting, giving him great, golden lighting. He rolls his eyes, embarrassed, and does a couple more poses for me. Then a car pulls up to the curb and out of the backseat climbs a pretty, curly haired brunette. She's wearing her hair down, and her dress, too, is completely black. It stops a little bit above the knee and has a slight slit in the side. It's very flattering on her small frame, and she is wearing bright white heels that look very uncomfortable, matching Warner's whole look.

I still feel like I expected Lyla to come out of the backseat of the car. I'm not even sure why. Warner has told me several times that he's taking some girl named Jessica to the dance.

"Nice to meet you," I say to her. "You look beautiful, by the way."

Jessica smiles at me and the car drives away. "Thank you. I'm Jessica." She holds out her hand and I shake it warmly. I'm glad she isn't one of those tryhards that goes in for a hug. I'm not much of a hugger.

"You can call me Miss Carpenter," I tell her.

"Mom," Warner complains.

I smile at both of them. "I'm just kidding. Call me Maddy."

Jessica awkwardly giggles. I tell her to go stand next to Warner so that I can take their couple photos together before they leave. They really do make a cute pair. Jessica has perfect tanned, olive skin that contrasts well against Warner's slight paleness. I could totally picture them winning homecoming king and queen. But apparently neither of them were even nominated.

I guess a lot of kids would have an issue with their homecoming king being a potential murderer.

Not that Warner is a murderer. I don't think he killed Sydney. I just think students at his high school still believe he did.

I snap all my pictures and play nicely with Warner's a little date. I have no idea how interested he is in her or if I'll even ever see her again. But she's sweet enough, so I'm going to definitely bug him about her later.

"Okay, you kids go and have fun," I finally say. "Warner, if you do anything afterward, *please* keep me posted on your whereabouts."

"You got it," he says, then I make him give me a hug, and I kiss him on the cheek, making him embarrassed again.

When they drive off in Warner's Jeep, a cold sadness expands in my chest. That was his last homecoming photoshoot ever. He's never going to have another.

I don't know if I have ever felt older. Especially when I can remember my homecoming like it was yesterday.

I hope he's safe. I hope he has a good time. And I hope he's honest with me if he goes anywhere after. I can't risk anything happening to him. It's taking a lot of my willpower not to just put a tracker in his phone. To make him share his location with me on it.

I am pretty proud of myself. I think I am getting better at trusting him. And I hope he realizes it and appreciates it.

I slowly get ready for my evening plans. *Slowly* because I'm dreading going to them. I have a planned girls' night with Nora at her rental house. And it's not that I don't like Nora and like spending time with her, I just hate the anxiety that fills me every time I do. I hate all the lies I'm constantly telling. I hate having to put on this fake act for her. I hate that I can't just be myself and let loose and unwind. I'm even afraid to have too much wine in case I let something slip that I shouldn't. The last thing I want to do is say the wrong thing to her and send her spiraling again. I don't want to get slapped by her like she did to Mia.

Eventually, I've wasted enough time and I finally make my way over to Nora's rental. It's not far from me, but it's an even worse part of Toxey. Probably because it's more affordable over here. I know she has my trust fund, but I also know that she is being very cautious with it. She told me so when I confronted her about how I thought maybe she had spent most of the trust fund money already and that's why she has such a banged up old car, why she wears used clothes, and why she had to stay at Mia's house instead of getting a place of her own in a nice hotel.

The rental exterior is a little creepy. It's wedged between two houses I think drug dealers could easily live inside of. Her front lawn is overgrown with weeds and is gated by a chain-link fence. The weeds pop through rocks—the owner's only use of landscaping. One of the steps on the staircase up to the front door is broken. I have to be careful as I clamber over it. And as I look through the windows to see if any lights are on in the home, I notice that some blinds on them are broken.

Looking around me, feeling uncomfortable in an area like this, I clear my throat and knock on the door.

Nora throws it open in an instant.

"Maddy!" she cries excitedly as she throws her arms around me. She nearly suffocates me with her hug and cinnamon scented perfume, and even when I try to pull away, it's clear she's not done yet. So I keep hugging her until she's ready to let go. And once I finally step back, I smell a little hint of wine on her breath. I think she has started this party without me.

"Come in, come in!" she cries.

"Cute place," I say, feeling better already. The interior looks *way* better than the exterior. The owner of this rental at least decorated the inside to the best of their ability. Cute, but probably flimsy pieces of furniture are in every room from what I can tell, and everything is very colorful and inviting.

"Thank you!" she says, like she's the one who decorated it herself. "I like it here. Kinda wish it was my house."

"Would you ever move back to Toxey?"

"No." She says it so suddenly and loudly that it nearly startles me. Then she's back to smiling bright and big. "Come on, let me pour you a glass of chard."

I go into the kitchen with her, a cute little space with the cabinets painted salmon pink and the countertops made of butcher block. The fridge is hand-painted lavender. It's all very... girly.

I take a look at the bottle of white wine on the counter and see that it's already halfway gone.

"And don't worry," Nora says when she sees me looking. "I have plenty more."

Great. She's trying to get me drunk. Trying to get me to spill my secrets.

I'm not going to let it happen.

I take my glass and we go over to the couch and start an old nineties rom-com. *Never Been Kissed*. A classic. Although, the relationship Drew Barrymore's character has with her teacher makes me think of Dean, and it kind of makes me wish I had chosen a different movie to watch.

"So, any more developments on what happened with Lyla and what's going on with Warner?" Nora asks me.

"Well I don't really know what's going on with Lyla," I say. "I'm not really filled in on her life. But Warner... everything seems to be going okay with him. I don't know. He's not exactly the best at telling me everything, either."

"Has Amelia reached out to you to try to get you to make a statement to the police or something ridiculous about how you *also* saw Carson in the woods? It would be *just* like her to try to force you to lie."

"No, I... I haven't talked to her," I say. I can feel my shoulders tensing and my palms getting sweaty. I haven't been here ten minutes and already, the lies have begun and I want to crawl out of my own skin.

I am in for a long night.

CHAPTER 35

LYLA

Upon dress shopping and suit shopping with Wrigley, I came upon a gaudy pink tulle dress with tulle off-the-shoulder long-sleeves and a tulle-covered corseted top. It reminds me so much of Glinda the Good Witch in *The Wizard of Oz*—our dance's theme is "There's no place like homecoming." So I think it's a perfect match, even though this might be the most girly dress I've ever been in in my entire life. Not only is there lots of tulle, but there's also little sequin hearts glittered about the whole thing.

Wrigley thought it would be a little too corny if he tried to match me and wasn't too keen on the idea of wearing pink, so I let him do his own thing and he decided to go with a beige ensemble: slacks and a silk button-down shirt. He even opted for no tie, but honestly, Wrigley is so hot that he can pull off any look. And during the pictures we took earlier, it was pretty undeniable how cute we looked together. The beige next to the Glinda-the-Good-Witch-pink works really well together.

"Are we ready to do this?" Wrigley asks as we sit in his car, slapping a hand on my knee. We didn't arrive at the dance with Audrey and her date because they had other plans to go with Ryan's senior friends. In fact, Audrey was picked up in a limo.

I'm not jealous though.

Okay, maybe just a little bit.

But I knew from the get-go that arriving in a limo was more than likely not Wrigley's style, even though his father is rich. It's like he has made it his goal to seem like he comes from no money at all. But he can't fool anyone here in Toxey. Especially not his classmates. We've all been to one of his house parties. We know the truth.

Still, I like that Wrigley isn't always trying to flaunt his wealth. I think it's one of his better qualities.

I'm lucky to even be getting to go to the homecoming dance with Wrigley at all.

"Did I mention how handsome you look?" I decide to tell him.

He grins from ear to ear. "And you... you're literally a princess."

He hops out of his car and scurries around the front of it so that he can open the door for me. The parking lot is full of other students arriving, and it's overwhelming to try to take in what everyone is wearing and who everyone's dates are. People say hi to Wrigley and me and we wave in return. Then, to my surprise, Wrigley even reaches out and holds my hand. I'm holding hands with Wrigley in public.

"Yo, Wrigley, the after party at your place tonight or what?" a kid in our grade asks.

"Can't, man," Wrigley replies, looking deeply disappointed about it. "Dad's home."

He and his date make noises of disappointment and then continue on their way.

"You haven't had a party in a while," I point out. "At least, compared to how often you *used* to throw them."

"Yeah, I have to lay low a little bit right now. Ever since someone broke into our house, my dad's been a little more on edge. He's talking about wanting to set up cameras and all of that. It sucks."

"Wow," I say, "Did you guys ever figure out who broke in?"

Part of me has this horrible feeling it was Carson Price. That he found out Wrigley and I have a thing and was looking for a way to ruin it somehow. And also, with his father dating Maddy...

"Oh my God!"

I snap my head and see Danielle rushing up to me.

"You look so stunning!" She hugs me tightly even though we hardly even talk anymore. She looks pretty, too, in a navy blue gown with her hair up in a bun. I am forced to push the thoughts away about who may or may not have broken into Wrigley's house.

I chat with Danielle and her date, Conner Schaeffer, for a little bit with Wrigley, and then we finally go inside the gym.

There wasn't much of a budget for the decor, so the gymnasium does look kind of bland, only *loosely* based off of *The Wizard of Oz* theme. Someone did a cut-out of the castle and taped it to the wall. There's a balloon arch full of yellow balloons and a fake yellow brick wall backdrop to pose in front of for pictures.

The music is loud, and the bass is vibrating in my chest. The only lights in the place are coming from the various strobes and disco balls hanging above. It makes it hard to see anything or anyone.

My chest tightens, but I take a deep breath and try to loosen up. It's just a school dance. Nothing is going to happen here. There are chauffeurs everywhere.

"So, what do we do first?" Wrigley asks. There are already people on the dance floor, but I don't think we're quite ready for that yet. "Take pictures? Go get punch?"

"I don't think there's *actually* punch here," I say, giggling. That seems like a thing done only in the movies.

"What?" Wrigley's shoulder sag. "How disappointing."

I roll my eyes and drag his hand over to a vacant table for us to take a seat at. "How about we just start here?"

"Here is good."

We chat with each other and mingle with some other classmates as more people arrive in the gym. I keep looking for Audrey's arrival, but either she's already out there on the dance floor somewhere with Ryan, or she's arriving late.

What I *do* find walking through the gym doors from the parking lot, however, is Jackson. My lovely ex-boyfriend.

And I can't believe who his date is. Physically, it makes my jaw drop.

"What's wrong?" Wrigley asks immediately. Then he follows my gaze. I hate that he's caught me even staring at Jackson in the first place. I shouldn't care at all about him and who he decided to bring as a date.

But his date just happens to be Sophia.

"I didn't know they were even a thing," Wrigley says with a shrug.

"Yeah," I say. "Tell me about it."

"Does that... bother you?" he asks. "Wasn't Sophia a friend of yours?"

"Once upon a time," I say. "But it's not like we're friends now. And it's not like I want anything to do with Jackson. So I don't care at all, actually."

I smile at Wrigley boldly just to show him *how* much I don't care.

Finally, Audrey and Ryan show up with some other seniors a little while later, and Audrey practically drags Wrigley and I onto the dance floor with her and Ryan. And while I had been expecting

Wrigley to not be interested the dancing part of homecoming, he gets *incredibly* into it. In fact, his moves make me, as well as others around him, giggle. It ends up being a blast having him as my dance partner.

But as we jump and jive in the middle of the crowd, I can't help the uneasy feeling I still have. I can't help that my eyes continue to wander around the gymnasium. But I don't know exactly who it is I'm searching for. What it is I am afraid to see.

When I see Jackson walking out some double doors into the hallway, something takes over me and I react without thinking.

"I'll be right back," I say suddenly. Then, so that I don't concern Wrigley or make him question anything, I smile at him and even give him a kiss on the cheek.

"Sounds good," he says, then he turns and dances with his class-mates.

I race out the doors into the hallway after Jackson.

Why am I doing this?

He's about to turn into the bathroom, so I yell his name to stop him.

He whirls around and looks surprised to see me quickly speed-walking toward him. We are the only ones in the hallway right now.

I'll admit: Jackson *does* look handsome in his full suit that matches Sophia's emerald green dress. They *do* look cute together. But it just feels all wrong. And I don't know why I'm bothered by it so much. Something is off about Jackson. And it has been for a while. And maybe I don't like Sophia much right now, but I still think she should steer clear of him.

"So, Sophia?" I ask, venom in my tone.

"What?" he asks, his tone devoid of any emotion. "It's not like you guys are friends anymore, right?"

"Right... but still..." I glare at him and shake my head.

He lifts his hand up. "What do you expect me to do?"

There's the emotion.

"I don't... I don't know," I say, crossing my arms. "There's a million other girls at this school, Jackson."

"What, you're seriously jealous?"

"Not jealous," I spit. "I'm here with Wrigley."

"Oh, the guy you cheated on me with."

"I did not cheat, Jackson," I say. "We Snapchatted. We became friends. Nothing ever happened between us. But you go ahead and believe what you want. Spread whatever lies you feel like spreading."

"Lyla." He takes two steps toward me. I don't back away. It's so weird that he's so strange to me now, when we used to be so close. "You know how unfair this is, right?"

"What are you talking about?"

"It's not fair of you to be mad at me for being here with Sophia."

"It's not? You're one to talk, Jackson. I broke up with you. So you can't be upset about who I choose to be with. I liked Warner. You know that. And you had to go and…" I don't need to finish the sentence. Jackson attacked him. Twice.

"That's different. He is my friend."

"*Was*. You guys stopped being friends a long time ago."

"Yeah. Because of you!"

This argument is pointless and it's going nowhere. "You know what, whatever." I turn to go back into the dance. But then his hand curls around my wrist, turning me back around, making my stomach lurch. Suddenly, he's only inches from me.

"I may be here with Sophia, but I'm nowhere near over you, Lyla."

His hands swiftly grip my waist, he gets even closer to me, and then he leans into kiss me.

I am quick to shove him off of me. The last time somebody I detested came that close to me, it was to put a chloroform rag over my face. Inside, I want to scream. I want to claw Jackson's eyes out. It takes all of me not to.

"What is the matter with you?!" I demand, fury raging in my veins. "You stay away from me, Jackson! I mean it!" Then, trying to not let the tears fall, I race into the girl's bathroom.

CHAPTER 36

AUDREY

When I see Warner, looking perfect and full of smiles as he stands next to Jessica Vaccari as they walk in to the gym, I am more determined than ever to show that I am unaffected by the fact that he has brought her to the dance. I am more determined than ever to prove I'm having the time of my life and to not care about anything other than the fact that I am here with the hottest senior at Blackfell High, Ryan.

In fact, I should be *thrilled* that I am Ryan's date. I hung out with him and his friends and their dates for dinner before we headed here—via *limo*—and I got to talk to some of the other senior girls, and they were all really nice to me. The ones on the cheerleading team, like Cami and Kiley, were especially eager to talk to me and treat me as if we had been friends for forever. It made me feel like I belong to a new clique. Like I am part of a new, popular crew. It's the high school dream, and I'm living it. So, I need to act like it.

"Are you having a good time?" Ryan asks me in the middle of dancing. We're probably about two hours into homecoming, and we're both sweaty from how long we've been on the dance floor.

"Yes!" I yell at him over the music. He chuckles and nods his head, and we keep dancing. When I can see over his shoulder, Warner dancing with Jessica, the two of them still all smiles, I rotate Ryan by grabbing his shoulders and moving him so that Warner is no longer in my view. Then I go back to having a good time again.

After Lyla told me that she was going with the whole Glinda the Good Witch theme for her dress, I opted for a baby blue dress that slightly resembles Dorothy. It has an asymmetrical hem and only one poofy sleeve, my other shoulder exposed. And I paired it with, of course, bright red sparkly heels. My hair is down and I've curled the pieces that frame my face. I have on a lot of bronzer and my makeup took hours.

But Ryan is the real showstopper in his baby blue suit. I feel like most other guys would not be able to pull that off, but Ryan completely rocks it.

And we look totally awesome together.

Even when Warner is no longer in my eyesight, I can't help that I'm now thinking about him again, since I had just been forced to see him. I'm thinking about Jessica again. About how I'm curious if she's the reason he turned me down. About how maybe, if she hadn't been in the picture, he would have told me he liked me back when I made my confession at *our spot*.

I try to lose myself in the music and forget about it. I raise my hands over my head and look at all of the strobe lights as I dance. I stay that way for a while, letting the bass thump powerfully in my chest, and when I finally go to lower my gaze back to Ryan, my eyes instead land on someone else.

Someone in the crowd who's not dancing. Someone just over Ryan's shoulder, a few yards away.

Someone wearing a black hoodie and a cartoonish mask.

And they're looking right at me.

All I can do is scream.

CHAPTER 37

WARNER

Jessica looks beautiful, and any guy would be lucky to be at homecoming with her. Including me. I know I'm lucky. But it's not stopping me from feeling slightly depressed still every time I look over and see what a good time Lyla seems to be having with Wrigley Hall. I can't help but think of them as an unlikely pairing. All Wrigley cares about is partying. He doesn't seem like he ever applies himself at school, and he doesn't seem like he cares to be too social or too active in anything high school related.

But maybe I'm just pointing out the fact that he is the polar opposite of me, and that's what has me so upset about it.

I also sort of just wish she would've told me she was interested in Wrigley and that is why she didn't want to be with me in the first place. It feels crummy to think that maybe she did want to be with me but just couldn't because of Jackson.

Lyla is a stunning vision in pink. She shines brighter than anybody else in the gym. The lights dancing around from the ceiling seem to mainly shine on her. Creating a tunnel vision and darkening out everybody else.

"Are you sure you're okay?" Jessica asks for probably the tenth time tonight. We're on the dance floor, and a slow song is playing, so I put my arms around Jessica's waist and we've been slowly swaying to the music. But I think maybe she's noticed that my eyes keep drifting elsewhere.

"Sorry, I'm just... nervous, I guess," I try, giving her a flirtatious smile.

She giggles slightly. "You seriously don't have to be nervous around me. I'm really happy to be here with you."

"Oh yeah?"

She nods her head nervously. "In fact, I don't know if you know this or not, but I've sort of had a major crush on you for like... a really long time now."

I did know. Jackson told me about it over and over again, and he told me how I should just go for her. And when I found out that Lyla had a date, I finally jumped on the chance. Is it really fair on my part? No. But I'm also hoping that maybe I can come to find that I like Jessica. As more than a friend. That maybe she will end up being just the distraction I needed. Like she was somebody who was right in front of me the whole time and I just missed it because I was so blinded by someone else.

"Oh..." I trail off. I have no idea what to say to that. "I—I didn't know."

She looks at me expectantly. Like she wants me to say I've had a crush on her for a long time, too. But it's just not the truth. And I feel I've already lied to her enough.

Luckily—but at the same time not really—a scream somewhere in the crowd drowns out the loud music playing, and it turns my head yet again, so I don't end up trying to come up with that lie for Jessica about how I've liked her for forever. I don't know who screamed, but as I scan the crowd of dancers, I do see something that sticks out.

A person dressed in all black. A hood over their head. A mask on their face.

My stomach lurches and I stop dancing immediately.

"What's wrong?" Jessica asks, following my gaze this time.

"Do you see that?" I ask, just to be sure I'm not going absolutely crazy.

"Oh my God, is that...?"

The figure turns away and leaves the dance floor.

"I'll be right back!" I call to Jessica, already running away from her through the crowd to follow the freak in the costume. It can't be the real Carson, can it? He wouldn't show up at school like this. Would he? It has to be an imposter. Somebody just wanting to freak us out.

The freak is still super far ahead of me, so he makes it out of the gym doors before I can reach him. I shove my way through people to try to get to him quickly enough. I burst through the gym doors out into the hallway, but when I look to my left, I see nothing. When I look to my right, I also see nothing.

Where could he have gone?

I walk a little to the right, but I don't trust my instincts. I just want to know who it was. I want to rip that stupid mask off their face and even if they were impersonating the real tormentor, I want them tossed in jail. It's not okay to mess with us like this. It's just what I had been afraid of happening now that it's close to Halloween. I knew people were going to start showing up in that same caricature cartoon mask. Just because it's getting popular on social media that that is what our tormentor wore every time we were attacked or messed with.

I turn around to go back into the gym, feeling defeated and angered, but then I jump at the sight of the figure standing suddenly so, so close to me.

It's Jackson Mullens.

"What the heck, dude?" I ask angrily. Where had he even come from?

"What's got you all spooked?" Jackson asks.

"I just..." I look over my shoulder again in hopes of seeing the masked figure. But they're not there. Does that mean...?

I turn back to Jackson. I find it all too suspicious that *he's* the one I see out here.

"What are you doing?" I demand.

"I was in the bathroom," he says condescendingly.

I don't know if I buy it.

"Are you good?" he continues when I don't say anything back.

"Why do you care?" I hate Jackson. I'm bitter. I'm sick of him attacking me over things out of my control. I can't believe we were ever best friends.

"You know what? I don't," he says.

"Okay then." I move to go past him. But he puts a hand on my shoulder and stops me, which instantly makes my blood hot.

"So," he continues, like he is wanting to have a conversation with me. "I see you finally took my advice and went for Jessica Vaccari."

"Whatever," I reply. "I see you're here with Sophia Key. What's up with that?"

"What do you mean?" he asks, his eyebrows clashing together. "I like her."

"Isn't she Lyla's friend? Doesn't it go against your rules or whatever?"

"They're not friends."

"Okay."

I go to move past him again. He squints at me as I move around him and open the gym door.

"I'll see you at practice," he says. But something in his tone seems sinister, almost. warning-like.

I don't answer him.

CHAPTER 38

AUDREY

Without any explanation to Ryan, without saying anything at all, I turn and book it out of the gymnasium. I don't go into the hall. I opt to go directly back into the parking lot outside, where the air is cold and instantly makes me start to shiver—even more than I already was at the terrifying sight I had beheld inside the school dance.

I half-sob and half-hyperventilate as I run far away from the gym doors and stand in the middle and the rows and rows of cars. There are a few students lingering around. And I know they're probably looking at me. But I don't care. I can't care. I'm too busy freaking out.

"Audrey!" a voice calls behind me, coming from the gym. I don't turn around. I know it's Ryan, and I'm already embarrassed enough as it is that this has happened.

Had I imagined who I saw in there?

Had it really been our tormenter?

Had it been someone who just felt like playing a practical joke on us?

Or maybe the mask was supposed to represent someone from The Wizard of Oz. The wizard or the scarecrow maybe. The way the dance lighting had been flickering and shimmering across everything, it did make it easier for my eyes to deceive me.

"Audrey, hey," Ryan's voice comes again behind me, closer this time. I sense that he's jogged to reach me, and when I hear his footsteps slow, I turn around to look at him finally. I probably look hysterical. I *am* hysterical.

"Th—that person," I try, "in the gym! D-did you see him?"

"Who?" he asks, closing the distance between us and putting his hands on my shoulders, rubbing them up and down my arms comfortingly. "You must be freezing out here. Are you okay? What happened in there?"

"I swear I'm not crazy," I say, trying to stop the tears and allow my breathing to slow. "But there was someone in a mask. A mask just like the one..."

I had been about to say "the one Carson wears."

But no word has been confirmed about if it really was Carson Price in those woods or not. And if I tell Ryan I, like my mother, believe Carson is the one doing this to us, would he think I *was* crazy?

"I...I didn't see them, Audrey." Ryan looks apologetic as he steps back. "But hey, you're okay, all right?"

I nod and put my hands on my hips as I focus on my breathing.

"No one is going to hurt you," he continues. He sounds genuine. It makes me want to believe it. "Not when I'm with you, okay? I won't let that happen."

"I just..." I don't even know what to say. But it's okay because he quickly wraps his arms around me and envelops me in a tight, big hug. One that I very much appreciate.

"You don't have to be brave around me, you know that, right?" he says into my hair. I pull away just enough so that I can look up at him. He has made me feel so much better already. Just with the few sentences he has said, and the fact that he's hugging me tightly right now.

"Thank you," I whisper. He wipes a stray tear from my cheek, and then in one swift motion, tucks some hair behind my ear.

I find myself leaning in, and then our lips touch.

Kissing Ryan is quick, but sweet. It sends a flit of butterflies swarming around in my stomach and gives me a head rush. And even though it doesn't last long, when we pull apart, I feel breath-less.

I just stare at him, no words coming to mind. But I'm grateful because for half of a second, I forgot all about the masked freak.

"Better yet?" Ryan asks.

"Definitely," I say, giggling slightly. I want to focus on the fact that I just kissed Ryan Copeland. I want to be over the moon with excitement and happiness. But as I stare at the trees across the street from the parking lot, I still feel this eerie sensation of somebody's eyes on me.

I'm still worried I'm being watched.

Lyla

After my conversation with Jackson, I am fuming, and I go back into the gym and try to find where Wrigley disappeared to. It's not hard to do—he hasn't moved from the spot on the dance floor where I left him. He's still dancing stupidly, my classmates throwing their heads back with laughter around him.

"Hey," I say a bit curtly when I reach him. He smiles at me and stops dancing.

"Whoa, are you okay?" he asks, apparently noticing that I have some sort of look on my face.

"I... yeah, I'm good," I tell him. "Want to go get a drink?"

"Definitely." He takes my hand in front of everyone, even the girls that had been giggling at his dance moves and leads me off the floor. We go over to the beverages and grab two mini water bottles. I chug mine until it's empty.

"So, are you having a good time?" he asks, but there's something about the tone of his voice that makes me think he suspects I'm not.

And it's true. I'm not. I feel like coming to the dance was a mistake. I am still heated about my confrontation with Jackson, and it bothers me that I'm *letting* it bother me. Who cares if he came here with Sophia? Who cares if it's unfair that he got mad at me for being with Warner? I am with Wrigley by choice.

"Do you want my honest answer?" I decide to ask. This isn't how the new old Lyla should be acting. But right now, I've forgotten that I'm doing that.

"Always, you goofball." Wrigley chuckles.

"I don't know what I was thinking when I asked you to go to the dance with me." It feels strangely relieving to finally be a little bit honest. To not be trying so hard at being the old me. But then the guilt settles in after my statement. This is what I had promised when

I was locked in the shed. And I was breaking that promise by being how I truly want to be.

He shifts uncomfortably and replaces the cap on his water bottle. He has only taken a little sip out of it. "What do you mean?" he asks cautiously.

"I'm glad I'm here with you, don't get me wrong," I say, but my stomach dips a little for some reason. "It's just that... coming to the dance had been a bad idea. I don't actually want to be here. Do you?"

"Lyla, I only came because you asked me to. Do you *think* I want to be here?"

I giggle. "No."

"So, what are we going to do about it?"

I tap a finger to my chin. "How about we ditch this stupid thing and go get some ice cream from Delilah's?"

"You've just read my mind."

CHAPTER 40

AMELIA

I'm beginning to think being left alone to my own devices isn't such a good thing. As I sit here in this house all by myself, all I can think about is how it's been a week since Lyla was rescued. Since *I* rescued her. Not the police. Me. Sure, I had the help of my daughter and Maddy and Warner, but it should've been the police who found her. They should've done a better job. They should have figured out a long time ago that Carson has been alive all this time. It would've saved me from a lot of guilt and Nora from a lot of heartbreak.

It's been a week, and it hasn't even been released to the public, except for on some blogs where people like to call me crazy, that it was Carson who kidnapped her. People are still saying they don't know who did it. They don't know who's behind it. And they're still looking for him.

Is anyone even looking? Are the police just relieved that Lyla is home safe and sound and they've decided to leave it at that?

It's not good enough for me. And it never will be. Not until Carson is caught. Not until he is locked away and put somewhere where he will never hurt my babies ever again.

Maybe it's the fact that I'm already in a bad mood about a million other things that makes me unable to think or do anything but sink even lower. Maybe the fact that I'm upset over so much going wrong in my life is what gets me off of the sofa. It's what makes me take my purse off the counter and put the strap of it over my shoulder. It's what propels me into the garage and gets me into my car. And it's what makes me drive all the way over to the police station.

I walk inside the department where unflattering fluorescent lights flood over me and make me acutely aware of how I should have probably made myself look a little bit more professional and approachable before coming in here. Thinking, *Oh well*, I walk up to the receptionist.

"Is Detective Craig Fritz in?"

"He is…" The receptionist, a woman in her early twenties who is side eyeing me, also looks over her shoulder toward where Craig's desk is. "But I think he might be a little busy at the moment."

"I'll only be a second," I say. It makes me wonder if he told her to watch out for a crazy blonde woman and to tell her that exact line.

"I understand, miss, it's just that—"

I roll my eyes, scoff, and decide to just walk right past her. I know where Craig's desk is, and I can see the top of his stupid gray-blond hair over his desktop in his cubicle.

"We need to talk," I say when I reach the opening and face his back.

He turns around in his chair. "Mia."

"Where is he, Craig?"

"What?"

"Don't look at me like that."

"Did the receptionist let you come back here?"

"It's been seven days."

"I understand. I know how to count."

"What are you doing just sitting here at your desk? Why are you not out there searching for him?"

"Searching for *who*? Who exactly do you want me to be searching for? The person who did this to Lyla, I get it. But you seem to think you have an idea as to who that is. The fact of the matter is that we have *no* idea who kidnapped Lyla. And in order to figure that out, we have to do some research that requires us to be at our computers at our desks."

"Bull."

"*Excuse* me?"

"You're not doing enough. And you know it's Carson who did this, Craig. I don't know why you keep trying to lie to yourself and to me and everyone in the public about him. Is it because you're all embarrassed that you failed to do your jobs all those years ago?"

"Mia, you can't just come in here and start talking to me like this. Not at my place of work." Craig gets to his feet.

"And you can't just deny what's right in front of you, Craig! I mean, *come* on! I know Carson was your friend in high school and you don't wanna believe it. You're like Nora. Accepting his death is easier than accepting the fact that he is alive and just didn't want to let you guys know."

"That's not it."

"Then *what* is it?" My voice is getting louder with each sentence I say to him. And his is, too.

"You need to leave." Craig looks angry.

Good.

"Not until you find him."

"What are you talking about? You're just going to stand here at my cubicle until I find Carson Price, who is *dead*, and bring him back here to you?"

"I just might."

He points a finger at me. It's close to my face. "You're being crazy, Mia. Maybe you should go home and get some sleep."

"Do *not* call me crazy!"

"Do not stand here and yell at me! Mia, get the heck out of here!"

A couple other bodies pop up over their cubicles. We draw the attention of other police officers. One of them being Officer Wilde. He quickly leaves his cubicle and walks over to where I'm standing.

"Mrs. Bailey, why don't you just come with me?"

"It's Ms. *Flynn*, actually," I snap, even though this isn't probably the time or place to announce that I am separated from my husband. I don't even think about the fact that I have officially outed it to the public. I'm just so caught up in my own feelings, in my own anger, that stuff is flying out of my mouth. "And I don't want to go anywhere with you, Officer Wilde. No offense. I like you, but you haven't been helpful, either!"

"It's time to go." Wilde's voice is deep and strong. The way he's looking at me isn't angry. It's just final. And for some reason, he is the only one I will listen to.

My shoulders sag. I shoot another glare at Craig. Then I follow Officer Wilde, where he walks me back over to the receptionist area by the door.

"You need some rest, Mia," he says to me. "You don't look well."

"What is that supposed to mean?" I ask, feeling offended. "It's not *my* fault you have poor fluorescent lighting in here."

He chuckles despite everything. "That's not what I mean. You seem tired. A little out of it, even. You've been through a great trauma. Are you getting the help that you need?"

It's the only thing he could've said to me that stops me from blurting something stupid out. I stare at him, my mouth hanging open, as I consider what he asked me.

Am I getting the help that I need?

I've spent so much time thinking that I needed to get Lyla into seeing a therapist again. That it's my daughter who needs help.

I never even considered the fact that maybe I need it, too.

CHAPTER 41

WARNER

I would have probably slept in so much later if it weren't for the fact that my phone kept blowing up, vibrating loudly on my nightstand over and over again, bright and early in the morning.

"Ugh, what?!" I finally complain loudly, after several attempts to just ignore it all and go back to sleep. Irritated, I harshly grab my iPhone and yank it off of its charger.

Then I bolt up in bed when I see just how many notifications I have.

It seems as if everyone I know has sent me a link to a video on TikTok.

My heart begins immediately pounding in my chest as I rub my eyes to make sure I am not just seeing things.

Do I even want to watch the video everyone has sent me? Something in my gut is telling me not to.

But I have to know what everyone else is seeing. I can't be the only one left in the dark about it.

Gripping my phone tightly, I go to the fist random text I see and tap on the link. My TikTok app opens, and I am taken to the page I had a feeling I would be taken to.

Toxeydramaenthusiast.

Great.

At first, I have no idea what I am looking at. All I see is a blurry massive crowd with colorful lights shining all around. When the camera clears, I realize that it's footage taken at the school dance last night.

"What is this?" I ask out loud as I squint and stare at the footage. What was I about to see?

The camera pans over the crowded dance floor. Then it pauses. The camera focuses and then zooms in on the person who had been wearing the mask.

Someone else knew that person was at the dance and this is what they decided to do about it? Record it on their phone?

"You should have called the police!" I find myself yelling. I'm yelling at the video poster, of course, but I am also yelling at myself a little bit, too. Maybe that's what I should have done, too, the moment I saw the figure in the mask. I think the reason I didn't is because I worried it was just a fake, playing a trick on us. Even then... it still would have been worth it to try, and I regret it.

The video shows how the person in the creepy mask just stands there, not dancing. It freaks me out how many of my peers are dancing around him, not even seeming to notice what's happening. Who's right next to them. How easy it would be for them to be attacked...

Suddenly, the figure whips around and starts pushing his way quickly out of the crowd. The camera zooms back out but doesn't lose sight of the person, whoever it is. Not until, a few seconds later, the camera pans over to me, instead, the camera moving from blurry to focused as it zooms in on how I am trying to shove my way through the crowd to get to him. Once I break free from everyone, I race across the wooden gym floor, and the camera follows my every move. I go out the same doors the person in the mask had gone through, and then the video ends.

"What was the point of that?" I ask angrily. I'm confused as to why so many people sent it to me, but then I quickly realize I need to read the caption of the video to better understand.

What's Warner up to? Who is he meeting with? Could he be plotting his next move?

"Oh, c'mon!" I grumble. That's what everyone is freaking out about? Because I followed the stranger into the hallway?

It was all a set up. The person in the mask *was* a fake. They knew they were being filmed. Maybe they were paid by the Toxeydramaenthusiast person. They did this on purpose. They wanted to be able to film me in a way that puts me in suspicious lighting. Like the masked figure and I are in cahoots or something.

Jessica's name pops up on my phone, and feeling nervous about what she thinks about all of this, I read her message:

Jessica: *Hey. Last night was wonderful. Thank you for asking me to go to homecoming with you. Ummm... so I saw the video going around. I just wanted to also say that I don't believe anything anyone is saying in the comments. You're a good guy, Warner. Just ignore them.*

I'm afraid to read the comments. I know I shouldn't.

I click my phone off, feeling proud of myself for being able to ignore it. I even get out of bed, stretch, and use the bathroom. But when I walk back into my room and see my phone lying face up on my bed, still vibrating and lighting up every so often like I am some sort of celebrity, I can't help but go back to the video.

Back to the comments.

"Warner?!" Mom is calling from somewhere out I the living room. "Are you awake already?"

I ignore her and read:

WHY HASN'T HE BEEN ARRESTED??
Notice how neither Bailey twin wants anything to do with him now?
I was standing right next to Audrey when she saw the guy in the mask. she FREAKED out. Someone needs to catch this person and I think the best way to do that is through Warner, who HAS to know more than he's letting on!
#Warnercarpenterisamurderer
Warner killed Sydney!
Warner didn't find Lyla, he was trying to keep Audrey from getting to her! The parents following them wasn't supposed to happen, so Warner had to improvise! He's her kidnapper!
#justiceforsydney
#justiceforlylabailey
Warner Carpenter is going to get what's coming to him.

The last one is when I finally click my phone off and toss it far, far away from me like it just burned me. It *feels* like I've been burned, anyway. Badly.

Some of these comments are from people who live in different states. Who don't know anything about me. It's like I've gone viral, in the worst way possible. I'm afraid that if I look on Twitter, I will see that *#warnercarpenterisamurderer* is trending.

I thought after Lyla was finally found, things would start to get a little better.

Apparently, they have to get much worse before that can happen.

CHAPTER 42

AUDREY

At the dance last night, Ryan and a bunch of his friends apparently came up with this plan to have them all get together at Delilah's this afternoon. Just as a normal thing they usually do on the weekends when they have no big plans. His group of friends consists of the most popular seniors at Blackfell High. They're basically all on the football or cheer team.

When they had all been talking in a group over by the beverage station in the gym, I had hovered next to Ryan awkwardly, looking over my shoulder every so often to make sure no freak in a mask was standing right behind me. I felt out of place by Ryan's side. Like I shouldn't be there. Like I was just a junior who wouldn't be joining them today and should just leave them all alone to talk.

But then one of Ryan's friends, Brandt White, nudged me with the back of his hand and gave me a smile and a head nod.

"You'll be there, right?"

I had instantly felt myself blush. So... I *was* included after all?

I looked at Ryan to see what he thought about it and saw that he was smiling at me hopefully.

"I'd love to," I said.

"Yay!" Brandt's date, Kiley squealed, grabbing my forearm and excitedly squeezing it. I giggled, astonished that she seemed eager to have me there. Usually the senior girls wanted nothing to do with the junior girls.

Or so I had thought. It was an idea Sophia had put into my head. She had probably made it all up because she enjoyed the drama and loved the idea of a rivalry.

It takes me forever to decide on a good casual-Saturday-at-Delilah's-hangout outfit, and eventually I decide on an oversized sweater, leggings, some white ankle socks, and white sneakers that are far from the white they were when I first got them because I have worn them so many times.

When Ryan picks me up, he's in Kaleb Frey's Ford Explorer, which is packed with a bunch of teens all carpooling over to Delilah's. Ryan gives me a big hug on the front porch in front of everyone, but he doesn't kiss me again like he had last night, and I am a little grateful for it. I wouldn't have wanted to have another moment like that in front of all these people.

Some of the guys in the car hollered out the window at us, and he waved them off like he didn't care if he looked whipped by me. I feel like I'm living a high school girl's dream. Like I have woken to find myself in some sort of teen movie.

I squeeze into the back seat middle row with Ryan, besides two others, and as I say hi to everyone while Kaleb starts driving, I vaguely think about how unsafe it is for none of us to be wearing our seatbelts. Then it makes me think of Trinity. I wonder if maybe the seniors just don't care about what happened to her. They don't think they could ever get in an accident. Maybe they think that, being seniors, they're invincible.

We get to Delilah's and hog two booths back-to-back. Everyone is loud and rowdy and laughing and having a good time, and no one tells us to be quiet, even the workers, who are teens at Blackfell High as well. And I have a feeling it's because it's just an unspoken rule that no one is allowed to tell the cool kids to be quiet.

As we all share desserts and gossip, I think about what a dream of mine this used to be. I suddenly have a whole new group of friends. I have a boy that might want to make me his girlfriend soon. I am hanging with a bunch of fun people at Delilah's on a Saturday, living the perfect life.

The thing is, I don't know if this is the life I want anymore. It feels like someone else's dream. Someone I used to know.

What is my dream now?

As I sit there next to Ryan, who causally has his arm slung over me, in the side of the booth that faces the window, I see movement outside. Quickly, I realize that movement is from someone familiar.

It's my aunt Nora, walking across the street.

"Hey, I'll be right back," I say quickly to Ryan, sliding out of his arms and the booth and getting to my feet.

"Taking off already, Bailey?" Chance Hobbs asks from the booth behind.

"I just… have to see something really quick." When I turn away from everyone and walk towards the exit, I feel the tips of my ears turning hot as I wonder what they're all thinking and saying about me now that I am not there.

I step outside.

"Aunt Nora!" I call to Aunt Nora's back as she walks down the sidewalk on the opposite side of the street. I begin crossing the road, not looking at traffic because I don't want to take my eyes off of her.

"Aunt Nora!" I call again, since she hasn't stopped to turn around or acknowledge me. It's a little frustrating because there's no way she can't hear me. There's no one else around, and I am not that far from her.

"Hey!" I yell, a little more aggressive than I wanted to be. It's just that I don't understand why it has to take an arm and a leg to get this woman to talk to me.

Finally, Aunt Nora turns to me. It takes her a moment to say anything, and I know it's because she is trying to determine which twin I am.

"Audrey," she finally guesses correctly. "Hello."

I'm still standing in the middle of the road. I had stopped walking in her direction when she stopped and turned to face me. I don't want to get to close.

"Hey, can we talk?" I ask as the bell on the door to Delilah's chimes behind me.

Aunt Nora scratches her head and looks over her shoulder. It's not a good sign. I can tell she wants to get away from me. What I don't understand is why.

"Please," I say, taking a step toward her. "I've been trying to get in contact with you for a while now, and I—"

"It's really not a good time right now," Aunt Nora tells me. "I have somewhere I need to be."

"It'll just take a second. Please." I continue approaching her.

"I'll give you a call or something when I have more time, Audrey, okay?"

"Why are you avoiding me?" I demand, my voice rising. I don't mean to sound rude, I am just fed up with being ignored.

"I'm—I'm not."

"Yes, you are. I just want to ask you a couple of things. It'll only take a second. C'mon, I'm your niece."

"You sure?" Aunt Nora asks, sneering at me. "Because right now you are reminding me more and more of your mother."

"And that's a bad thing how?" I snap.

Aunt Nora stands there, unmoving, and glares at me.

At her own niece.

"What is your problem with Audrey?" a voice asks as an arm goes around my shoulder protectively. I look up and see Ryan has come to the rescue. "Come on, Audrey," he tells me. "Let's get out of the middle of the road." He urges me along to the same sidewalk Nora is on, his eyes not leaving hers.

"Mind your own business, you tool," Aunt Nora says to Ryan.

"*What?*" I gasp. "You can't just call him that!"

Aunt Nora turns and starts to walk away from us.

"Aunt Nora!" I snap loudly. I want her to turn around. I want to confront her and make her demand to tell me what her issue is with me.

But she doesn't turn back. She just keeps going.

CHAPTER 43

AMELIA

I pop my meds and wait for Maddy to arrive. She asked if we could see each other this morning via text, and she had seemed concerned, which had filled me with anxiety. Did she have bad news to tell me? Had there been developments with the Carson situation? Had she seen him? Had he done something? Something to her or to Warner maybe?

Maddy rings the doorbell and then I hear her open the front door on her own.

Had I not locked it? Had it been unlocked all night long?

As I stand from the couch and wonder, I also realize I don't even remember when I went to bed last night. What had I been doing before I did go to bed?

I can't think on it for long because before I know it, Maddy is hugging me tightly.

"Did your girls have a good time at the dance last night?" she asks. "I *have* to show you pictures of Warner. He looks so freaking handsome, Mia. Like a little grown adult. I can't get over it. His last homecoming dance ever..."

"Oh." I haven't even gotten an update on how the girls' dance had gone. Not from them, anyway. I only got text updates from Gentry letting me know they had returned home to his house last night at some point, safe and sound. "Yeah, they had a blast." I lie because I don't want Maddy to think my girls don't care about me enough to want to tell me how their night went, although that's exactly how I am feeling in this moment. Maybe it's my fault. I hadn't reached out to them to even ask.

"Here." Maddy pulls her phone out and shows me a photo of Warner and his date, a girl I don't recognize.

"Cute," I say with a fake smile. I haven't received any pictures of the dresses my girls had picked out yet. The reality of it stings a little, and I turn from Maddy and go into the kitchen. "Want some tea?"

Maddy follows me and takes a seat at the big farmhouse style table. "Yeah. Uh... you okay, Mia?"

"Fine. Why?" I ask. I open a cabinet full of plates and bowls, realize I'm in the wrong cabinet, and then open the right one to get two glasses out.

"You seem quiet."

"Just tired." I get the pitcher out of the fridge and pour us each a glass. Then I get some precut lemon wedges from the fridge and drop them in.

"I haven't really been sleeping all that well, either" Maddy says as she accepts her glass from me and takes a sip. I sit at the head of the table and sip mine as well.

"No?" I ask, not surprised.

"No. Um, I guess it's hard to when he's still out there, ya know? I just keep waiting for more bad things to happen."

"*Did* something happen?" I ask.

"What do you mean?"

"Is that why you wanted to come over? You sounded like you needed to tell me something on your text..."

"Oh. That." She sets the class down carefully. "Nothing happened. Except... I did get a call from Craig Fritz."

My stomach lurches. What was Craig doing calling her?

"Really?" I ask, narrowing my eyes. "Why?"

Maddy looks uncomfortable. "He, uh, told me about how you went to him at the police station last night and screamed at him—his words. Not mine."

I roll my eyes, but I can't hide the embarrassment I feel. I would have preferred Maddy—or anyone—to not know what I did last night.

"He's full of it," I say, slightly lying. "I just went to check in on how it's going with his search for Carson, and—"

"Mia." Maddy leans over and grabs my hand firmly. Then she looks me dead in the eyes. "Are you sure, like absolutely positive, it was Carson in those woods?"

This again?

I snatch my hand away, immensely offended by her question.

"I'm sorry," Maddy says immediately. "It's just that… I've been dong a lot of thinking, and when I talked to the police—not even just Craig, I sort of—"

"Just great." I get to my feet and wander into the kitchen. "Have you been hanging with Nora again or something? Because you're sounding a lot like her right now. Or have you started seeing Craig again? Has he convinced you to somehow be on his side instead of mine?"

"Mia, I—"

"*Are* you dating him again?"

"No!" Now she is the one who looks offended.

"No? Why? Because you've been spending all your time with *Dean* instead?"

"Dean? What are you even—?"

But the words don't stop coming out of my mouth. "Is it *him* you're interested in? Did you ever stop having feelings for him after high school? Have you been hanging on to hope that you'd get back together all this time? Because newsflash, Maddy: he doesn't want to be with you. He just wants to be in Warner's life. So if you think he's trying to get closer to you, it's only to get to Warner, okay?"

Maddy stands. "Gee, thanks, Mia. I really came here hoping you would be able to clear that up for me."

"I'm just saying."

"Look, I didn't come here to be talked to like this by you. All I asked was a simple question. I don't know why you're freaking out on me all of a sudden."

"You two shouldn't be together."

"Me and Dean? Or me and Craig?"

I glare at her.

She shakes her head. "It doesn't even matter. I am not with either of them, Mia. And I don't plan on being with either of them either, okay? Despite what you may be thinking right now—that you can't trust anyone and that no one is on your side—you're wrong, okay? I just want to help you."

"You want to help me?" I bark out a sarcastic laugh. "Then help me find Carson, Maddy!"

"I'm trying!"

"No, you're not! You don't even think he's alive!"

"I never said that!"

She doesn't have to say it, though. I know it's what she's thinking.
I don't have anyone on my side.
I'm all on my own.

CHAPTER 44

MADDY

I don't sleep easily that night after my fight with Mia. It wasn't at all how I wanted our conversation to go with each other when I went over to her house yesterday. I hadn't expected her to react so defensively. So... irrationally.

In all honesty, I'm actually worried about her. I know that there was a good long time where Mia and I weren't friends, but I have known her for a long time still. And even when we weren't friends, I knew the kind of person she was because Toxey is a small town. People talk.

And Mia definitely is not acting like herself.

This whole thing with Lyla must've really messed her up.

After I spend the next morning doing some housework and paying some bills, I make sure Warner is home and that he doesn't need anything from me, and then I get in my fancy borrowed car from Steven and drive over to his house to hang out with him. When I knock on the door, I'm nervous that it's going to be his son who answers. Luckily, Steven opens it wide and gives me a big smile. Then, to my delight, he greets me with a kiss before letting me in.

I feel flustered from the kiss as we walk through the foyer into his living room. He has a bunch of snacks set out on the coffee table and Netflix loaded onto the TV. He also has my favorite type of bubbly water that's sweating slightly in the can on its coaster, letting me know that it's nice and cold.

"Well, this is incredibly thoughtful of you," I say with a smile. But my head is still elsewhere. The thoughts of my fight with Mia are still prickling their way to the front of my mind. I want to reach inside my own head and pull the portion of my brain out that has any thoughts whatsoever of Mia. Just so I can be able to fully enjoy my time with Steven.

We sit down and get comfortable: he puts his arm over me and I tuck myself into the curve of his body, fitting perfectly.

"What do you feel like watching?" he asks me.

"Anything happy," I decide.

We opt for some lame comedy. But it's lame in the way that it still makes me laugh. I've always appreciated that blatant, dry humor in movies. And I like finding that Steven has, too.

"You doing okay today?" he asks halfway through the movie. I guess I've been kind of quiet and I haven't really picked on the snacks too much. I am on my second flavored bubbly water though.

I love the stuff.

"Yeah," I reply automatically, like one does when someone on the street asks, "How are you?" but continues on walking and it's an unwritten rule that you're just supposed to say "Good, thanks."

When I look over at him, he has a thick caterpillar eyebrow arched.

I falter. "It's nothing I really wanna get into," I say. Maybe venting about Mia would feel good. But I feel sick to my stomach thinking about it. I wish I could turn back time and make it so the fight never happened. But when Craig contacted me to let me know that I needed to keep my crazy friend away from him, it frankly concerned me.

"It doesn't have anything to do with your ex, does it?" Steven asks.

I shake my head quickly. "Definitely not. Hey, where is Wrigley today?"

"Who knows where that boy goes off to? He's probably been all over town. More than likely hanging out with his homecoming date."

"Lyla?"

"Yeah. I haven't gotten to meet her yet. She seems nice."

"She's a Bailey," I feel the need to point out.

"Does that mean she's not?"

I don't know what it means. I don't know what I'm saying.

"No, she is..."

When Stephen gathers that I'm not going to finish my sentence because I don't know how, he changes the subject. "You know who else I haven't met?"

"Who?"

"Warner."

My stomach dips. "That's true." Why do I feel so panicked inside all of a sudden?

"I'd like to," he tells me. "You've met Wrigley."

"I have, but that was sorta an accident."

"What is the hesitation?"

"It's just that..." I pause to let out a prolonged sigh. "Warner and I sort of have this deal. He doesn't wanna meet any of my significant others unless it's... unless it's something super serious. And... well, I don't know what you and I are yet."

"I see." He scratches his stubbly chin. "Well, I've loaned you one of my cars. So, I like to think we're pretty serious."

"You don't give cars to all of the girls you casually date?" I joke.

He tickles me and I squeal.

"I'm serious," he says. "I want to be in a relationship with you. I want to be able to call you my girlfriend."

Girlfriend.

When was the last time I was seriously considered as that to someone?

I take in the features of his face. I smile at the piece of hair sticking out on the side of his head that he probably doesn't know about. I melt at the almost-smile he's wearing on his face as he waits for me to answer him.

"Well, okay then," I say, biting my lower lip and smiling shyly. "I'm your girlfriend."

"Which means...?"

"Which means I will talk to Warner and see when we can set up a date."

He leans over and kisses me softly on the lips again. I instantly grab the back of his neck and let the kiss sink deeper, but only for a moment. I pull away because a thought has come over me.

I'm pretty sure Steven isn't aware yet that Warner now knows who his father is.

I had told Steven, my *boyfriend*, once upon a time that I didn't know who the dad was.

So, I guess it's something, on top of the other millions of secrets I seem to be harboring from him, that I need to clear ASAP.

I just don't know how.

CHAPTER 45

AMELIA

My mood doesn't improve at all the next day. It doesn't even matter that the kids are going to be home from Gentry's tomorrow after school and that it's finally going to be my week with them. I should be happy that I'm about to have them back. But the situations I've had to deal with this week have been preventing me from feeling so.

My slap from Nora. Dean avoiding me. Then the weird confrontation I had with him that didn't lead anywhere. My conversation with Craig. And then my fight with Maddy. The fact that Carson Price is still out there somewhere and there's no saying when he's going to return to continue with his torturing of our families.

The kids were supposed to return home to me tonight, but Gentry texted me and explained that he wanted to spend his day off with the kids and that they wouldn't be home until tomorrow. It annoyed me because hasn't he had enough time with them this entire week? But then I think about how he works so much, and he probably didn't get to see them as much as he would've liked. So, I let it slide.

Besides, it gives me some more time to lock myself up in the study and continue with my... work.

But I find it hard to focus today. I feel uncomfortable in my skin; I find myself wanting to peel it off of me to see if that'll make me feel any better. Any more relaxed. If it will prevent me from doing another stupid thing.

It's too bad that I'm stuck in this skin. That leaving it isn't an easy thing to do.

Because I'm definitely going to do another stupid thing.

I've taken a shower. I've had my pills. I've had my coffee. I've even hydrated and sat out in the backyard for a little bit to get some sunshine.

I've been trying to take the steps to get myself in a better mood. To get myself more calm. To get myself to try to think more even headed.

But I am sorry to say that none of it has worked.

As I work in my study, I'm not getting anything done I want to. I'm not getting the answers I'm searching for. I'm not satisfied. And I won't be until Carson Price is behind bars. But I don't think I can figure out how to get him there on my own.

I call him. Naturally, he doesn't answer. So, I call him again. And again. And on the fourth try, he finally picks up.

"Mia, what's going on?" Dean's voice is icy. "It's really not a good time."

"Dean. Please. You started helping me figure out everything that's been going on with my family and Maddy's family. With *your* kid. We still don't know if—the police still haven't found anyone. And honestly, I don't trust them to figure it out. They're not doing a good enough job, Dean. And unless we figure out where Carson is and why he's doing this and how we can stop him, he's going to keep coming after Warner and my girls. After me and Maddy. You were willing to help me before. Can you please just help me now?"

Silence.

"Dean."

I look at the phone screen to make sure he hasn't hung up on me. He hasn't.

"Please," I whisper.

Finally, he talks. "I don't know how to help you, Mia. I don't know how to hunt down Carson—whoever did this."

"It *was* Carson."

"Even so. I... I can't help you. I promise you that the police are still out there looking for who did this. Just—you need some rest, Mia. You need some time to recuperate after the horrible situation you went through. Can you please just lay off a little? Take a break?"

"You want me to take a break when the person who kidnapped my daughter and held her in a shed for a week is still out there?"

"I know it sounds like an impossible request."

"Why would I listen to any of your requests anyway?" There's an edge to my voice. Venom. Who does he think he is asking me for this when he won't even help me with what I need?

"I'm just... I'm worried about you, okay?" he says.

"Well, that's not fair," I blurt out. "You've lost any right to be worried about me."

Again, he sighs. And I hate the sound of it.

"You know what?" I spit out, my hand shaking as it grips my phone. "Fine. I'll find him, and I will figure out what happened to Megan Young myself."

"That's literally the opposite of what I am asking you to do, Mia."

"I don't care."

"Well, I do," he says, his voice getting tighter. "C'mon, Mia. You can't just go running around searching for him and what happened to Megan Young yourself. It's not safe out there. And you... you need a break. I just—"

"Well, you won't help me. And I'm not going to rest, Dean. So don't worry. I'll figure it out. Whatever it takes."

"Mia, don't do anything reckless. It's not safe and you need to let the police just handle it."

"Not a chance."

"Promise me you'll let. The police. *Handle* it. I need you to say that, Mia. I need to hear it out of your mouth."

"Goodbye, Dean."

"Mia!"

I hang up.

Immediately, he calls me back. I ignore him.

He calls me again.

I ignore him.

This goes on and on. He calls me so many times I lose count. But I refuse to give him to what he wants.

So, I guess I'm just going to let him suffer.

LYLA

I am at school with a case of the Monday blues—even though I'm concealing it well— when my English teacher, Mr. Reeves, approaches me in the hallway. The bell for first period has not rung yet.

"Hey, Lyla," he says with his hands in his pockets. His face is downcast. I can tell something is bothering him.

"Hi, Mr. Reeves."

I think about how at one point, we considered him to be the person messing with us.

"Hey, so, this is a little unorthodox of me..." He looks around to make sure—I don't know why, actually. To make sure kids aren't listening? Other teachers aren't listening? It makes me nervous for whatever he's about to say to me. "But have you heard from your mom?"

"My mom?" I raise my eyebrows. I have my suitcase in Audrey's car, and we're planning on going to Mom's to spend the week with her after school today. But I haven't been home yet. And... I guess I haven't really talked to her, either. Not even to tell her how homecoming went.

But she didn't even ask.

"Yeah," he says, shuffling his feet slightly.

"I... I haven't. Why?"

"I'm sure it's nothing. I just had a question for her and I'm having trouble reaching her."

"Oh. Yeah, she is probably just busy at work or something."

"Right. Well, I'll see you in class."

"Is everything okay?" I ask, sensing something may be bothering him he wants to get off of his chest.

"Everything's fine, Lyla. Enjoy your morning."

I walk slowly to my locker, replaying the conversation with him in my head. Now I feel more off than I did when I first arrived at school. More uncomfortable. Concerned, even. But before long, Wrigley has approached me looking like an excited puppy dog, and I forget all about Mom for a second as I spend the morning with him.

It's only when I am left alone to myself again, in class, when I should be paying attention, where I'm thinking about Mom again. I send her a text, and she doesn't reply to it. In between classes, I try to give her a call. She doesn't answer her phone.

Each time a call goes unanswered, or text goes unreplied to, I get more worried. More nervous.

So, when lunch falls around, I march up to Audrey in the lunch-room. She is sitting at the senior table next to Ryan, giggling at something some senior cheerleaders are saying to her. Ryan has a hand on her shoulder, squeezing it in a friendly way as he talks to his buddies. Ryan is incredibly good-looking, but I guess I don't really understand the appeal of him. Why Audrey is so interested in him. He seems like a typical superficial jock.

"Audrey, can I talk to you?"

Audrey snaps her head to me, and the smile falls off of her face. And I think, *Geez, is it really so bad to talk to me?*

"Of course," she says, standing from the table and walking away from everyone. We go and stand over by the window where there are fewer people around. Outside, the air is gloomy per usual. The clouds are thick and dark, and there's a slight breeze in the air, making me wonder if a storm is coming.

"What's up, Ly?" she asks me.

"Hey, have you heard from Mom?"

"No. Why?" She looks over her shoulder, back toward the table of people she was sitting with. I wonder if she thinks getting back to them is more urgent than whatever I have to say to her right now. If she's worried that they're judging her for needing to have a conversation with her tragic sister.

"Mr. Reeves came to me today asking if I had heard from her. I told him no, but then I tried to contact her, and she hasn't been answering me. You haven't heard *anything*?"

"I'm sure it's fine, Lyla." Still, she seems distracted. And she has a giant smile on her face, like she wants everyone to think the conversation we're having is a good one.

"This is serious, Audrey," I say darkly. "I'm worried."

Finally, her brows furrow and she seems more concentrated on what I'm saying. "Wow," she mutters, crossing her arms. "This is the most normal I've seen you act since you returned home."

"What are you talking about?"

"You've been like, this perfect, smiling, happy robot. It's nice to see that you have a normal side again. I was really starting to get freaked out by it."

"Are you not hearing me?" I demand.

"I hear you, Ly." She bobs her head up and down. "I'm sure everything's fine. She's just not answering cuz she's busy working or something. There's nothing to freak out about until we know for sure. Just... wait until we get home. okay? If she's not there, and she's not at her office still, then there will be more cause for concern. But let's just wait."

I squint at her for a long while. Then I finally bite out a single, "Fine."

What other choice do I have?

CHAPTER 47

WARNER

Football practice today is going better than it has in a while. I feel focused. I am barking out all the right instructions and ideas to my teammates. Even Mr. Reeves—Dean —and I are working well together. The sight of him doesn't exactly make me want to pull my own eyeballs out of my sockets. For some reason, I'm able to handle it. We even have a decent time together, and when Dean cracks a couple of jokes, I find myself laughing at them.

It seems a lot like how it was before all of this drama started. Before I had any idea that he was my father. And before I found out he was my father; I had always liked him as a coach and a teacher.

And as practice continues, I feel more and more relaxed. Would it be crazy for me to wonder if things were finally getting back to normal—albeit slowly? Sure, the school still thinks I am some sort of killer, and that TikTok page is still very much active, and I don't know who the owner of the account is, but in other areas of my life, like my relationship with my mom and with Dean, is the air finally cooling?

When I see Jackson glaring at me as he mutters something to somebody during a water break, I change my mind.

Things are never going how they were. Never again.

In the locker room after practice, I grab all of my stuff and then start to walk out to my car. I walk with my phone out and aimlessly scroll through social media as I stroll through the parking lot, the sun setting already because it's getting later into the year, the heavy clouds in the sky making it darker than it really would be without them.

As much as I didn't want to, I eventually decided over the weekend to follow the Toxeydramaenthusiast's TikTok page. I figure it's better to just stay on top of these creepy videos regarding my life, then to be texted links to them later, the last to know.

Always the last to know.

As I walk to my Jeep, I see on my TikTok feed that there is indeed a new video posted by the account. Just the sight of their name on my screen makes my stomach roll and I freeze in my step.

"What could be Madeline Carpenter's part in all of this drama surrounding the disappearance of Lyla Bailey and the murder of Sydney Hutton?" the voice over says in the video. At first, there's only black on the screen, but then a blurry camera focuses on a woman getting out of her car and walking into a grocery store.

The woman is my mother.

She's not even doing anything suspicious. She's just going to the dang grocery store. And still, Toxeydramaenthusiast wants to post about it? Why?

I feel sick. I feel angry. For the first time since discovering this account, I find that I desperately want to get all these videos to stop. That I want to do whatever it takes to make sure it happens. The videos can involve me, sure. They can involve my friends, whatever.

But my mother needs to stay out of this.

I'll do anything to protect her.

CHAPTER 48

LYLA

It's late. I am a shaking, terrified mess when I sit in Audrey's car as we drive to the police station.

"It's okay," Audrey says to me. "Mom is going to be okay."

I sit there and continue shaking, not saying anything to her. I knew something was wrong. All day long I knew it. And Audrey told me to wait. I want to scream at her. I want to shove her. To claw at her. To tell her this is all her fault.

And poor Joey... he's in the backseat. He shouldn't even be here. He shouldn't be dealing with this.

None of us should be.

Audrey pulls into a parking spot right up front by the door to the station. I throw the car door open and leap out.

"Joey, stay in the car!" Audrey yells as she gets out after me. Her voice is severe, and I don't think Joey is going to disobey her.

I don't even think about Joey though as I dash inside through the glass doors.

"I'm here for my mom, Amelia Bailey."

Audrey is right behind me.

"Just a moment." The receptionist motions for us to have a seat. Then she gets up and walks back into the station somewhere.

Audrey goes over to a chair and sits down. I don't.

"They found her, and that's what matters the most," she says to try to be reassuring to me. I watch her glance out the window to make sure Joey is still in the car.

No, it's not! I want to scream.

Instead, I just ignore her. I wish she knew how loud I was screaming inside my head, though. Can twins tell that sort of thing?

Minutes that feel like hours go by and then the receptionist returns, and behind her is Craig Fritz, Officer Wilde, and my mother. My mother, who looks completely pale. Who has dirt smudges on her face and hands. Who is trembling, worse than I am. Who looks like she has no idea where she even is.

"Thanks for coming," Fritz says.

"Mom!" I run over and hug her. She just stands there, still trembling. I wish I could get the shaking to stop. I squeeze her harder as if that will help.

Audrey hugs her as well. But she puts her arm around me a little bit, too, and I want to shove her off of me.

This is your fault.

"What happened?" Audrey asks Fritz and Officer Wilde.

"A camper saw her in the woods," Fritz says.

"What does that mean?" I ask, stepping away from Mom and Audrey.

Saw her in the woods.

"Exactly what I'm saying," Fritz says slightly condescendingly. "They said she was babbling incoherently and shivering, and she had no jacket on... as you can tell."

I look at her again and see that she's wearing a jacket from the station. Underneath it, she seems to only have on a simple black tank top.

"How...?" I'm afraid to even ask a question. My throat is tight.

"How long was she out there?" Audrey asks for me.

"All night," Wilde says, his voice deep and grave.

"I'm fine," Mom manages to squeak out.

"Look, I didn't *want* to send you kids to come get her," Wilde explains, "but she insisted it being you two instead of her husband."

"They're separated," I say, not caring if Mom wanted it to be a secret. I don't really know who it even is that I'm mad at right now. My anger feels very displaced. I don't know where to put it. All I know is that I'm angry.

How could this have happened? What on earth was Mom doing out there?

"Is she free to go?" I ask.

"Yes. She's all yours." Wilde looks as if he doesn't think it's the best idea for us to be home alone in a house with her. But I ignore the look and I take Mom by the elbow and guide her out of the station. I open the back door and plop her into the backseat with Joey.

"Where were you?" Joey asks in a high-pitched voice as he hugs her.

"What are you doing here?" Mom snaps. Then she turns to glare at Audrey and me as we get in the front seat. "Why would you bring him?"

"What did you expect us to do?" Audrey asks. "It's our week with you, remember? Joey got on the bus and rode it back to your house. And we know you don't want him home alone anymore right now..."

"You should've... had his dad come get him or something," Mom says.

"Does Dad know about this?" I ask.

"No," she replies. "And I'd rather he didn't find out."

I cross my arms and shake my head.

"Then it's a good thing we *didn't* have Dad come get him," Audrey informs her.

"Where were you?" Joey asks again.

"I was just... I got lost. I'm okay, Joey," Mom says.

"You don't *look* okay."

Agreed.

"I am."

The car ride back to the house is silent after that.

Initially, Audrey and I freaked out when we got home and saw that Mom's phone was here. Just on the counter, abandoned. No sign of her anywhere. Her car gone. We still don't know where her car is, somewhere in the woods parked along the side of the road that we're going to have to go retrieve at some point.

It had been Officer Wilde who had called us to let us know they had our mother and that they had taken her to the police station. He didn't tell us much else besides that. I don't know what I had been expecting to have happened to Mom, but it's not this.

Something is seriously wrong with her.

I pick up her phone and see she has a million missed calls and text messages from Dean Reeves. He must have really started to freak out when he couldn't get ahold of her. Or he has something really important he needs to tell her.

While Audrey gets Mom settled on the couch and hands her a cup of water and a blanket, which replaces the police jacket she borrowed, I use Mom's password and get into her phone, and then I grab Mr. Reeves' phone number and decide to send him a text from mine:

Me: *We found my mom. She's safe, but she's in bad shape.*
Mr. Reeves: *Where is she?*

His reply was immediate.

Me: *We're here at home now.*
Mr. Reeves: *Is it all right if I come over?*

I look at mom. She's still so out of it. If Dad were here, he would take control. He'd be the man of the house. He would know what to do. So with that in mind, I reply to my English teacher:

Me: *You'd better.*

CHAPTER 49

AMELIA

When Dean gets here, which I would have preferred not to have happened, I shoo the girls and Joey upstairs so that I can talk to him alone.

I'm feeling a little better than I was when I was first found. When the camper had found me—I don't even remember what his name is—not only had the police arrived, but the paramedics checked me out, too. It was freezing in the woods last night. The paramedics asked me a bunch of questions, but I hadn't really been able to give them any answers. I was just... I don't know.

Numb. Cold.

I was out of it.

I don't know how to describe it. I don't know how to explain it.

"What are you doing, Mia?" Dean asks as he sits next to me on the sofa. He keeps his distance from me. My sectional is L-shaped, and while I am seated in front of the windows, he sits on the part that backs up to the kitchen.

"I was looking for him," I say dully, averting my gaze.

"Oh yeah?" he asks, his voice sarcastic and a little high-pitched. "Out there in the woods in the middle of the night, all by yourself? Tell me, did you find anything good?"

"Don't patronize me, Dean."

"I'm sorry," he says. Then he reaches out so that he can put a hand on my knee. "Look. I am. Seriously. I am sorry." He looks more sincere and a little bit calmer now. And when I meet his eyes, I can see that he's being genuine.

"I just wanted to get to him so badly," I say. "I just wanted to find him."

"That's not the way you go about it." He lets go of my knee. But I still feel his hand where it just had been. It's like it's burned me.

"I don't know what else to do," I say.

"You scared me to death, you know that?"

"I don't understand why."

"What do you mean?"

"You don't care about me, Dean. You don't want anything to do with me. Honestly, I don't even know what you're doing here right now. Why *are* you here? Don't you wanna be off ignoring me, trying to live out your happy fantasy with Madeline and Warner?"

"Mia, you just don't get it."

"Sure." I don't even want to bother to ask him to help me understand it. Help me make sense of it. He doesn't want to be with me and that is that.

"Have you even— have you checked your phone at all? Do you know how *badly* I wanted to get a hold of you? I hardly slept. I..." He looks away from me and shakes his head. Dean really does look miserable. It almost makes me feel guilty.

Almost.

"I forgot my phone at home," I explain.

"How convenient."

It truly had been an accident. I was so scatterbrained, and I had set my phone down so that I wouldn't have to endure Dean's continuous calling and texting me and telling me not to do something stupid. So, when I finally left my house, I simply left it on the counter.

"Dean," I say, not knowing what else there is that I can talk to him about. "I'm fine. I'm safe. I won't go anywhere. I'll try to be less stupid. You can go. Really."

"Here's what I'm gonna do instead," he deadpans. "I'm going to make you some tea. Coffee. Whatever you want. Then I'm going to go check on your kids. They are terrified, Mia. Lyla told me she's never seen you like this. So I'm going to calm them down and make sure they're okay. And then I'm going to make sure *you're* okay."

"So... you're staying?" I don't want to believe what I am hearing. It sounds too good to be true. Impossible.

Still, Dean gives me a stern nod as he gets to his feet. "I'm staying."

CHAPTER 50

Audrey

When Dean Reeves comes up to check on us a little while after talking to Mom, all of us are hanging in Joeys room. Together, we decide that maybe it's best that our grandmother, Susan, comes over and takes us for the night. It *would* be easier just to call Dad and let him know what's happened, but I know how upset Mom would be if we did that. Susan is the next best choice. Especially since Aunt Nora won't even talk to me.

When our grandmother arrives, it's getting pretty late. Yet, Dean is still at the house. He doesn't seem like he wants to leave Mom's side, and it's sweet. It makes me wonder how deep rooted his feelings for her are. If Mom feels anything for him, too.

"Well," Grandma Susan says with a sigh as we all linger around in the living room together, our bags packed. "Ready to go?"

"Yes," Joey and I say together. Lyla is too busy looking at Mom with sort of a blank expression that I don't understand. I can't help but wonder what's going through her mind. She has been pretty much dead silent all night.

"And you're sure you'll be all right?" Grandma Susan asks Mom.

"Yes," Mom mutters. I can tell she's embarrassed. I don't think she likes Grandma seeing her this way. Heck, I don't think she likes *anyone* seeing her this way.

Grandma Susan turns to Dean. "And *you're* going to make sure of that?"

"Yes," Dean says soundly.

We all hug Mom goodbye, and I notice how stiff she is in my arms. Then we all trudge outside together and clamber into the back of our grandma's Buick.

I don't remember the last time I went to Grandma Susan's house.

I don't even remember where it is. What it looks like. If she even has anywhere for us to sleep. If she's the kind of grandmother who will even have anything for us to eat. I really don't know Grandma Susan that well at all.

"Grandma Susan, can you tell me something?" I decide to ask after a few minutes of riding in silence. She doesn't even have the radio on. I wonder, if she did have it on, what kind of music would be playing. What kind of music does my grandmother like?

"Of course," Grandma Susan says.

I swallow. "I was just wondering... about Aunt Nora."

"What about her?"

"What—I, um, I'm sorry—I guess I'm just wondering what happened to her when she was a teenager. After Carson Price went missing or—or died—or whatever."

Grandma Susan drums her fingers on the steering wheel, still looking relaxed, but the expression has changed on her face, something I can see in a review mirror as she drives.

"It was a tough time for our family," she says. I'm glad she seems willing to release the information to me. I want to hear it from her. I want to know her side of the story.

I want to know the truth.

Grandma Susan continues. "Your aunt Nora, on the night of a school dance, found—or so she says—Carson Price's body in the woods. Carson was her boyfriend. Her first one. Her first relationship. And... no one ever found a body. To this day it seems that nobody really knows what the truth is of what happened to him at night. Did he die, or did he live?"

"What do you think happened?" Lyla asks.

"It doesn't matter what I think," Grandma Susan says. "Regardless, Nora fell apart. We started out just letting her stop going to school. We homeschooled her. But then, she just got worse and worse. Depression, you know. Talking nonsense, even. And so, everyone thought it was best if she went and stayed at an institution."

"That must have been horrible for her," Lyla says.

"Lyla," I scold her for judging her grandparents' choices.

"No, it's okay," Grandma Susan says. "It was horrible for everyone. But especially for her. You know... I don't know how much your mother has told you, but your great grandmother Patty, well... she suffered from depression and... other...mental illnesses... as well. And one of the main reasons your grandfather and I wanted to put Nora in the institution was because... well, because we were worried that she passed down those genes to Nora. Grandma Patty needed help in an institution as well. And so it's what helped us make the decision to take Nora to the same."

"So, craziness runs in your family?" Joey asks in the middle of Lyla and me. No one opted to sit in the front seat with Grandma Susan, and now that I think about it, I'm not exactly sure why. Maybe all of us are afraid to be too close to her since we hardly know her. We are all just more comfortable being next to each other. Maybe we want to be close after what we just dealt with.

"Joey," I say, "just because some members of our family have mental illnesses does not make them crazy."

"Does Mia have a mental illness then? Is that why she got lost in the woods?" he asks. I notice how Joey always switches between wanting to call Amelia "Mia" or "Mom." His mood is what sways which version of her to go with.

"I..." I trail off.

What do I say to that? In all actuality, I have the same question Joey does.

What if everyone spent so much time worrying that Nora had gotten our crazy great grandmother's genes that in reality, it had been passed down to our own mother instead?

CHAPTER 51

Maddy

Steven is going to be leaving for out of town again soon, so I want to soak up as much time with him as possible. I make sure over and over again that it's okay with Warner that I leave again this evening, and then I drive over to Steven's house. I have to pick a day for Warner and Steven to finally meet. I haven't even asked Warner yet if that is something he would be open to doing. It's just hard because I've spent so much time getting Warner back on my side. Back to liking me. Or at least not ignoring me all day long and looking at me like he wished I would fall off the face of the earth. So, I'm afraid to ask him because I don't want anything to happen to where I have suddenly pushed him into a corner and he's back to how he was acting before.

Thankfully though, this time when I go to Steven, he doesn't bring it up. I can tell that he's probably waiting for me to bring it up first. To tell him, "Hey, by the way, I was thinking *this* date would work perfectly for you to come have dinner over at our house and meet my son."

But it is not going to happen. If he ignores it, then I am going to ignore it, too. If he really wants to meet Warner, he's going to have to push me into doing it.

We're doing the same thing we did the last time I was here. Wrigley isn't home again. It seems a lot to me like he doesn't really care to be home when I'm here. But it also makes me wonder if he just doesn't care to be home with his dad is. Maybe he is *never* home. What do I know? I've only met him a couple of times.

All of the lights in the house are off except for a small lamp over on the kitchen island and some candles lit on the end table next to the sofa. There is the glow from the TV, too, of course. But other than that, everything in his massive mansion is pitch black. To the left of the TV there's a long hallway, and someone could easily be standing in it, watching us, and I wouldn't even know.

I wince at the thought and try to push it away.

Besides, what am I doing being afraid, anyway? We're watching another comedy. Steven has his arm around me. We're both sharing a blanket. There is a massive cheesecake on the coffee table in front of us, but we're both nearly too stuffed to eat it because of the magnificent steak dinner he cooked before we started the movie.

There's nothing scary about this atmosphere. I'm safe here with Steven, in his arms. I need to chill.

And just when I try to listen to myself, that's when a shrill loud noise makes me cover my ears and jump away from him.

"What is that?!" I yell over the noise. It's still going off. An alarm of sorts.

I don't feel any better when Steven looks distressed. When his eyes get big, and he looks behind the couch and all around the room. "I had cameras and a security system installed. You stay here, okay?"

"Steven," I try. I reach for his hand so that he doesn't leave me, but I only manage to grip the tips of his fingers and miss as he leaves me there on the sofa, alone, while the alarm continues to blare.

The masked figure, Carson, whoever it is, had warned Steven to stay far away from me.

And Steven hadn't listened.

And now an alarm is going off.

My blood runs cold. The hairs on the back of my neck stand up. I'm very aware of how alone I am in the middle of Steven's massive house.

He's back.

That has to be what this is.

"Steven!" I call, realizing I hate that I don't know where he is and what's happening to him. I get myself off of the sofa, my adrenaline the only thing moving me along. "Steven!" I scream louder. I hate this. What if Carson has attacked him? What if Carson does *worse* than just attack him?

If it is Carson, and he wants his revenge because of what we did to him all those years ago, who's say he won't kill my boyfriend?

"Oh God," I whisper, trying to figure out which direction Steven went.

I take a right into the dark hallway on a whim, and I slam into something bulky, solid, yet soft on the exterior.

A person.

I scream.

"It just me, just me!" Steven's voice says. I grip his shirt tightly and bury my head in his chest.

"What's happening?!"

He only has one arm around me. I look up and see it's because he's using the other one to punch something in on the pad on the security tablet mounted to the wall. The alarm stops.

"Just stay with me," he says. "The police are on their way."

The police arrive in record time. Steven gets me seated on the couch while two officers I don't know search the place. Steven goes with them. I don't like that I've been left alone again, but I suppose I should feel safe since the police and Steven are all here. No one will try anything with all of that around to protect me, would they?

Eventually, the police officers and Steven return to the living room where I am picking at my cuticles nervously. I get to my feet when I see them.

"So, what happened?" I ask. I feel freezing. But I also feel too afraid to move my body enough to pick up the blanket and put it around myself.

"I can't find anything," one of the officers says. "It happens some-times, but I think the alarm malfunctioned or an animal triggered it. There's no one here."

Steven walks over to me and hugs me to his side. I know he's trying to calm me down, but it's not exactly working. "Are you sure?" I ask the officers.

"We're pretty positive," one of them says. "We've checked every-where. Steven can confirm that."

"It was just a false alarm, Mads," he says into my hair.

"Oh... okay."

It takes another ten minutes or so for the officers to finally leave me and Steven to ourselves again.

"Steven, I need to tell you something," I say. I don't know why I suddenly feel that now is the time. I have this need to be honest with him. But the thing I need to be most honest about is difficult for me. So maybe that's why am choosing *this* honest truth instead. "I lied to you when I said I don't know who Warner's father is."

"What?" Steven looks completely confused. I don't blame him. This isn't exactly an opportune time to bring it up.

"I... I should've been honest with you before. But I was keeping it a secret, not only from you, from everyone I could. For Warner."

"Oh... kay..." He waits.

"Um." I tuck some hair behind my ear. "His father is actually one of the teachers at Blackfell High School. His name is Dean Reeves."

"Dean Reeves. The English teacher?"

"That's the one."

"Wrigley has him."

"Yeah. I know."

"And... you said you were trying to keep it a secret from everyone..."

"Even Warner," I admit. I feel so ashamed. "But you have to understand Steven, I was only doing it to protect him."

I expect Steven to get mad at me. I shouldn't have lied to him. I shouldn't lie to my own kid.

So, I'm surprised when, instead of lashing out and telling me to leave, he cups my face with his large hand and caresses my cheek with his thumb. "I get why you didn't tell him," he says. "It's okay."

"You're... you're not mad at me?"

"At you? Impossible."

I can't even believe it. He's not mad at me. He's being understanding. *Comforting*, even. Like he knows it had been a hard decision for me to make. Like he understands why I would want to keep Warner's father's identity a secret from him for most of his life.

Well, Steven, you're the only one in the whole universe who seems to understand.

What on earth did I do to deserve a guy like him?

CHAPTER 52

AMELIA

When I walk down the hallway the next morning, I see a figure standing in the kitchen and I scream at the top of my lungs and drop my phone.

"Geez, Amelia, it's just me!" Gentry sticks his hands up in surrender.

"What the heck is the matter with you?" I snap, bending over to pick up my phone.

Cracked screen.

Great.

"I'm sorry, you haven't changed the locks yet."

"That doesn't mean you can just come in here whenever you feel like!"

"I know, I know, I'm sorry," he says. "But we have bigger problems than me deciding that I wanna come in here unannounced."

"What are you talking about?" I'm in my robe. I look like death. I pull it tighter around myself and walk barefoot toward Gentry. I let the kitchen island separate us and stand by the barstools as he stands on the other side.

"What happened last night?" he asks. He looks angry. Which means he knows what happened. Which means him asking me this is basically pointless. Because he found out. He found out even though I didn't want him to.

"Nothing," I say, looking up at the ceiling. "Everything is fine. I am fine. The kids are fine. Seriously, I cannot believe you came all the way over here."

"You can't? Really? You *can't*, Mia?"

"No, I *can't*," I whisper-hiss. I don't know why I don't just full-blown yell at him. It's not like there's anyone else in the house.

"You think having your mother take the kids for the night means everything is *fine*?" He's only getting angrier as we speak. "Your mother, who they hardly know? Whose house we haven't been in in years and don't know the state of? *You* never even like going over there. And yet you sent them, instead of just letting me know." He grips the countertop. His knuckles are white.

"My mother was happy to do it. It's not like she lives in some sort of toxic waste zone. Chill out, will you?" I'm exhausted from the long morning I've already had, even though I just woke up, and I sit down on the barstool and rest my elbows on top of the counter.

"No, I will not chill out," Gentry snaps. "Are you out of your mind?"

"Don't. Ask me that!"

"Why? Because it seems like you are!"

"I'm not!" I slap my palms on top of the counter loudly. Enough so that it stings my hands. But I welcome the pain.

"That's a load of crap," he spits. "Do you wanna know the main reason I came over here this morning?"

"Please. Enlighten me." I roll my eyes.

"I came over here to tell you that after that little stupid stunt you pulled last night, there's no *way* that you're going to get Joey. You know that, right? No way, Amelia. And... and I'm going to get the kids from your mother and they're staying with me another week. And don't even try to fight me on it, got it? They shouldn't be around you right now, and you and I both know it."

He has stunned me into silence.

Joey. My kids. Taken away from me. For a whole other week.

Maybe even more for Joey.

Joey?

Never get to see him again?

Joey, under custody of Gentry? Of Gentry instead of me?

"Say something so that I know you're understanding me clearly," Gentry demands. His voice is dark. Scary, even.

"You... you can't..." I'm barely even whispering.

"What was that?" he asks, leaning over the counter, getting closer to me. I don't like it.

"I..."

"Tell me you understand. Now!"

"Fine," I gasp out.

He stands there, his reddened face still too close for comfort, and nods his head a couple of times, his long hair making him look slightly crazed in the current state he is in. "That's what I thought."

CHAPTER 53

AUDREY

I wake up early at Grandma Susan's, much earlier than I normally ever wake up, to my phone ringing. It's Dad calling.

"Hello?" I ask, my voice thick and groggy with sleep.

"Audrey?" Dad asks. "Put me on speaker and get your sister and your brother."

He has a tone in his voice. A tone that lets me know better than to even ask him questions.

Lyla, Joey, and I had a sleepover in the living room at Grandma's. She dug out an old dusty air mattress from the closet and some bedding and quilts and we made ourselves comfortable. Lyla and I slept on the air mattress and Joey slept on the couch behind us. The TV is still on from when we watched a movie last night. It's the only source of light in the room because it's still dark outside since it's that. Freaking. Early.

I shake Joey and Lyla awake. They look at me with concern and confusion.

"Dad's on the phone," I say, putting him on speaker.

"Dad?" Lyla asks. "Why?"

"Hey, Dad," Joey says groggily.

"I'm coming to get you guys. And I'm bringing you back to my house. Understood?"

"Wait, why?" I ask.

"Mom needs some alone time right now. It's not a good week for you guys to be staying with her. You'll spend another week with me."

"How did you... Who even..." I'm afraid to ask him how he found out where we were and what happened. Because that would imply that we had purposely been trying to keep it a secret from him. And I don't like keeping secrets from my parents. It's already stressful enough that I have to keep the secret about Carson Price's supposed father from Mom.

"Your brother texted me, terrified, late last night, and I woke up to find it," Dad explains to me.

I shoot Joey a look.

"I wanted him to know," Joey says quietly. "I didn't want to stay here last night."

I don't exactly blame him. Grandma Susan's house is old. Grandpa David hardly talked to us. It's as if he had completely forgotten that he had children once, and he has no idea how to coexist with them now. It makes me wonder if he ever even leaves this old, creaky house anymore.

"I'm sorry I didn't see your message sooner, buddy," I hear Dad say.

"S'okay," Joey replies.

"Why didn't you?" Lyla asks. "Are you with your girlfriend or something?" Her tone is harmless. But I know she's trying to cause him pain and frustration. Trying to make him feel bad.

"No. I was asleep," Dad says.

None of us say anything.

So he continues. "Anyway. I'm on my way to your grandmother's house. Get everything together and let her know, cuz I'm going to be there soon."

He hangs up without even saying goodbye. That's how I know Dad is *extremely* angry.

"Why did you have to go and do that, Joey?" I snap. "Mom didn't want him to know!"

"It didn't seem right to not tell him!" Joey complains. "I was scared last night, okay? I've never seen her like that before, have you?"

"It doesn't matter. It wasn't your place to rat her out like that!"

"Well, somebody needed to!"

"Can you guys knock it off?" Lyla barks.

"Do *you* think he should've called him and told him?" I ask Lyla. I just want her to be on my side.

"It doesn't matter. Both of you shut up."

Her harshness stings a little. It brings me the realization that she is still mad at me. Mad at me for telling her we didn't need to be worried about Mom yesterday when we definitely should have been.

"Ly, I'm sorry, okay?" I try.

"What?" She squints her eyes and shakes her head quickly. "It's... That's not even... Just shut up."

I open my mouth to tell her not to talk to me like that, but I quickly decide against it. Maybe I deserve it. Maybe this is all my fault.

Maybe everything always is.

CHAPTER 54

LYLA

om is losing it.

Audrey and Joey need to get it together. I'm not their mother—not that *their* mother is doing a good job at keeping them from fighting each other either. But I'm already stressed out enough without me trying to constantly break up the two of them bickering with each other about what we did. Yes, what we did was messed up, but there's no changing it. There's no taking it back. What happened happened, and we just have to deal with it now. Mom went a little crazy and Dad knows about it.

I'm sitting in class now, pretending like everything is fine. Pretending like I'm paying the slightest bit of attention to what my teacher is saying to me. To the rest of the class. But it's not the truth. It's all an act. It always is with me these days.

Instead, I'm thinking about this morning. I'm thinking about the car ride after Dad came to Grandma Susan's to pick us up. How silent and uncomfortable it felt. How I pretended like it wasn't uncomfortable at all. How I even offered to sit in the front seat next to Dad. Dad, who gripped the steering wheel so hard. Who had his jaw clenched so tight. Whose eyes didn't look anywhere except straight-ahead the entire drive back to his house. And I was too terrified to speak. To ask him what he was thinking about.

And as I sat there, trying to have a pleasant presence in Dad's car, no one's noticed that I was digging my nails so hard into my underside of my forearm—when I finally pulled them away when Dad turned into his driveway, I had drawn blood. Literal blood. It hurt a little, but almost in a good way. It gave me something else to focus on. Something besides how horrible everything else in my life seemed.

In class, I peek again at the bloody nail marks on my forearm that have now dried up, then I pull my sleeve down and try to remember that I should probably keep them covered so that nobody else sees it.

That's when my phone buzzes.

Making sure my teacher is paying zero attention to me, I sneak my phone out and hide it under my desk so I can see what was sent to me.

I don't recognize the phone number. It's not even our area code. But in the text message, there is a video that is begging for me to press play on it.

Do I really want to?

It could be him. The person who kidnapped me. Carson. Whoever.

I can't open the video in the middle of class. But I have this ache inside of me. This pull in my stomach nearly ripping through my skin that's telling me to get out of the classroom and go somewhere where I can watch it.

So silently, I get up from my seat and I walk over to the bathroom pass. Without asking, I grab it off the hook and wordlessly slip out.

It's echo-ey here in the hallway, which will make the video play too loudly if I watch it with sound on, so I dive into the girl's bathroom and shut myself in a stall even though it's empty in here. As I am pulling my phone out again so that I can finally watch whatever was sent to me, another message appears up underneath the video. This one has words in it:

I can hurt anyone you care about. Anytime. Anywhere.

My chest constricts. My face flushes. My blood goes cold.

I press play.

It's Wrigley's car. The back of it. The video was taken from somebody else's car, through their windshield. The footage shows that they're following Wrigley. Then it skips to another scene: Wrigley walking up the school steps. The video looks like it's taken from the school's parking lot. And while there are so many other kids about on campus, the video is zoomed in and only focused on the back of Wrigley's curly haired head.

Then it skips to another scene. Wrigley, walking on his own, somewhere I don't recognize. But he's all alone, that much is clear. And he doesn't know that someone is following him. In this scene, it looks as if his stalker is simply just walking behind him, a few feet back.

I read the message again:

I can hurt anyone you care about. Anytime. Anywhere.

I don't know if it's a threat or a promise.

I look over my head repeatedly as I walk to where I asked Wrigley to meet me after school. I don't see anyone anywhere who looks like they're filming. No suspicious cars with suspicious people poking their eyes out of their slightly unrolled, tinted window.

I climb into the passenger seat of Wrigley's Honda. Wrigley is already there in the driver's seat. He gives me a smile, but it's tight. Forced. Granted, nobody exactly likes getting a text that says, "We need to talk."

"Hey," I say softly, feeling the urge to dig my nails into my skin again. I hate this. I feel like an idiot. I don't know what I was thinking starting anything up with Wrigley in the first place. I know how dangerous my tormentor is. I experienced it firsthand. Inside that shed. And what? Just because I like a boy, I am willing to risk the same thing happening to him?

No.

"What's going on, Ly?" he asks. He looks relaxed in his seat, but I think it's an act. An act just like the one I'm always trying to put on.

I sigh. And he tenses.

"Look, Wrigley..."

"What is going on? What is happening right now?"

He knows. He has to know.

Still, I try and get the words out. "Um... I really like you, okay? But I just think..."

"Lyla, what are you doing?"

He's squinting at me. Challenging me. He doesn't look mad, exactly. Just defiant.

My chest constricts. My veins close up. I feel lightheaded.

What *am* I doing?

"I don't think you and I are really such a good idea after all." There. I said it.

"Yes, we are," he replies. It's simple. Direct. And it sounds true. He sounds more honest than what I told him did.

"Wrigley," I try.

"Lyla," he deadpans. His gaze burns into mine.

We're silent for a while.

I sigh yet again.

"I don't know why you're doing this," he says before I can say what I was about to. "I'm not letting you go. I won't. I can't. I'm not kidding, Lyla. I—you like me, don't you?"

"Yeah, that's why I said I did..."

"Then ending it is stupid. Because I like you, too."

"But there's somebody after me!" I'm exasperated. I just want to keep him safe. Why does he have to be so stubborn about it? "Don't you get that? They want to ruin my *life*, Wrigley."

He begins driving.

"Where are we going?" I ask, falling back into my seat. I had planned on just getting this conversation over with and then hopping out of his car and then maybe running home in tears. I don't really know.

"The park," he says.

We drive in silence. And when he reaches out and holds my hand, I let him. It's impossible not to.

We pull into the small parking lot of a park in one of the neighborhoods near school, and he hops out quickly. I have no choice but to follow him.

"Why are we here?" I ask.

"You need some fresh air. It'll help you think better."

I roll my eyes. Still, he walks over to a patch of grass surrounded by trees, and I watch as he flops down on his back.

I stand there, not wanting to join. I have to break up with him. I have to end it with him. It's for his own protection.

He looks up at me with squinty eyes because surprisingly, the sun is out today. I stand over him so that I cast a shadow and he doesn't have to squint anymore.

"Come on," he says, patting the grass next to him.

"Wrigley. I really can't."

He lets out a frustrated sound and sits up. "What happened?"

"What do you mean?"

"What happened between homecoming and now? Who said something? Who did something? You have to tell me, Lyla. You can't just keep me in the dark."

Do I show him the video? Whoever sent it didn't exactly tell me what the repercussions would be if I did...

Scared to do it, I take my phone out anyway and go to the video.

Then I show it to him.

I stand there frozen as he watches the video. As he reads the text message underneath it.

"Does it make sense now?" I ask when he finally looks up from the screen.

He reaches a hand up. I know I'm supposed to take it, but I'm hesitant.

"Come on," he urges. I take it. He pulls me down and I sit next to him. Our knees touch. We sit crisscross. He clicks my phone screen off and hands it back to me. I set it on the grass.

"Lyla," Wrigley says, seeming as if he's searching for the right words. Searching for a solution. He picks at some dying pieces of grass.

I grip both of my knees and wait.

"I—it doesn't change anything," he finally says. "I'm not going anywhere. Whoever is doing this, Carson or whoever, it's messed up. They want to isolate you. They want you completely alone so that you're an easier target. I'm not gonna let this freak scare me, okay?"

"But, when somebody broke into your house, I sort of think that—"

"It doesn't matter. I'm not going anywhere. You can try to break up with me all you want. But I'll only leave when your reason is because you simply don't have feelings for me."

My head is screaming to say it to him. *I don't have feelings for you! I don't like you! You repulse me!* But it's all lies. And I don't want to lie to Wrigley. I physically can't bring myself to do it.

Does that make me a coward? Does that mean I'm willing to risk something happening to him?

Instead of saying anything back, I collapse and fall into him. He holds me as I lean against his chest. We lay back in the grass. He strokes my arm. He seems more relaxed now. As if he can tell that I've caved. That I am not breaking up with him after all.

"I'm right here, Lyla, okay?" he breathes in to my hair. "I'm not going anywhere."

And even though I'm scared, I'm glad he's said it.

CHAPTER 55

WARNER

I'm trying to have a lovely, casual, fun, *normal* date with Jessica Vaccari at Delilah's after school when the bell to the ice cream parlor chimes and in walks Freaky Fritz in full uniform, looking tired and strung out.

I hunch my shoulders and keep my gaze lowered. Maybe he won't recognize me.

"Are you good?" Jessica asks across from me. Her back is to Delilah's entrance, so she hasn't seen him come in.

"Yeah. Totally," I say, trying to throw her a smile. She smiles back and takes another bite of the banana split that we've decided to share.

I like Jessica. It's easy to be with her. She's sweet. She laughs at my stupid jokes. There's nothing complicated about our relationship. It's a good thing I'm with her and not... someone else.

"Whatever you say," she says, rolling her eyes as she puts her spoon down. "You seem all... squirrely all of a sudden, though."

Jessica is also always blunt and direct. It's a quality I admire.

I'm about to relax and sit up straight, but then Freaky Fritz stops right in front of our booth. He has a smile plastered to his face, like it's his lucky day.

"How can I help you, Detective?" I ask in my best formal voice. He's spotted me, clearly, so I sit up as straight as I can now, wanting to look brave and unaffected by the fact that he's here to undoubtedly torture me. It's one of his favorite past times.

"On a little date here, Mr. Carpenter?" Fritz asks, his hands on his hips. He looks at Jessica and smiles headily at her. "What's your name?"

"Uh, Jessica Vaccari."

"Vaccari. I know your parents. Good people."

She nods slowly, like she could care less. She's making it very clear with her expression that she doesn't understand why Fritz is talking to us and that she wants him to leave us alone.

It makes me like her a little bit more.

"Did you need something?" I ask, my voice devoid of any emotion.

"Just checking in," Fritz tells me. "How is your mom?"

Why would he ask me that?

I instantly think back to the video. The video that had her in it. And the way Freaky Fritz is looking at me...

Is he Toxeydramaenthusiast?

"Why would you ask me that?" I challenge.

Craig rolls his eyes, looking playful. "Oh, come on. We used to date. I'm just checking in. You don't have to act so... worried."

I side-glance at Jessica, who is not even looking at me because she's too busy giving Detective Fritz a dirty look. She doesn't like him already. And I like that she doesn't.

"She's... she's fine," I say. "Yeah. Fine. So if you don't have any other questions..."

"You know," Fritz says abruptly, quickly switching his gaze back over to Jessica. "I'd stay away from this one if I were you." He points a finger at me and wiggles his eyebrows. "He's nothing but trouble. A harborer of secrets. Dark ones. Scary ones. He's dangerous, you know. I don't think your parents would be too thrilled about the idea of you guys together."

And I have officially heard enough.

I get up from the booth and storm out of Delilah's. Freaky Fritz is out to ruin my life. Why would Jessica want anything to do with me after that? After the threat of Freaky Fritz going to her parents and letting them know all about how I'm all wrong for her? It's pointless. Why did I even try to move on from Lyla? Why am I even bothering to try and find a girl for myself anyway? I need to just give up until I can move out of this crappy town and start new, somewhere where nobody knows my name. Nobody knows my background. Nobody knows what I've been through.

I don't make it very far before I hear Jessica's melodic voice calling, "Warner!"

I keep walking. I'm just worried she's only chasing after me to tell me that Fritz is right and that we need to just be friends. I don't want to hear it. I'm sick of hearing that.

Just friends.

The title I'm doomed to have the rest of my life.

"Warner, wait!"

I can't ignore it anymore, especially since I can hear that Jessica has started running now. I stop on the sidewalk and turn around to her. I look over her shoulder toward Delilah's and see that Craig hasn't followed her out. That's good at least.

She stops in front of me, her brows furrowed. Her long, curly hair is blowing back in the breeze. The sun is slowly setting behind her, casting a glow. She's luminescent.

"Why did you run out like that?" she asks me.

"You heard him," I say dejectedly. "He's...he's right. I don't know what you're doing with me. I'm sorry for wasting your time."

Suddenly, her hand is on my shoulder. She clutches it tightly. "Warner. That cop back there? I'm not worried about him. Besides. My parents already know I've been hanging out with you, and they're okay with it. Seriously. I've already told you before: I'm not buying into all that crap about you. I know you're a good guy. We've gone to school together our whole lives. You haven't done anything wrong. Despite what everyone keeps trying to put out there."

"Are you sure about that?"

Her other hand goes on my other shoulder. She shakes me a little. "*Yes,*" she groans crabbily. "Stop letting people try to ruin this for us. I like you, Warner. Like... a lot."

I can't help the slight grin that forms on my face. Even after all of that, even after the threat Fritz made to tell her parents, Jessica doesn't care.

She likes me.

I still almost sort of don't want to believe her—not until I see that she's started to lean in. That her eyes are fluttering closed. That the distance between us is getting smaller.

I'm the one who closes the gap.

And Jessica and I kiss.

I am in a daze when I get home and close the front door behind me. I'm thinking about Jessica. About our kiss. About how I liked it way more than I thought I would like kissing her. Not just because I've been so hung up on Lyla, but I guess I hadn't ever even really thought about kissing Jessica before. Not until it happened.

And I want it to happen again.

"Hi, Warner."

"GAH!" I yelp out, startled. "Mom!" I hadn't had any idea she was standing right there in the kitchen staring at me. Too much in my own world. Too much in my head about Jessica. About that kiss. About those full lips of hers.

"Sorry. I thought you saw me," Mom says.

"Yeah well... I didn't." My voice is a little snappy. I hate being startled like that. And I hate that she just caught me with whatever stupid expression must've been on my face as I thought about kissing Jessica.

"You okay?" she asks, her voice thick with concern. "You seem upset."

So maybe she didn't notice the dumb look on my face. Thank God.

"Yeah, I'm good. Sorry." I try to lessen the annoyance in my tone. Mom and I are getting along these days. I sort of want to keep it that way.

"You sure? Because I have to talk to you about something, and I don't want to talk to you about it now if you're already in a bad mood."

I throw my head back, look up at the ceiling, and groan aloud. "What *now*?"

"Oh, *so* dramatic," she says. Even though I'm not looking at her, I know she's rolling her eyes. "It's not that big of a deal. We just... we have dinner plans."

"Who is 'we?'" I look at her now and see that she is biting her lower lip nervously.

"Me and you..." she starts.

"I am sensing another 'and' in there..."

"Right. Me and you... and Steven and Wrigley Hall."

My eyes widen. "Oh. *Those* kind of dinner plans." The "meet the boyfriend" dinner plans. That means Mom is serious about Steven. Because she knows our rule.

But that means having dinner with Wrigley. Whom I don't like.

But I want to be supportive of Mom. Even if it's hard. Even if I hate her boyfriend's offspring.

"Great," I say. "Sounds like a fantastic evening."

"Watch the sarcasm."

"Sorry."

"Steven really wants to meet you, Warner. And I want you to meet him, too."

"Sure, sure." It will be weird going to dinner at Wrigley Hall's. I've only ever been inside that house to go to one of his massive parties. What will it be like without all of the loud, happy, teenagers inside of it?

"And... you should know," Mom continues. *What else?* "Wrigley is going to have a date at the dinner."

"A date?" I don't know why I ask it so stupidly.

"Yeah..." she trails off. I think it's because she knows that I already know who his date is. It's obvious.

Lyla is going to be there. She's Wrigley's date.

CHAPTER 56

LYLA

I am at Wrigley's, having gotten the okay from Dad to be here, and we're hanging out in his game room. We've already played a few rounds of air hockey, and I'm a little sweaty and out of breath from doing so. I tried really hard to win. But out of the four games, I only won once.

"So you're giving up, then, right?" Wrigley asks with a chuckle from the other side of the air hockey table.

"I just need a break," I say, panting. He doesn't even sound out of breath. It had been effortless for him to beat me. "It's not fair. You're the one who owns this table. You probably play it all the time."

"With who?" he asks. "Dad?" Then he barks out a sarcastic laugh. We walk over to a pub table and sit on the barstools. He fiddles with the air hockey puck in his hand. "You know, I'm thinking about throwing a party soon. Dad is going to be headed out of town again."

"A party?"

He cocks an eyebrow. "Yeah. You know. Those things where our peers come over and trash my house. Where people break up and get together and there's a bunch of gossip. Where all the *stuff* happens."

But Wrigley hasn't thrown any parties since we started our... whatever this is that you call our relationship. It's strange to be on the other side of it. On the side where he's planning on throwing one.

"Why *do* you have parties?" I ask carefully.

"What do you mean?"

"I mean... you don't even seem like you *like* most of the kids at our school. Why have them come here? Why risk your dad catching you?"

He shrugs. But that's when it hits me. Maybe Wrigley *wants* his dad to catch him. Maybe he has these parties in *spite* of his dad. Maybe it's his way of getting back at him for always being gone.

My heart saddens for him.

"You know what, it sounds fun," I say quickly. I don't want to make him talk about something he isn't ready to.

But the thing is... the way Wrigley's looking at me now... I sort of wonder if maybe he *does* want to talk to me about it. About his poor relationship with his father. He opens his mouth, and it looks like he's going to say something, but then all of a sudden, a head pops into the room.

"There you are, Wrigley." It's his dad. Steven pauses when he notices that I am in here with him. "Oh. I didn't know you had company over."

"Is that okay?" Wrigley asks.

"Yeah..." Steven scratches the back of his head. He's a very handsome man. I totally see where Wrigley get his good looks from, and why Maddy wants to date him. He's datable even without all the money.

Wrigley is, too.

"It's just that... Maddy is sorta coming over for dinner. With Warner. So I can meet him," Steven slowly explains.

"It's cool," Wrigley says with a casual shrug. "Lyla and I will just stay in here."

"No, you won't," Steven deadpans. "You're needed at the dinner. Maddy wants to get to know you, too, ya know. And Lyla, you're more than welcome to stay."

"Oh..." I say awkwardly. "That—that's okay."

"No. She'll stay," Wrigley says. I shoot him a pointed look. He just grins at me.

His dad leaves the room, and Wrigley and I talk about how awkward the dinner is going to be, but the fact of the matter is that Wrigley really doesn't know the half of it. He doesn't know about Warner's and my past. He knows we're friends, but he thinks that's as far as it's gone. Which, technically, is true.

Wrigley's dad grills up some delicious meat and vegetable skewers for dinner, and we all sit in the formal dining room. I've never been at such a fancy table. I've seen it during Wrigley's parties, but even then, the formal dining area looks so fancy that most of the kids usually stay out of this room.

I am sitting next to Wrigley, across from Warner, who is next to his mom. Steven is at the end of the table.

"So, Warner," Steven says, trying to get to know Warner better. "You are on Blackfell's football team?"

"He's captain," I find myself blurting out. *Why did I say that?* I stab at my meat.

"Captain?" Steven raises his eyebrows, impressed. "Good for you."

"Thanks," Warner says, looking up at me through his lashes as he tries to focus on his food as well. We made quick eye contact, and then I look down at my plate again.

"Dad wishes I would get more into sports," Wrigley says to no one in particular. Steven then shrugs.

"It's just good to stay active," he explains. "And I always did sports when I was in high school."

"It's never been my thing," Wrigley replies.

"It's not for everyone," Warner says flatly.

"I used to be in cheer," I throw in even though no one is asking. "But I quit. I guess I'm not so active, either."

"Yeah, but you sorta have been through a lot," Warner says. "Enough to make anyone want to quit the things they used to enjoy doing."

I smile slightly. Maddy looks back and forth between us. It makes me uncomfortable. I shift in my seat.

"Um." Maddy clears her throat. "The food is delicious, Steven."

"Agreed," Warner and I say at the same time. Then we laugh a little about it. Next to me—maybe I'm going crazy—but I feel that Wrigley is growing tense in his seat.

"Thanks," Steven says as he wipes his mouth with a cloth napkin. That's right—*cloth*. Then he keeps talking. "But, speaking of people who have been through a lot, you've been through a lot, too, Warner."

Warner shrugs. "Still going through it."

"Right," Steven nods with sympathetic eyes. "How are you holding up?"

"We really don't have to talk about this," Maddy says awkwardly.

"I'm fine," Warner says, addressing Steven and ignoring his mom. "Nothing I can't handle. Nothing compared to what Lyla went through."

Mr. Hall then looks at me. "Right. How are *you* holding up?"

"I'm okay," I say slowly. "I'll be better once whoever did it is caught."

This is not suitable conversation. And Maddy agrees. I can tell because she's the one who does something about it.

"Let's just change the subject," she says. "Warner, why don't you tell Steven a little bit about what you want to do after you graduate?"

The rest of the dinner goes like this, teetering on the edge of awkwardness. There's long pauses of silence. Moments where you can only hear the sounds of our silverware clinking and our mouths chewing. Small talk is made. And if anything, too controversial of a topic is brought up, the subject is quickly changed. Warner and I keep meeting each other's eyes across the table. And I keep trying not to look at him.

Then finally, the torture is over, and Wrigley and I are excused to go somewhere else in the house... Anywhere that isn't where Maddy, Warner, and Steven Hall are.

We retreat to Wrigley's bedroom.

It's fancy. He has an industrial theme going on. One brick wall. The other ones are painted gray. He has a concrete desk with an expensive camel leather rolling back chair tucked underneath it. He has a massive bookcase filled with books that I am curious if he's ever actually read. The light fixture from the ceiling looks expensive. The blinds are remote controlled. And his bed is king sized, like mine at Mom's.

At Dad's, I have a twin bed.

I sit down in his rolling back chair. It's so cushioned that I could fall asleep in it.

"Well, that was practically awful," Wrigley says, sitting on his bed, hunching his shoulders a little bit.

"Yeah," I laugh out, "super-awkward."

Wrigley nods and looks away from me.

"Are you okay?" I ask. I can sense that he's not.

"It was just... weird," he tells me. "Warner is... weird."

"How so?"

Wrigley won't meet my eyes when he says it. "It's just that... I can tell he has a crush on you. That's all."

CHAPTER 57

MADDY

After the dinner, I drive Warner back home and ask him what he thinks of Steven. To my delight, Warner says he likes him. And that we look cute together. Then he gets out of the car and tells me to go have fun at Steven's restaurant. It's where Steven and I have agreed to meet to get some quality time *alone* to digest the evening we just shared with our boys—and Lyla.

"Be safe," I make sure to tell Warner before I drive away. "Keep all the doors locked!"

He rolls his eyes, but I know that if I don't remind him to do it, he'll probably leave everything unlocked.

I drive to The Viper and get seated in a special booth by the host. Steven has some small business things to attend to, but then he comes over to join me when he's finished. I still can't get over how hot he is every time he first gets in my presence. He's like a movie star. Like somebody way, way out of my league. And yet, he wants to be with me.

Before he sits across from me, he holds out his hand. I take it and get to my feet. Then he wraps his arms around me and suddenly, he's kissing me. It's deep and passionate and he even dips me slightly. When he pulls away, I'm breathless, and he has the biggest grin on his face.

"That's one way to greet me," I say, blushing as we finally take our seats across from each other.

"I just like you so much, you know that?"

The butterflies are going nuts in my stomach right now. "I like you so much, too."

"And dinner went well, don't you think?"

"I do." Even though it was clear to me that Warner and Wrigley aren't the biggest fans of each other, Wrigley was at least nice to *me*, and Warner was nice to Steven, and I think that's more important than whatever rivalry those two have going about Lyla right now.

"Warner is a good kid," Steven says.

"So is Wrigley." But I'm more proud of Warner. Of how involved he is in school and how good his grades are. How he has plans to go to college and Wrigley hasn't made up his mind yet. I don't say this to Steven, of course.

"Yeah, he is..." Steven trails off, looking almost troubled. "I'm trying my best. You know?"

"I do," I say, nodding. "What does he think of me?"

"I didn't exactly get a chance to ask him yet. He was still hanging with Lyla before I left. The two of them... they spend every minute together."

It bothers me slightly to hear it, and I think it's in defense of Warner. I know my son likes her, despite the fact that he has been seeing that Jessica girl. I watched him look at Lyla at dinner. I could see it all over his face. I wonder if Lyla can see it, too. And why she doesn't want to be with him in return.

"That's okay," I say, waving it off and taking a sip of my martini.

"I want to have a lot more dinners like that," Steven says. "What do you say?"

It reminds me of Dean. That's my first thought. Of Dean and how he wants to do family things together. *The three of us.*

It sounds so much more appealing to do stuff with Steven.

"I'd love that," I say, meaning every word.

"Me, too," he agrees, sipping his whiskey drink. "You know, Mads. I just—you're the first woman in a long time who's made me feel hopeful. Who's made me see a future. One that can really work. I just... I hope you see that, too."

My mouth opens.

Then it closes.

Then it opens again.

Then I smile nervously and sip my martini. Or gulp.

I do see a real future with Steven. Truly. But... there are still secrets. Stuff I need to tell him.

I need to tell him about Carson.

And you know what? What a better time to do it than now?

Just get it over with, Maddy.

"Steven, listen..." I start.

"Uh oh," he says immediately. "That doesn't sound good."

I quickly shake my head. "No no, I really like you. I do see a future with you. That much I'm certain about."

"Okay..." He waits.

"I just wanted to tell you—"

At that exact moment, a staff member swings up to the table looking frantic. "I need you in the kitchen," she says to Steven. "Stat."

Quickly, Steven gets to his feet. He looks apologetically at me. "It'll just be a minute," he says.

"No worries," I say, waving him away.

And just like that, the moment to tell Steven the truth about Carson once and for all has again slipped through my fingers.

CHAPTER 58

WARNER

I try to get some homework done after my dinner with Mom, Steven, Wrigley, and Lyla, but I keep getting on my phone and scrolling aimlessly through social media instead. My endless scrolling is much easier to pay attention to than the homework that I need to get done. It's too hard to focus when I keep replaying how the dinner went in my head over and over again. The way it felt to see Lyla sitting across from me, as Wrigley's date. How I couldn't help but picture having her be there as *my* date instead. How I couldn't help picture Wrigley having to be in my shoes. Sitting alone, continuously looking at Lyla and wishing he were me.

"What is wrong with you?" I ask myself now that I've caught myself thinking about the dinner yet again. I'm with Jessica. I *like* Jessica. We have fun together. And that kiss had been great. Amazing. I shouldn't be bothered by Lyla at all. I shouldn't be plagued by thoughts of her. I am moving on. I *have* moved on.

But of course, while thinking about that, I get a TikTok update from Toxeydramaenthusiast's page. They posted a new video. I tap on it, being immediately one of the video's first viewers.

It's a video that was taken at some point during the daytime. Maybe even earlier today. The person filming is far away, in a parking lot or parked on the curb, zooming into two people who are sitting in the grass with each other at a park. They both wear troubled expressions on their faces. They're both talking to each other and looking unhappy about something.

Those two people are Wrigley and Lyla.

They're much too far away to even know what it is they're arguing with each other about. But I don't like the distressed look in Lyla's eyes. And I don't like the angered look in Wrigley's.

The video isn't long. There's not even any voice over. All that goes along with it to give it any context is the caption:

Trouble in para-DIE-se?

It makes my stomach lunge. The caption is one thing, but I don't like that we're being followed. That Lyla is being followed. And that she was arguing with Wrigley about something not long before the dinner I just had with her.

Instinct takes over and I quickly send her a text message:

Me: *R U home?*
Lyla: *Yeah. But I'm at my dad's.*

Thanks to TikTok, I know where her dad lives. I don't even reply to her. I don't want to risk her telling me not to come. I have to check on her, though. I have to talk to her. When Wrigley isn't around.

When I roll into her neighborhood where her dad lives, my phone vibrates. I pull over to the curb and see that she's texted me again:

Lyla: *??*

I park and walk to where I'm standing on the sidewalk in front of her house. I feel a bit like a creep. But I know she doesn't think I am one. It's just everyone *else* who does.

Me: *Come outside.*

It takes a couple of minutes, but then Lyla unlocks the front door and tiptoes out of her house. It's late. We should both definitely be in bed.

"What are you doing?" she asks in a whisper-yell.

"Hello to you, too," I say.

She approaches me and we meet in the middle on the driveway. Her hair is damp from a fresh shower. She smells like berries. It's captivating and I have to try hard to ignore it.

"Whatever you have to tell me couldn't be said over text?" she asks.

"I saw the recent TikTok video," I say.

Red blooms in her cheeks. "Oh."

"Are you okay?"

"About the fact that I'm being watched everywhere I go? No. But... with Wrigley..." She pauses so she can sigh and shake her head.

"The person who is following us knows how to make things look completely the opposite of what they are. I'm fine."

"Are you sure?" I guess I just want her to say that she's *not* fine. That she doesn't want to be with Wrigley. That she's worried Wrigley is the one who is responsible for all of this. If the answer could just be that simple. That easy.

If only.

"Yes, Warner," she says. I look at her. She looks at me. There's no denying the chemistry we still have between us. So what if she is with Wrigley? So what if I am with Jessica? There's something here. Between us. She's chosen to ignore it. Which has left me with no other option but to do so as well.

I keep trying. "But like... are you *really* okay?" I'm grasping at straws now. I also just want to be certain she's being honest with me. I want her to know that she can be. That she can tell me anything.

"Why are you asking me?"

"Lyla, you... you were kidnapped. And you act like you weren't. I just, I don't know. I worry about you. All the time."

"You don't need to," she says quickly. She crosses her arms and shivers. She's wearing long sleeves and sweatpants, but it's not enough to keep her warm because her hair is still wet. I wish I could get my jacket out of the car and throw it around her. I hate seeing Lyla suffer.

"I do, though," I say confidently. "And... I miss you. I feel like I haven't seen you since... you know—that thing with Jackson. Are we even friends anymore?"

"Of course." She reaches out a hand like she wants to touch my arm. But then she changes her mind. She's back to crossing her arms. "Of course we're still friends."

"Good." Relief blossoms in my chest and warms my insides. "Then *as friends*, we should hang out more."

"I agree," she says, even offering a smile. One that I eagerly return. We talk a little more. About everything and nothing. And then, before she finally goes back inside, saying she's about to get hypothermia, we've agreed that her and I, along with Wrigley, Audrey, and Jessica, are all going to hang out at the Halloween carnival together tomorrow.

It might hurt a little, but I'd rather have Lyla in my life as a friend then not have her in at all.

At least this way, I can keep an eye on her. I can try to find out if she is really, truly okay.

AUDREY

Today is a day. It's officially Halloween. I have to endure people dressing up at school, even though technically we were told we are not allowed to. I have to endure people dressing like the masked figure who torments us. People playing pranks and practical jokes on each other. People trying to get a rise out of everyone. People trying to scare each other.

Trying to scare us.

When Lyla and I arrive at school, I internally groan as I see how excited our peers all seem to be in the student parking lot. And I can see, over on the football field, where they are setting up the carnival for tonight. They do it every year. Usually, Mom volunteers at a booth, running a game or selling treats. This year, she hasn't even brought it up. It kind of makes me wonder if she even remembers that it's happening. If she knows what day it is. But thinking about Mom also makes me sick to my stomach, so I force myself to focus on something else. *Anything* else. Like this couple leaning against the trunk of a car giggling and flirting with each other. Or the guy wearing a cape and pretending to spook his classmate. I think he might be a vampire.

"I thought we weren't allowed to wear costumes," Lyla says.

"No one likes to follow the rules," I complain. I can tell she's just as uneasy as I feel about it.

Still, Ly and I hang out before the first bell rings, then we go to our separate classes. I keep my eyes peeled everywhere for that familiar cartoonish mask. I also keep my eyes peeled for a camera aimed in my direction. Toxeydramaenthusiast's camera, to be exact. Everywhere I go, I still can't shake this feeling that I'm being watched.

I see the first cartoonish mask at lunch, in the cafeteria, a few tables down from where I sit with Ryan and his buddies and some of the senior cheerleaders. Ryan is the one who points out to me. I sit there frozen once I see it. I think, for a moment—just a single, quick moment— *What if it's really Carson? What if he's here at school?*

Then the wearer takes off his mask and reveals he's just some stupid freshman. He sets the mask down on his lunch table and dives into his food with his friends, all of them laughing, thinking that his little costume is genius.

"Do you want me to go say something to him?" Ryan asks me with his jaw set tight.

I still feel frozen and afraid. And I'm glad that Lyla doesn't typically come to the cafeteria anymore. That she's off hanging with Wrigley somewhere. I stare straight-ahead at nothing as I answer him. "No. It's fine."

I manage to make it through the rest of the school day without seeing another mask. But there's talks of it. Some of my peers and friends come up to me and ask me if I've seen it. They tell me how messed up it is. It's like they *want* to see what my reaction is. It's like they want to see how terrified I am. They want to see my PTSD take hold of me.

I wonder if anybody really cares. Or if they're just looking for some gossip or drama to keep them entertained.

I am more than relieved when the final bell rings and I head to the parking lot to meet Lyla at my car. I don't have cheer practice today because of the carnival. It starts soon. There's barely going to be enough time for us to go home and get ready and come back with our dates. Lyla and Warner filled me in last night about how we're going as a group together. I sort of want to skip it. But I don't want to come off as an insecure baby. If Lyla is going to be strong, then I will be, too. And I have to go where she goes. So I can keep tabs on her.

I dig around in my backpack for my keys as I approach my Mini Cooper. When I look up, I freeze in my step. Just a few cars away, there's a familiar man standing in the parking lot. He's laying against an unfamiliar car. And he's too old to be here. He's definitely trespassing.

The man is Eric. Carson Price's father.

I want to pretend like I haven't seen him and get in my car and speed away. But I'm still waiting for Lyla. And besides, I'm pretty sure Eric has already seen me see him.

What do I do? I ask this to myself over and over again. I teeter between getting into my car or going to talk to him. Does he want to talk? Is that why he's here? For me?

I get my answer when he nods his head in my direction. I sulk over there, my pulse gaining speed. I feel creeped out. I feel nervous. I feel uncertain. My stomach is telling me to turn back around and run. But then another part of me is saying that it's fine. That Eric is harmless and he's just looking for his son.

My mouth opens and words come out despite all of my internal battle. "Have you been following me?" The question doesn't stem from just right now. It stems from all the times I've felt like I was being watched. From the fact that I don't know who owns the Toxeydramaenthusiast TikTok page. From when I saw somebody on the bleachers watching me underneath them. From the person at the homecoming dance who wore that stupid cartoon mask and stood there in the middle of the dance floor, staring at me.

"Following you?" Eric immediately steps away from the car, looking concerned. "Of course not. This is where Carson Price went to school."

"I know that." I say. "Like, years ago. Why are you here?"

"I'm still just trying to piece everything together. I'm still trying to find him."

Maybe it's because I've already been wary all day, but something about Eric seriously freaks me out. I don't like that he's here. I don't like that he shows up randomly when so much is still unknown about what happened to Lyla. What happened to us.

"You know, I'm actually glad you're here," I say, half lying, "because I've been wanting to tell you—that whole thing about seeing

Carson Price in the woods... I'm not really so sure about it anymore. It might not have actually been him."

"What... what are you talking about?" he asks. Immediately, I watch his body language turn defensive. "You said you saw him. Your mother thinks she saw him. He... he was there that night. He had to be."

"I'm sorry, Mr. Price. I don't know what you want me to say. But I can't help you. I really hope you get the answers you're looking for."

"Why are you just now deciding to say you don't think he's alive anymore?" He steps toward me. "What happened?"

"N-nothing," I stammer. And then I watch as his face twists with anger. He points a finger at me. Then, he sees something over my shoulder. It stops him from saying whatever he had just opened his mouth to say. Instead, he angrily throws his car door open, gets in, and drives off.

That's when I finally turn around to see who he had been looking at. Although, before I even do so, I have a feeling I know who it is.

And sure enough, Lyla is standing there, and she's with Warner. And they both have looks on their face that let me know I have some explaining to do.

CHAPTER 60

LYLA

A witch, a fairy, a bumblebee, a character from the TV show, *The Office*, a Batman, and an average teenage boy and all cram together in a red Jeep Wrangler and drive over to the school carnival together later in the day.

I am the witch. It's a very last minute costume and mainly consists of just a pointed hat and some dark purple, glittery eye makeup. Wrigley told me he never got a costume, but I don't see him as the type of guy who'd want to dress up on Halloween, anyway.

I sit in the back with Wrigley and Audrey and Ryan on the way to the school. I can tell that Wrigley is being quieter than usual, and I'm pretty sure it's because he isn't thrilled about being here with Warner.

The carnival is cute. There are rides. Lots of lights. A corn maze. A pumpkin patch. People of all ages are allowed to attend, including little kids. There's music and laughter and the sounds of screams—but screams that are full of excitement instead of terror.

Jessica, the bumblebee, says she desperately wants a snack from one of the food booths, so she, Warner, Ryan, and Audrey walk up to the line together. Wrigley and I stay back.

"Are you okay?" I ask for probably the fifth time tonight. "You've been quiet." Wrigley is usually kind of a quiet guy anyway. But not around me.

"Lyla, I just got to say: you know what I think about Warner. About him having feelings for you. So I'm not really the biggest fan of being here, forced to hang out with him."

My stomach twists. This is part of the reason why I have no appetite. No want for a snack at the food booth like the others do.

I should have known this was coming.

"I get that," I say. "But also, you have to understand. Warner and I have been friends for a while now. We were friends before you and I became a thing. So, I kind of need you to be okay with it."

"But he doesn't want to *be* just friends with you."

"He knows how I feel about him. And how I feel about you. So it doesn't matter. He's also... he's tied to everything that's been going on. Like, I honestly feel that I have no choice but to have him in my life anyway."

He snaps his jaw shut and looks straight ahead, nodding dismally.

"I'm sorry. It was his idea for all of us to come together. Maybe we can ditch them?" I offer. Maybe I just need to only hang out with Warner when I'm not with Wrigley. That might be the best solution. When I look over at Warner with the others in line, and I see the way he casually swings his arm around Jessica's waist, I try to ignore the strange feeling it gives me.

"Yeah. Maybe," Wrigley says. "I'm sorry, I'm not trying to be that guy. I just... with all that stuff going around about him, I don't trust him."

"All that 'stuff' going around, it's rumors. Lies. Warner is a good guy."

"I think maybe you're too trusting."

"You're entitled to your own opinion."

This is weird. Wrigley and I don't normally have bickering moments like this. It feels like a first for us. A first that I never wanted.

Finally, the rest of the gang comes back.

"I was thinking we should do the maze first," Audrey, the fairy in beautiful glittery wings and a frilly skirt of pastel colors says.

"Sounds good," Wrigley quickly agrees. He takes my hand and leads the group, and after getting tickets and handing them to the person working the maze, we all enter.

The maze is made from stacks of hay that tower over our heads. It's huge. It's placed right on the greenbelt next to the football field where the rest of the carnival is, and it backs up to the forest. One time, my freshman year, I remember we had to do a search and rescue for one of our peers who got lost inside of it for too long.

More than just there being several twisty, confusing paths, there's also fog machines and people dressed in creepy costumes whose whole job is to scare us. I used to think it was fun, to be scared by the actors. Now I wonder why anyone would willingly put themselves through this. And I am wondering why I even agreed to come in here at all.

Oh yeah. Because this is the sort of thing the new old Lyla would do.

I try to be lighthearted at first, giggling with the girls and squealing and pretending like I'm not having an internal panic attack. Then, we come to a fork in the maze, and right behind us, a man dressed up like a werewolf starts chasing after us, and I dive to the left, thinking that that's the direction everyone else is going, too. I scream and run and run, and I don't stop.

"Lyla!" a voice calls behind me. "He's gone, he's gone!"

It's Warner. And we're the only two that decided to go left.

I stop running and put my hands on my knees, panting while Warner catches up to me. "This was stupid," I say, feeling like I can be my normal self around him. "I want out."

He looks half amused. But I don't see what's so funny. And I don't have a good feeling about how Wrigley is going to react to finding out that Warner and I have split off from everyone else. "Let's get you out of here, then," he says to me. I nod and hold the stitch on my side while we continue walking through the maze. I stay a little bit behind him so that if anything pops out in front of us again, Warner will be the first to face them.

"You having a good time with your date?" Warner asks after we walk in silence for a bit.

"Yeah," I say, a little bit too quickly. "Why?" I try to make my face look like it's silly that he would even ask.

Warner shrugs casually. "He seemed a little quiet. Just like he was at the dinner at his house. I don't think he likes me very much. His dad's kinda cool, and whatever, but I really kind of hope we don't become stepbrothers someday."

I shudder visibly at the mention of it. "Oh my God, how weird would *that* be?"

"I'm trying not to think about it."

I laugh. "He's fine," I reply. "He's just... I think we're having an off night." Why did I tell him that? It's none of Warner's business.

Still, I look to see what his reaction is to it.

"Oh yeah?" He has an eyebrow raised. Part of me thinks he's a little bit excited to hear the news.

"Yeah. But it's nothing that won't pass."

He nods, and we walk in silence some more. Then he blurts out randomly, "Don't you think it's weird that Jackson went to the dance with Sophia?"

I should've known it was a matter of time before that got brought up. That Jackson made it clear it wasn't okay for Warner and I to be together, but then he went and got with one of *my* friends. *Ex*-friends. Whatever. Same thing. He and Jackson are ex-friends now, too.

"The more that I think about it, the more I think they're kind of perfect for each other," I say with a mouth full of bitterness. Jackson and Sophia are both very concerned with their image and think they're in charge of everything.

"Yeah. I guess," Warner says.

"Jackson has changed a lot," I say. We come to another fork, and Warner waits to me for me to pick which way to go. I choose left again. It's getting quieter and quieter as we get deeper and deeper into the maze, close to the forest. I don't even know where the exit is. Part of me wonders if there even *is* one.

"He has, hasn't he?" Warner agrees.

"Like, not in a good way, either," I say. "It's like, when this whole thing with Sydney went down, maybe even earlier, when I got my car accident, I started seeing this whole new side of him."

"I think when he saw that he was starting to lose you, he tried harder to hold on."

A bit of guilt swims through me. The last thing I wanted to do was hurt Jackson. But maybe that's not exactly true. The last thing I wanted to do was *stay* with him.

"I don't know why I even listen to his stupid demands," I admit. "Why I let him have some semblance of control over my life still. I guess... this new Jackson... he kind of scares me."

Warner stops walking. I don't notice for a little while. Not until I turn around and see that he is a few feet behind me.

"What?" I ask.

Warner doesn't say anything. But that's when I realize he doesn't have to. I know that look on his face. I know what he's telling me. And I realize that I've just admitted the only reason that I told Warner I wanted to stay friends with him was because I was only listening to Jackson's demands. Because I was too afraid of what would happen if I didn't.

I think Warner now knows about the feelings I have for him.

CHAPTER 61

Audrey

pparently, when the werewolf man attacked, I was the only one who had the instinct to run the *opposite* direction of where he was going, back in the direction we had all come from. Because when I stop running and look over my shoulder, I see that nobody came with me. I see that I am suddenly very alone in the maze.

"Ryan!" I call. He doesn't call back to me. "Shoot." A shudder ripples down my spine. I am an idiot for wanting to do this. It's just that, once upon a time, I remembered the maze being so fun. And I thought, with Ryan by my side the whole time, that I would be well protected. I hadn't even considered that we could get split up from one another.

I try to turn back around and go in the direction I think Ryan went. But the more I walk, the more lost I get. Every time I call his name, he doesn't answer. I even call for Lyla and Warner, and I don't hear from them, either. And no one has passed me—not another classmate, or a kid, or a family—in a long while, either. It's as if I'm suddenly all alone in the maze.

I hear a rustling behind me. The scuffle of footsteps. I tense up, hoping that I'll see my friends rounding the corner when I look. Or at least another family. Anything except for another one of the actors in a costume trying to scare me.

I turn and look at the figure rounding the corner.

Stones drop in my feet. Everything turns cold and hot at the same time.

It's someone in all black. All black, and that stupid, terrifying mask is covering their face.

He's here.

I let out a wounded animal sort of sound and then take off at a run. He starts chasing me.

I look over my shoulder and I see the knife in his hand. It glistens in the moonlight. I scream. I scream and I keep running. I turn corner after corner. I push past other families and groups of people when I—*finally*—come across them. I go as fast as I can in attempt to lose the masked man inside the maze.

"Get me out of here!" I yelp out at no one.

Eventually, I've had enough trying to figure out how to get out of this wretched place, and I run straight at a towering stack of bales of hay and jump up. I desperately climb, getting endless splinters and snags in my costume, and make it to the top of the haystack. Then I jump over the other side, where my ankle rolls and I fall back on my back, pain searing through me.

But at least I'm out of there.

With the air knocked out of me, I scramble to get to my feet, my ankle throbbing. I look to my right and see that the exit of the maze wasn't too far away from where I had decided to just climb out instead. I run the opposite direction, thinking that the masked man is going to come out of the exit any second and continue on chasing me, maybe even leading me straight into the woods, where he can try and kill me in private.

When I make it back to the football field, where the rest of the carnival is, people generally avoid getting in my way as I sprint, but there's one body that steps in front of me and, not seeing them in time, I slam into them.

Arms wrap around me. They're warm.

It's Ryan.

I sob into his chest, so relieved to be where I am safe. "He... he was in there! Inside the maze!" I look over my shoulder. I don't see the masked man anywhere. He didn't follow me back to the carnival.

"Hey hey hey, it's okay," Ryan says in a soothing voice, holding me.

"He had a knife!"

"It was probably one of those fake ones," he tells me. I don't know where anyone else from our group is, which leads me to believe that Ryan got led astray from them as well. "It was probably just a kid playing a prank on you, Audrey. The real guy wouldn't come here. There's no way. All kinds of people are wearing that stupid disguise. You saw that one in the cafeteria today. People just want to mess with you."

I look over my shoulder again. Then I wipe my eyes and force the tears to stop. Maybe Ryan is right. Maybe I am being completely ridiculous.

Or maybe I had just escaped an attempted kidnapping.

After all, I'm the one he wanted in the first place.

CHAPTER 62

WARNER

When Lyla and I make it out of the maze, I see Wrigley waiting for her at the exit. She quickly goes to him and they hug, and she acts relieved, as if he's some sort of great hero of hers or something. I tell them I'll see them later and that I need to go find my date, and Wrigley says he lost her inside the maze when he went looking for Lyla.

I send her a text, but she doesn't reply. So I wander back to the carnival and search everywhere for that yellow and black striped costume Jessica has on. It's ridiculously cute on her. And with my Batman costume, we look good together.

That's right, Warner. Just focus on her. Your date. Don't think about anything Lyla just told you in that maze.

And finally, I spot Jessica. She's standing outside of the fun house. She is underneath a light pole, and she's crying.

That can't be good.

As soon as I notice the tears, I jog the rest of the way to her. "Jessica, hey!" I call. The only thing I can think that might've happened is that when we were all separated in the maze, maybe Wrigley said something to her to make her think that I didn't actually want to be with her. But he wouldn't do that, right?

When Jessica looks up and sees me, she gets these terrified, deer-trapped-in-headlights eyes. Then she quickly turns and starts speed walking away from me.

I rip my stupid Batman mask off. "Jessica!"

"Stay away from me, Warner!" she yells over her shoulder. I run so that I can catch up with her. I have to know what happened. I have to know why she is suddenly repulsed by me.

"What?! What happened?!" I ask as I jog to reach her.

She glances at me again over her shoulder as she continues speed-walking. "I mean it!" Her voice is shrill and loud. It's unrecognizable. "Stay away for me I'm going to call the police!"

Her words make me freeze in my step. And it's then that her speed walk turns into a run.

"The police?" I whisper to myself.

What exactly happened inside of that maze?

CHAPTER 63

MADDY

When Dean shows up at my doorstep, I'm immediately suspicious. He and I both know that Warner isn't here. That he's at the school carnival with his friends, dressed up in his little Batman costume with his date, Jessica the bumblebee.

"Dean?" I ask through the screen door. I haven't opened it to let him in yet.

"Hey, Mads."

"What...?"

"Have time for a quick chat?"

"With you?"

He looks over his shoulder. "I don't know who else it would be with," he replies.

I itch my head and open the screen door to let him inside. "Did something happen?"

"No, everything's good. Fine."

Yet, I can sense he isn't telling the truth. Something is bothering him. Deeply. "Okay..." I trail off. He takes off his coat and walks over to the living area. It's late enough in the evening to where we won't be interrupted by any more trick-or-treaters. "Can I get you a drink, or something to eat?" I ask, feeling weird offering it. Why is Dean Reeves in my house?

"No. I... I shouldn't stay too long."

I nod and walk over to the living area to join him. We both sit down on the couch. I would've taken the chair, but I have a bit of laundry piled up on it at the moment.

"What's going on?" I ask. My voice is soft and level.

He shakes his head and looks at his hands in his lap. "I don't know."

"Whaddaya mean?" It's weird seeing him like this. Seeing him not sure of something. Because ever since he came back to Toxey, I've gotten to know the Dean Reeves who is completely certain of what he wants. And what he wants is to be in Warner's life. I sort of let that start to happen, so I know this has to be about something else.

He sighs. "Earlier this week, I saw Mia."

"You saw her? Where?"

"At her house. Did you—did she tell you what happened?"

I shake my head.

"She's a mess, Maddy."

"What happened to her?" So, this is what has him so upset? His worry over Mia?

I feel a bit of a constriction inside my chest. Buried somewhere deep. Deep enough to where I think maybe I can try to ignore it. Ignore the way it makes me feel.

"She went looking for Carson Price in the woods all by herself," he explains. She got lost and was found by a camper. And she was... she was out of it, Mads. Like seriously—something is wrong with her. I don't know."

This is news to me. "She was... found by a camper?"

"She nearly froze to death. I don't know what she was thinking."

I don't know what to say.

He notices the look I must have on my face. "She didn't say *anything* to you about how she wanted to go and find him?" he asks, his voice full of skepticism. "Is he even out there, Maddy? I mean, seriously. What do you honestly, truly think?"

I think it's weird that you're in my house talking to me about my best friend when you're the father of my kid.

"I... I think Carson *could* be out there. Somewhere. Otherwise, I don't know how else all of this happened. Who else could be behind it all."

He shakes his head and says nothing.

"She's okay now, though, right?" I ask. I need to call her.

"Yeah." He turns his head to look at me. "She's okay." Then he just keeps staring. He looks like he has a million thoughts racing through his brain, and he doesn't know what to say or do next. I stare back, waiting for something to happen. Waiting for him to vent about how worried he is about her. For him to suggest that I talk to her for him. *Something.*

What I don't expect, is when he suddenly leans in and plants his lips directly on mine.

I'm too stunned to even move at first. I am still as a statue, trying to process the fact that Dean is kissing me right now. It doesn't take too long before my brain catches up with me and my reflexes react. I shove him away. "Dean!" I cry out hysterically.

Dean quickly leaps to his feet. "Maddy. I'm sorry. I... I don't know what I'm doing."

"Yeah, me neither!"

"I... I should go." He walks over and grabs his coat. He then throws the door open, but something makes him freeze before he can leave. I'm about to ask him *why* he's still here, maybe even hit him or yell at him or something, because what the heck just happened?! But then I see that he stopped because Nora is standing on our front porch.

Nora and Dean. Two former best friends. Two people who haven't seen each other in a very long time. Forced to face each other now.

"Dean," Nora says. Her tone is even, but a bit icy.

"N-Nora." Dean sounds completely caught off guard. Maybe even a little bit terrified.

"I... I didn't know you would be here," Nora says, sounding as if she is carefully choosing her words. Oh God, does she have any idea what just happened? Could she have seen it through the window maybe? I don't want anyone to know Dean just kissed me. *Ever*.

"I was just leaving," Dean says.

"Okay." She still sounds unfriendly. "Well... I'm here to see Maddy."

"Right." Dean goes outside, around Nora. Nora trades places with him and comes inside. But she turns and looks at him again. And Dean turns and looks at her.

"What?" Nora asks him.

"Nothing. Nothing," he quickly says. "Nice to see you, Nora." Then, as I stand in the background, I watch Dean practically stumble down the steps in his hurry to get away from the both of us.

Nora turns back to me, and when she closes my front door, I don't miss how loudly she does it. And I can't ignore that angry gleam in her eyes.

"Nora," I say calmly. "I have no idea why he came here just now."

"Do you think I care about that?" she snaps. "I don't. He's your kid's father. Whatever."

"Oh gosh. Okay... then what's wrong?"

"What's *wrong*?" Her voice raises an octave with each word. "What's *wrong*, Maddy?

All I can do is stand there and nod my head.

"What's *wrong* is that I just found out that you and Mia have been friends *all* this time!"

Oh no.

No no no no no.

"Nora." I take a step toward her. "Just, hear me out."

"No!" she screams. "Thanks to a *lovely* conversation with my mother, I finally learned the truth! What kind of friend *are* you?!"

"It's not that easy to explain," I try.

"It doesn't matter, because I don't even want to hear you try! You've been on her side this whole time, haven't you?"

I don't know what to say.

So she screams louder. "*Haven't you?!*"

"Yes!" I cry out.

She looks like she can't decide whether she wants to cry or spring forward and hit me. I'm equally terrified of both options.

"You know what, Maddy?" she sneers. "Y-You're insane. You're just as crazy as my sister! Do you hear me?! You're both psychos! I'm done with you! Both of you!"

"Nora, please!" I try to reach out and grab her arm to stop her. She is so fast to yank it away from me that she nearly falls over. She gives me one last, pained expression, and then she flies out the door and down the steps just as Dean had done.

And I am thinking I'm starting to really hate Halloween.

CHAPTER 64

AUDREY

"It's... nice up here," I say to Ryan, a little embarrassed. We are stuck at the top of the Ferris wheel, overlooking the rest of Toxey together. It's dark up here. Quiet. Just the two of us. No freak in a cartoonish mask anywhere in sight.

"Yeah?" Ryan asks, bumping my knee with his.

I blush and look away from him. "I'm sorry about earlier. And about how I freaked out at homecoming. And that you had to see the way my aunt talks to me that day at Delilah's... I guess I'm kind of a mess."

"I don't think you're a mess," he's quick to say. "You and your family are all going through a lot right now."

"I guess. Still. Thank you."

"Thank you for what?"

"I don't know. I guess... you're the only person in my life that makes me feel a little bit normal."

He smiles at me. And it makes my stomach flutter. It's good to be with Ryan. It's good to feel that sense of normalcy. It gives me hope. Hope that I can get over Warner after all.

After we finish our ride on the Ferris wheel, I tell Ryan to wait on a bench so that I can run and use the restroom next to the bleachers. He smiles and tells me he won't move an inch. I walk through the dense crowd of costume-clad bodies.

"Lyla, why are you ignoring me!?"

Suddenly a hand is on my shoulder, spinning me around forcefully.

I'm looking right into the eyes of Jackson Mullens.

"Crap," he says when he realizes I'm not, in fact, Lyla.

"Jackson?" My face instantly darkens.

"Sorry," he says, letting me go. But I can still feel how tightly he had been gripping me. How tightly he would've gripped Lyla. And I don't like it.

"What do you want with my sister?" I demand immediately.

"I... nothing. None of your business." He starts to walk away. I grab his wrist just as tightly as he had grabbed my shoulder. He looks down at it, surprised at what he's seeing. Like he hadn't expected me to be able to be so tough.

"No," I say. "What do you want with her?"

"Dude. Leave me alone."

"No. You know what? *You* leave Lyla alone. Stay out of her life, Jackson. She doesn't want you to be a part of it anymore."

He glares at me. Darkly. And it makes me wonder what my sister ever saw in him. It makes me wonder why I ever hoped they wouldn't break up.

"What's going on here?" Ryan had seen the whole thing from over on the bench I had left him on. And now here he stands, looking back-and-forth between Jackson and me. I let go of Jackson's wrist and step back. Jackson shakes his head, rolls his eyes, and leaves me there.

"What was that about?" Ryan asks.

"He... he just thought I was my sister. That's all."

Ryan nods, but I can tell he knows there's more to it. And I can tell he doesn't like that I don't want to talk to him about it.

After I go to the bathroom, Ryan and I play some carnival games and he wins me a stuffed pink bunny that I carry around triumphantly. It's moments like these where I feel like I'm in a cute teen movie, and where I feel like I can just forget about the rest of my life and just be here with him.

But then there's the other moments. The ones that remind me I'm actually in a horror movie.

Ryan is in the middle of another game—the one where you have to use the gun to aim a stream of water at the target in order to get your horse to win the race. I watch him excitedly, until I get a notification from TikTok on my phone. Then I move my attention to the newest video from Toxeydramaenthusiast.

It's a video of the school's parking lot. There are red and blue lights everywhere. And Sophia Key is talking to a couple of police officers, mascara all down her face as she cries in front of them.

The voice changer shield's whoever is doing the talking in the video. "Earlier tonight, it seems that somebody attacked Sophia Key. Somebody who was wearing a costume very suspiciously similar to the one that the person who kidnapped Lyla and tormented Audrey wore. Is it the same person? Does he have a new target on his agenda? And why? How does Sophia Key tie into any of this? What does this person want? And who is it?"

As Sophia is wiping a snot bubble from her nose, the video ends.

"I... I need to find my sister," I say immediately to Ryan.

He turns from his game and looks at me, losing his concentration, and the water starts spraying everywhere except for on the target. And he doesn't win.

"Better luck next time!" the person running the booth says. Ryan gets off the little stool, still looking concerned. "Wait, what? What happened?"

I don't have time to fill him in on what I just watched. I hand him my phone and let him see the video for himself. Then, I hope he has the ability to multitask, because I take off, not waiting to see if he is going to follow me or not. I race over to the parking lot, where there are still police cars about. I can see Sophia with a blanket around her, Olive comforting her. Other classmates have arrived on the scene to check out what's happening.

Is one of them Toxeydramaenthusiast?

Ryan hands me back my phone after watching the TikTok, and I call Lyla and tell her to meet me. When she arrives, she has Warner and Wrigley with her.

"I knew he was here," I say to Lyla immediately.

"What are you talking about?" Lyla asks. I fill them in. Ryan stands next to me with his hands in his pockets.

"He's here, and he attacked Sophia." I feel horrible. Miserable. "Probably because he lost me in the maze and out of anger, he went after her instead since she's my friend!"

This is my fault.

It's all my fault.

CHAPTER 65

MADDY

Exhausted and overwhelmed over such a long, confusing night, I opt to go to bed extra early. I don't regret it until I wake up the next morning and check my phone and see that I have a new message.

It had been sent to me late last night.

I yawn. I slowly sit myself up. I rub my eyes and I stretch a little. My whole body is stiff. I had slept like the dead. I think I woke in the same exact position I had fallen asleep in. And now everything hurts.

With my eyes less sleepy and more able to focus clearly, I finally open the message. I am quick to learn that I was sent a photograph.

At first, I don't understand what I'm looking at. I see the outside of a house. I see a window with the blinds open. But it's dark. It's dark and hard to tell what's going on.

Seconds later, I realize that it's the front of *my* house. That the picture is taken of *my* window. I'm confused as to why this was sent to me, and how. But then, things start to make more sense.

They weren't taking a picture of the house.

They were taking a picture of what was going on *inside* of it.

Through the open blind slats, I can see my messy living room. I can see the arm chair that's buried in laundry I need to put away. And I can see the side view of our sofa, with two bodies sitting on it. And those two bodies belong to me and Dean.

And we are clearly kissing.

"Oh my God!" I can't help but call out loudly, slapping a hand so abruptly over my own mouth that it stings a little. I'm in shock. I'm in complete shock.

The photo. It wasn't sent from an anonymous person.

It was sent to me from Steven.

Immediately, I try to call him. He doesn't answer.

I text him:

Me: *Steven, please call me. Let me explain. That is not at all what it looked like.*

I can't stop staring at the photo. It was taken at the perfect time. I think that our tormentor sent it to him. Because if Steven had been here, standing right outside of my house, he would've seen how quickly I pushed Dean off of me. Because I had been quick to do it, hadn't I?

So, then. Three people showed up at my house last night around roughly the same time. First Dean. Then Nora. Then the tormentor. Or Steven.

I feel a coldness around me. Had Carson Price been here? Had Carson Price been just *feet* away from Nora and she hadn't even realized it? Had he been seconds away, just a whisper of a word away, from showing Nora that he's been alive all this time?

And what would Nora have done if she saw him and learned the truth?

Steven texts me back, and I notice that he would rather text me than call me. It's not a good sign. Because Steven always prefers phone calls.

Steven: *I swung by to check on you. I was worried because I saw that car outside and I knew it belonged to Dean Reeves.*
Steven: *To think I was about to barge in and save you.*
Steven: *I would've looked like a complete fool.*
Steven: *I guess that's what you do. You're good at making fools of everyone. Me included.*

I begin shaking. I feel panicked. Anxious. My stomach is rolling. Even though I should be hungry for breakfast, food is the last thing I want. All I want is to fix this with Steven.

Me: *That's not true! I pushed him away, Steven!*
Me: *Didn't you see it?*

I see the three little dots that show that he's replying. But then they disappear.

And they don't come back.
I text him again.

Me: *Steven, please.*

Still, I get nothing.

CHAPTER 66

AMELIA

Everything has slipped from my grasp. Right through my fingers. It's in a pile, broken and shattered on the floor by my feet.

But I can fix things. I have the power to fix things.

And I have to fix this.

I observe the work I've done one last time in the study inside of my home, then I leave in a hurry, because I've made up my mind, and now that I have, there's nothing that can stop me from doing this.

On my way to my car in the garage, I toss back more of my anxiety medication. I'm almost out, and I'm not due to get a refill for a while. I know I'm not supposed to be taking this much, but they're just not working.

Why aren't they working?

I make a mental note that I need to contact my doctor and let her know that I need my dosage upped or maybe even my meds switch to something stronger. Something that'll help me more. Because I can't take this anxiety. I can't take feeling this crazy. I just want to be the old me.

I know I look frazzled, especially when I see a glimpse of myself in the rearview mirror as I'm reversing down the driveway. I tried to get myself to look a little more put together when I woke up this morning, but I didn't have the energy to fully get ready. And it shows. I put my hair up in a sleek bun, but there are flyaways everywhere. I threw some mascara over my lashes, but I still have dark circles under my eyes. I moisturize and washed my face and brushed my teeth, but my skin still looks a ghoulish sort of sickly green color.

I don't feel beautiful. I don't feel normal.

I don't feel like Amelia Flynn.

But, I guess I've been Amelia Bailey for so long that I don't even know who Amelia Flynn is anymore anyway.

The entire drive over to Joey's school, I drum my fingers anxiously on the steering wheel. I constantly look down at my phone, expecting a call, but from who? Why? No one needs me. I'm the one in need.

I swerve all over the place. I don't use my turn signal. I roll a bunch of stop signs and then slam on my break once I realize it.

"Focus!" I yell at myself. It's a miracle when I finally make it into Joey's middle school parking lot.

I go inside the front office and I sign him out. I say that he has a doctor's appointment. Nobody questions it. But I do notice the hesitant looks I'm getting. I chalk it up to just being the news that everyone has been watching. To the fact that everybody knows the trauma I've gone through. I decide to not believe that it could be because of the way I am erratically behaving right now.

I sit in a chair and jiggle my knee the entire time until Joey finally arrives with his things. I smile big and give him a huge hug.

"Mom?" he asks. "What are you doing here?"

"Did you forget?" I giggle nervously and side-glance at the front office ladies. "You have that appointment, remember?"

Joey opens his mouth to report something probably along the lines of, "No I don't," but before he can, before I'm found out, I drag him out the front door.

We get to the car, and I hug him again. It feels so good to have this boy in my arms. My son. My Joey.

Mine.

"I miss you, bud," I say, tussling his hair and opening the car door for him. He climbs in, looking at me the whole time. "I miss you, too."

"Okay, so I'll be honest," I say when I get into the driver's seat and start leaving the parking lot. "You don't have an appointment. I just figured it would be fun to play hooky for the day. Go get ice cream and hang out or something."

"Seriously?" Joey asks. His face lights up. "Are we going to go get Audrey and Lyla, too?"

I smile at him through the mirror. I keep wanting to look at him through it. To make sure he's really there. To make sure I'm not imagining that this is all happening.

It's real. I have Joey. And Joey is mine.

"No, I figured you and I could use some one-on-one time. Does that sound okay?" I ask him.

Joey shrugs. "Sure."

I turn on the radio and we drive in silence for a beat.

Okay, maybe for more than just a beat.

"What ice cream place are we going to?" Joey asks eventually. We're on the freeway, and we're headed out of Toxey.

"A special one," I say, giving him an encouraging smile. It's one that I throw over my shoulder at him.

"Whoa, the road!" Joey yelps. I quickly turn and face forward again and notice that I'm swerving into a lane, about to hit another vehicle. I correct the car and wince.

"Sorry, sorry."

"Are you okay?" Joey asks.

"Of course I am!" I say, smiling big again. "Don't worry about me, Joey. Everything is fine. I'm just happy to finally be spending some time with you. It's hard to get used to not getting to see you guys every single day."

And it will be impossible to get used to never seeing him again if Gentry takes him away from me.

But I can't think about that.

I keep glancing at Joey in the rearview mirror to see his reaction to what I'm saying to him. He just shrugs again and then pulls his phone out.

Quickly, I exit the freeway.

"Where are we?" Joey asks. But I don't even know. This isn't where I intend on stopping. I just need to pull over really quick.

I pull into a gas station and stop the vehicle. I put it in park and get out, then I open Joey's back door and I hold my hand out.

"Watt?" he asks, arching one of his bushy eyebrows.

"Joey, I'm going to need your phone." I am sure to keep smiling at him. To keep smiling and acting positive. To make him think there's nothing to worry about. Because there *is* nothing to worry about.

Everything is going to be fine.

I wiggle my fingers, signaling at him to do what I've asked. "Come on, Joey."

"My phone? Why?"

"I just need it, all right?" Shoot. I sounded a little too snappy there. I try and fix it. "I just... you know how important you are to me, right?"

"Yeah?"

"I can't lose you, Joey. I love you, so much. And I just,"—I reach out and pluck his phone from his hand. He is quick to try and grab it back from me—"need,"—we start this tug-of-war thing between us over it—"your phone!" Finally, I'm successful, and I get the iPhone out of his hand. The second I saw him pull it out, it reminded me that he's more than capable of calling Gentry. Of texting him and telling him what's going on with me. Like he did when he was staying at my mother's. And I can't risk that again. I can't risk him ruining everything.

Joey belongs with me. Not Gentry.

Geez, these dang pills should have kicked in by now!

"Give it back!" Joey cries. But I shut the back door and climb into the front seat again. I keep his phone in my back pocket.

"You'll get it back," I say in a sweet voice. "I promise." And then I keep driving.

CHAPTER 67

Audrey

Lyla is in the kitchen working diligently on her homework, and I am in our shared room at Dad's, texting Ryan while I do some stretches to work on my flexibility.

There's hardly any carpet space in between my and Lyla's twin beds that flank two walls with two matching nightstands that sit right under our one window. It's weird to compare this room to the rooms we have back at Mom's house. It feels like I live two lives. One where my family has money. And one where we're struggling to get by. But I know it's not the case. I know my dad has money. He has a great job. This is just a temporary situation.

There's a knock on my door, and then Dad pops his head in. I lower the volume on my Bluetooth speaker, which is blaring a Harry Styles song.

"Audrey." Dad has a fearful look in his eyes, and it immediately makes my stomach churn.

"What is it?" I ask, rolling out of my left splits and sitting on my knees, ready to get up at a moment's notice if he needs me to.

"Joey..." Dad clears his throat, like it's a struggle to get the words out. "Joey never got off of the bus today."

I open my mouth to ask, "*What?*" but no sound comes out. It's as if all of my voice has completely left me. As if *more* than my voice has left me. Immediately, my heart constricts.

Dad continues. "I am going to go try and figure out what's going on. I need you and Lyla to stay here, okay?"

I still am incapable of moving. Of breathing. Of thinking anything except for how I've been giving Joey the silent treatment ever since he threw Mom under the bus. I've been giving Joey the silent treatment, and now he could be in danger.

Sophia was attacked. Who's to say that our tormentor, whether it be Carson or not, is attacking everyone and anyone they can get their hands on that we have any ties to?

I just have a sick, sick feeling that it's him who did this. That he somehow got to Joey, wearing that terrifying costume.

I picture Joey being locked in a shed identical to the one Lyla was in. I'm worried I'm going to be sick right here on the floor of our shared bedroom.

"Audrey. Do you hear me?" Dad asks. Lyla appears behind him, looking pale and horrorstruck. I think he's already told her the news.

"Yes," I manage to croak out.

"I'm... I'm sure everything is fine," Dad tries. "Let's just try to be positive." Then he gives me a stern nod. He turns and sees Lyla there and gives *her* a stern nod. Lyla throws her arms around him in a quick hug. He lets go too fast. Then he's out of both of our sights.

Lyla stopped working on her homework. I stopped doing my stretches. Suddenly, neither one of us can do anything but sit there and wait. We hardly even talk. We hardly even think. We hardly even move from our spot on the sofa. Not until there's a knock on the door and it makes Lyla jump.

"I'll get it," I say bravely. I'm just dying for something to do other than sit here in the paralyzed fear.

I go to the door and look through the peephole. It's a pretty woman I don't recognize. Confused, and against my better judgment given everything that has happened recently, I answer the door.

"Hi, I'm Heather," the woman says. "I am... I am a friend of your dad's. He asked if I would come and... hang out with you guys?"

Heather.

I look the woman up and down. And then it hits me as to why she looks familiar. Dad showed us a photo of her. Even though we didn't want to see it—or *I* certainly didn't.

Heather is Dad's girlfriend.

"Actually, we are okay," I try, standing in front of the doorway so that she can't let herself in. She has long, chocolatey hair that's in waves around her shoulders. Her eyes are almond shaped and the color of them matches the gray in the sky. She's wearing a maroon sweater and designer jeans. She looks very put together and like she does yogalates five times a week.

Already, I have a dislike for her.

Because she's nothing like Mom.

Suddenly, I can hear Lyla breathing behind me. "Dad texted us," she says. "We have to let her in. He wants her to babysit us, apparently."

Heather looks embarrassed. "I'm sorry about all of this," she says in an endearing voice. She keeps the smile plastered on her face. Maybe there's a chance she thinks this is just as uncomfortable as I feel it is, but it doesn't make me like her any more.

Not feeling like I have any other choice, I step aside, and Heather enters the home. She has this walk about her as she sets her purse on the counter in the kitchen that tells me she's been here often. But how can that be true if Lyla, Joey, and I have been staying here since Dad moved in? How often does Dad have her over here when we're at school? Or does he sneak her inside after we've gone to bed?

"So, let me guess which one of you is Audrey and which one of you is Lyla," Heather says. So many people have played this stupid game with us. Already, we know what to do. We stand side-by-side and let her quickly look us up and down. She scrunches her face up and then points a finger at Lyla. "You are Lyla."

I wonder what gives it away. I wonder what specific things my dad told her about us that made it obvious which one of us is which.

"Bingo," Lyla says lifelessly.

Heather smiles. Then she looks at me. "That means that you must be Audrey."

"Guilty as charged," I say with a heavy sigh in my voice.

"Have you heard anything about Joey from my dad?" Lyla asks.

Heather's smile falls. "Not yet. But I'm sure he'll find him. It's probably all just some misunderstanding. Maybe he missed the bus. Or maybe there was a mix-up on if he was going to a friend's house, and he told his mom and not his dad or something."

It's possible, sure. But I still feel sick.

Beside me, Lyla being much more personable with this Heather lady than I am. "Yeah. Maybe," she says. "Uh... it's nice to meet you. My dad talks about you all the time."

The smile is back on Heather's face, and all I can think is, *How can she smile at a time like this?* "It's nice to meet you, too. Both of you."

When her smile reaches me, I don't return it. I don't like this Heather lady. I don't like her one bit.

CHAPTER 68

LYLA

The only reason I'm being the slightest bit nice to this stupid Heather lady is because of the promise I made when I was in that shed. I am being the model daughter. The poster child for a perfect kid. It might be killing me inside slightly, but I feel I have no other choice.

The thing is, on top of being a perfect daughter, I also want to be a good sister. I want to be somebody who does the right thing. And I'm not going to just sit here in silence with Heather and Audrey while we await news of what could've possibly happened to our poor, small, innocent little brother.

So I'm quick to devise a plan. It's one I can't really tell Audrey about because she sitting right next to me as the two of us hang out in the living room with Heather. And I get the feeling that if I try to get Audrey away from her so I can fill her in, Heather is going to get suspicious, and I can't allow that.

Quickly, I go on this graphic design app I have and make a fake appointment confirmation from my therapist. Then I email it to myself.

"Crap," I say suddenly, breaking the silence in the room. I stand up off the couch, the email open on my phone. "I completely forgot. I'm supposed to be at therapy in, like, ten minutes."

"Oh..." Heather trails off, looking already uncertain. I knew this would happen, so that's exactly why I show her the email I received. The email that shows my fake confirmation of my fake therapy appointment. She looks at it, and it looks like she wants to read it word for word, but I quickly pull it away before she can. What if there's a typo or something? I can't chance it. This has to work.

"It's literally just right down the street." I explain. "I usually take my bike there anyway. The appointment is only an hour. I'll be back right after it. I'll text Dad and let him know."

"Your dad said that you guys should stay here," Heather says uneasily.

"Well, yeah. But not when it comes to my therapy. He specifically told me he doesn't want me missing any of my appointments. I won't be gone long."

"But Lyla—" Audrey says, but I shoot her a look and she shuts her mouth.

Still, Heather looks worried about it. "I just don't think—"

I'm not even going to stick around to listen to her try to convince me to stay. "I'll be right back! Thank you!"

Then I'm out the door.

I hop on my bike and a pedal as fast as my feet will allow me to go. I know exactly where Aunt Nora's rental is because she's texted me before and asked if we can meet up and hang out. She sent her address along with the message. The only reason I haven't gone yet is because I've had quite a bit going on.

But maybe Aunt Nora has been texting Joey the same thing. Maybe Joey went to her house after school. And maybe Mom is there with them, too. That's why I didn't want to say anything about it to Dad or to Dad's girlfriend, since Dad isn't a fan of our aunt. I just want to tackle this hunch on my own. Maybe Nora asked Joey to hang out with her but also made him promise not to tell Mom or Dad because she's not getting along with either of them right now.

It doesn't take long to get to her house. I throw my bike to the ground, in too much of a hurry to even bother putting the kickstand up. The outside of her rental is creepy. Unmanicured and in a bad part of town. And with the gloomy weather outside, the sun starting to set—earlier every day now that it's getting colder out—it makes the place feel even more eerie.

Still, I carefully climb up the broken steps. I ring the doorbell and then knock on the door, to be extra efficient. I hear a creak. It's loud and it's sudden and it's to my right.

When I snap my head to it, I scream.

The masked figure. The person who kidnapped me. The reason I was locked in a shed for a week.

They're here. Feet away from me, right on the front porch.

Where did they even come from?

I turn to the left and fly over the railing. I try to land on my feet but I am not that graceful so I fall and roll on my back. I catch a glimpse of the masked figure and see that they're right behind me.

I scream some more.

I yell for help.

I scramble to my feet as they, much more gracefully, are able to hop the railing and chase after me.

I run around to the back of the house.

"Nora!" I scream. "Help!"

He must've followed me. I can't recall ever bothering to check over my shoulder the entire time I pedaled my bike over to this house. I've put me and my aunt in danger now.

What else can go wrong?

I clamber up the back porch steps and try the back door. Thankfully, it opens. "Aunt Nora!" I scream. *Please let her be in here.*

I'm in the kitchen of her rental. I take a barstool and quickly throw it down in front of the door as I see, out the window, the figure coming up the steps in that creepy mask. I run through an arch and scream even louder. Quickly, I am shoved by somebody, and I don't even know who until I fall into a coffee table.

The masked figure gets into the house. They push the barstool out of the way and they run through the arch, into the living area where I'm on the ground, and then I look up just in time to see my aunt Nora, who was hiding around the corner, slam a bat into the masked figure's rib cage.

"Let's go!" she shouts at me, grabbing my hand and pulling me up from the ground. Then she's yanking me out the front door. Out to her car.

We both get in in a hurry, and my aunt Nora drives us away from the house.

CHAPTER 69

AUDREY

I'm furious at my stupid twin sister.

How could you leave me alone with this horrible, wretched woman, Ly?

I know that her therapy excuse is total boloney, and it makes me even angrier that she couldn't come up with an excuse that also included getting *me* out of here.

So, I guess I'll just have to figure my own way out.

"If it's okay, I really do have a lot of homework I need to get done," I say to Heather. We're both still sitting in the living room, some random TLC show playing on the television. "I'm just gonna head to my room and work on it. It's better to keep myself distracted, or else I'm gonna go crazy worrying about my brother."

"Yeah, of course," Heather says in a sweet voice. Maybe it wouldn't be so hard to like her if she weren't my dad's girlfriend.

But she is. So...

I start walking down the hall. My phone rings.

It's Dad.

"Dad?" I say when I answer. "What's going on?" *Please let it be good news. Please let Joey be found safe and sound. Please let this all be some crazy misunderstanding.*

"Audrey. I have to be straight with you, okay?" Dad's voice says.

"What?" I feel sick.

"It's not looking good. Your mother kidnapped him. She kidnapped Joey."

"Kidnapped?" I say it incredulously. Like it's impossible to put "kidnap" in a sentence that has to do with my mom and Joey. She's his foster mom. How is it even possible to kidnap him? "What are you talking about?"

"I don't know where she took him. But she took him. It's a long and complicated story, but your mother knows that I want to adopt Joey after the divorce is finalized, and she doesn't want to risk losing him. She is not in her right mind, Audrey. I don't know what's been going on with her, but she needs help. We need to find her."

"Where could she have gone?" My heart is pounding in my chest.

"I don't know. I don't have any idea. Do you?"

Think, Audrey. Think.

"I-I don't know!"

"Your sister is with you, right? Why didn't she answer her phone?"

"She just doesn't have it next to her," I lie, surprised Heather hasn't already texted him to tell him Lyla left.

"Heather is still there, right?"

"Yeah."

"See if she'll order you guys a pizza or something. I don't know how long it's gonna take me to get home, Audrey. Just stay there. And let me know if either of you thinks of any place your mom might have taken him. All right?"

"Dad—"

"I have to go."

The call ends.

My mom kidnapped my brother.

My *mom* kidnapped my *brother*.

I fill in Heather, who has a questioning look on her face when I turn around, then I continue to my room and close the door. I grab my keys out of my backpack and frustratedly figure out how to get this dang window open. It takes a lot of muscle to pull it up, and I don't even bother being careful with the screen as I kick it away from the window. Then I climb out. I run to my car instead of walk calmly, in case Heather has heard the commotion and is coming after me.

I can't sit around and let Dad handle this by himself. Lyla probably doesn't even know what happened. Someone has to help dad. And who else knows Mom besides him? Who else would be capable of figuring out where she might have brought Joey besides him?

Her daughters. The other people who know her best.

I speed away, my tires squealing on the pavement, from Dad's house and drive over to Mom's. I pull into the driveway, too impatient to wait for the garage to open all the way so that I can park in there. I fling my car door open and race to the front door, where I let myself inside.

"Mom?!" I know it's pointless because there's not a chance she would take Joey here, but I call out to her just to be sure. Maybe there's a tiny bit of hope in me about her being here. But I know it's stupid.

Where would Mom have taken Joey? Where would she have left a clue about where she might have taken him?

I go to his room. A bag has been packed. Clothes have been taken out of the closet and the dresser. Wherever she's taken him, apparently they plan on being gone for a while.

"My God, Mom," I breathe, putting a hand to my heart. Then I shake my head and swallow the lump in my throat and continue with my search through the house. I go into Mom's room and see that she's packed a bag as well. And in her medicine cabinet, her pill bottles are gone.

There has to be a clue somewhere.

I leave her room and then stop when I land in front of the study. The study that she's all of a sudden decided she prefers to keep locked. I turn the handle on the door harshly, expecting to find it locked and ready to kick the door in if it is.

But to my surprise, it swings right open.

And what it reveals behind it is truly horrifying.

I step into the room slower than a sloth. My jaw drops open.

Covering every surface of every table are pictures of Carson Price. Are news articles about him. Blog posts. Fact sheets. Pinned up on the wall are the same things. Sticky notes are plastered everywhere with little hand-written captions from Mom. This room makes her seem like a person obsessed.

I'm pretty sure she *is* a person obsessed.

This is what she's been doing all this time? Looking for Carson? Researching Carson? Finding out anything and everything she can about him?

I even see pictures of Eric. *So she knows about him, then?*

For a moment, I've completely forgotten why I've come home at all. All I can do is stare around at all of this Carson Price information, feeling afraid. Feeling worried. Feeling confused.

I walk over to the desk. Upon picking up some of the many, many papers and pictures of Carson, I nudge the mouse, and the computer comes to life.

What I see, right there on the computer screen, chills me more than anything else here in this room.

Chapter 70

WARNER

When I get to Audrey and Lyla's—their mom's—house, I wonder why Audrey needed me to meet her here when I know she's supposed to be staying at her dad's. I'm only slightly worried because the tone in her voice had been high-pitched and panicky when she said, "I need you to come over. To my mom's. now." And she hadn't really told me much else other than that.

Before I even knock on her front door, she pulls it open and throws her arms around me, and I stumble back with her as I hold her. I squeeze tight, sensing that she needs it.

When she pulls away, she looks pale.

"Hey, what happened?" I ask. She just shakes her head at me, and I don't know what that is supposed to mean.

"Just come look," she says. She turns, reminding me of a floating ghost, and reenters her house, expecting me to follow but not looking back to see if I am. I step inside the house. It's quiet. Still. Too still. Goosebumps break out down my arms.

I follow her down a hall to the left, a part of the house I have never been in before. I follow her to a black wooden door that is cracked open. She pushes it open wider and steps inside. I follow in behind.

"Oh my god," I whisper. Right away, I know what it is she wants me to see.

Carson Price's teenage face is plastered everywhere. Over everything. There are news articles. Pictures of other people that I don't recognize but wonder if they're his family members. His *real* ones. Not his foster ones.

How much did Amelia find out about him? And how much time has she been spending since Lyla's kidnapping doing this research?

"She's obsessed with him," Audrey breathes, looking everything over with me, like she is seeing it with a fresh pair of eyes. Outside, thunder rumbles at just the right time, and I shudder. "She's obsessed with catching him. With getting everyone to believe it was him who kidnapped Ly."

"There's even this," I say, pointing at a paper that shows what Carson Price would look like if he were still alive today. It's creepy. I don't even want to know how she got that information. How much money she has put into all of this research and digging. I wouldn't even be surprised if she has been working with a private investigator.

If Amelia is really that convinced that it was Carson Price who kidnapped her daughter and who has been messing with us, then I think I am inclined to believe her.

Audrey nods, letting me know she's already seen the aged-up photo of him. "There's also this." She walks over to the computer and nudges the mouse to wake up the screen. I walk around the desk so I can see what it is she has to show me.

It's just a bunch of photos, and at first, I don't quite understand what it is I am looking at.

There are pictures of an old truck. It's parked in the middle of the woods. There doesn't appear to be any road around it. There are pictures of it taken from several angles. In some of the truck's windows, blankets hang, covering the interior, and I begin to get the feeling someone lives inside of it.

Then, below those pictures, I see what has Audrey so freaked.

There's a tuft of blond hair in one pic. The scruffy profile view of an oddly familiar face in another. The back of the person, wearing all black and putting some tinder to make a fire in a circle on the ground in another. Then lastly, a full frontal view of them, looking unaware that someone was hiding in the trees, snapping their pictures.

It's Carson Price.

There's no mistaking it. Not when I've just seen the photo showing what he would look like if he were still alive today. The AI technology had been accurate. This picture is definitely of him.

"M-my mom," Audrey chokes out, sounding strained. Stressed. "She got proof. She found him, Warner. She found him."

"I don't understand," I say, swallowing audibly. For some reason, I have to turn away from the photo of him. I don't want to see it anymore. I don't want to look at the eyes of the person who kidnapped Lyla. Who chased after Audrey with a knife. Who put a bomb in my mom's car. "Wh—why hasn't she gone to the police, then? Why doesn't anyone seem to know about this except for… us?"

She shakes her head slowly and crosses her arms like she's cold. I hear raindrops hitting the window behind us. "I don't know. My mom—all of this—it's making her… I don't know. She's losing her mind, Warner."

"Where is she now?" I ask.

She opens her mouth to reply, but then my phone vibrates loudly in my hand, and I look at the screen.

"Who is it?" she asks.

"I don't know," I tell her. "It's a text. From an unknown number."

Even though opening it is the last thing I want to do right now, I know I have to.

Unknown: *Go to the indoor pool of Blackfell High School. Bring Audrey. Come alone and not a word to anyone.*

"What's it say?" Audrey asks, her voice squeaky. I don't want to tell her. I don't want to show her. I click my phone off.

"It's nothing. Wrong number." I try to put it back in my pocket, but then it vibrates with another text. I let out a noise of desperate irritation and open it.

Unknown: *Do it or your mother dies.*

The room quickly begins closing in on me. There's a loud, pounding sound in my ears that's drowning out everything else. I think it's my own heartbeat. My chest is tight. My knees are locked.

And still, another message comes in.

Unknown: *Don't believe me?*

I shake my head. Over and over. It's the only part of my body I can make move. I think I hear Audrey's voice, but I have no idea what it is she's saying to me.

A picture shows up underneath the last text.

It's of my mom. She's in the kitchen, doing the dishes—which isn't like her. But that's not the part of the picture that doesn't fit. The part that doesn't fit, that makes me want to vomit, is the fact that I can tell the photo was taken by someone from directly inside my house.

My phone is ripped from my hand before I can do anything about it. I fall back into the desk chair, my entire body shaking.

How can this be happening?

"I'll go."

I look up. It was Audrey who spoke.

"What?" I ask, having hardly heard her. I can still even barely focus on anything other than that sentence. *Do it or your mother dies.*

"I'll go, Warner."

Now I get it. Audrey is telling me she'll go to the pool at school.

"No." I shake my head. "No."

She clasps my forearm. It's strangely comforting. Like I didn't know how comforting Audrey's touch could be until this exact moment.

"Yes. I'm not going to let anything happen to Maddy, okay?" Her hand leaves my skin. Her body starts to leave the room.

I get myself out of the chair. "Audrey, no!" I'm suddenly realizing what it is she is willing to do for me.

She ignores me and disappears down the hall.

I chase her. When I get close enough, I take her hand and spin her back to me. "No, you're not going there." My voice is loud, strong, firm. "You're not going anywhere near there."

She looks deeply into my eyes. Then she yanks her hand from my grasp. "You can't stop me. Not from this." And then she is speeding away from me again, right out her front door.

And I have no choice but to go after her.

CHAPTER 71

Audrey

I do the driving. Warner sits in the passenger seat, complaining about how I shouldn't be doing this. About how I need to pull over. About how there has to be another way to stop this freak from hurting—or killing—his mother. I won't hear any of it, though. My life is not worth more than someone else's. It's not worth more than Madeline Carpenter's. Warner needs his mom. Dean might be a little more in the picture now, but for most of his life, Warner always only ever had Maddy. And I won't let her get taken away from him just because we decided not to listen to the demand of this sicko.

"How do we know he's not just going to—I don't know, try and kill her anyway?" Warner asks, his phone to his ear as he tries to call his mom for the third time. "Ugh, why won't she *freaking* answer?!" His loud tone makes me jump in my seat a little. But I keep driving. I have to get to the school. To the indoor pool. Why our tormenter wants us to go there, I have no idea.

"Audrey, can you say something?" Warner asks me. "Please? I am freaking out right now. Seriously."

"It'll all be over soon," I tell him, not sure exactly what I mean by that. How will it end? I gulp. "It has to be."

"Please." He is literally to the point of begging. "Just stop driving." His voice is a whisper. "Pull over, Audrey."

I don't listen. I don't stop this car until we pull into the vacant parking lot, in the rainy, dark night, outside of Blackfell High School.

I turn off my Mini Cooper and get out of the car. I start walking straight for the school. Warner is a few steps behind me, but then he jogs a bit to catch up.

"This is insane," he says. "We should call the police. Set a trap. Think about what we're getting ourselves into first before we just *go* in there!"

I say nothing and try the door handle of the front entrance. It's unlocked.

"Audrey!"

"There's no time, Warner!" I throw over my shoulder. "He was *in* your house. He was steps away from your *mom*. He said to tell no one. We have no choice. We have to play by his rules."

This shuts him up. For now, at least.

We go inside and walk until we turn a corner. The only sounds I can hear are our jagged breathing and our wet sneakers squeaking on the linoleum tile.

There are two entrances from inside school into the indoor pool. I walk to the one closest and put my hand on the handle. It's cold to the touch and sends a shiver through me.

I have to do this.

I open the door. Warner follows me in.

The lights on the ceiling of the indoor pool are on. The water inside of the pool is still. The rain and wind batter against the foggy windows on the far side of the room. The smell of chlorine floods my nostrils.

I don't see anyone else in here.

"Where is he?" I ask out loud.

"I... I don't see anyone," Warner says in a cautious tone. He stands right next to me, shoulder to shoulder, even though there is plenty room for us to spread out. He doesn't want to leave my side. He doesn't want me to get hurt. It's understandable.

But it might be inevitable.

Didn't Carson always want *me* to be the one who was taken anyway?

I'm about to ask Warner what we should do next. But then I hear the creaking noise of the second door, on the other end of the pool, opening.

And there.

He.

Is.

He lets the door close behind him. Then he just stands there, the mask over his face. Staring at us.

"Here, Carson!" Warner calls, his voice surprisingly strong. "She's here, okay?! What do you want from us now? Where is my mom?!"

Carson, underneath his completely unnecessary mask, now that we know he's alive, doesn't move. Nor does he speak.

He's still just staring at us.

Then Warner's phone blares. It echoes loudly through the pool room.

And that's when the chaos arises.

Carson starts running, his silver, sharp blade out, right in our direction. Warner doesn't see it at first because he's trying to get his phone out. I shove him to get him to move, and then we both sprint toward the door we entered through.

It doesn't open.

"How?!" I shout. It's not like the door locks from the inside!

We turn away from the door and see that Carson is close to us. So close.

But he told Warner to bring *me* here. Which means he doesn't want him.

Just me.

I shove Warner. Hard. He flies forward and hits the ground. I keep running, my fingers crossed that I am right, and that Carson is going to run right past Warner and continue after me instead.

"AUDREY!" Warner bellows. Then he cries out like an angry, feral animal. I look over my shoulder as I run and see that I made the right call. Warner is still down on the ground, his face twisted. Now it's just Carson and me.

I go to cut around the corner of the pool, but it's slippery; there is water everywhere, like someone recently just went swimming, and my foot falls and it brings the rest of my body into the pool with it.

I'm at the diving end. The water is deep.

But I don't sink far. Because Carson is quick to reach a gloved hand in and pull me up by the hair.

Then his hands are around my neck. And I get one single gulp of air in before he pushes me back under the water again, kneeling over the side of the pool.

I don't resurface.

CHAPTER 72

MADDY

When Warner answers the call I am finally returning after I didn't realize he had been trying to get ahold of me, I don't understand what he's saying to me. All I hear is a muffled sort of sound, like he's accidentally butt-dialed me.

"How?!" a girl's voice calls loudly. Now *that*, I could hear. Warner is somewhere echo-ey, like a gymnasium or concert hall.

"Warner?" I try. But I don't get any response. I hear more of a shuffling noise. Then I hear a series of thuds and thumps. Then Warner's voice is clear.

"AUDREY!"

And right after it, he screams. He screams like he's been hurt.

"Warner, what's going on?!" I demand, my pulse instantly picking up speed. There's more shuffling noises. I think maybe I hear what sounds like a splash.

When Warner talks again, his voice is clearer and quieter. He's whispering, but he also sounds like he's in a great deal of pain. "Pool. At school. Carson." He grunts out the words.

"Warner, are you okay? Tell me you're okay. Now!"

"Audrey, no!" Warner shouts. "STOP!"

A dry sob escapes me. I've pieced it together. Warner is somewhere where Carson Price is. And he's been hurt. And now it seems like Carson is hurting Audrey. And Warner is telling me so I can do something about it.

I have to do something about it.

"I'm coming, Warner, I'm coming. Just—hang on!" I don't want to hang up. Because then I will have no idea what's happening to my baby boy, but I have to. I press end and call 911 as I rush to my borrowed car. I freeze, only momentarily, when I reach my front door, because I have found that it's wide open. Wide open like someone just waltzed right in here—or out of here—without me even detecting them.

Dispatch picks up and I bark out that they need to send officers to the school ASAP. I'm shaking all over and I know I am in no condition to drive, especially in this thunderstorm, but I do so anyway. Because I have to get to my son. I have to save him. Save Audrey. Besides, Craig Fritz works for the police. And Craig Fritz and Carson Price were best buds in high school. So I don't feel I can trust the cops to take care of it.

I might have to try and save my son and Audrey all on my own.

LYLA

"What do we do now?" I ask Aunt Nora as we drive in her old, rattling car. It's been some time now since we left her house in a narrow escape from my kidnapper. "Should we go to the police station and tell them what happened?"

Aunt Nora looks clueless as to what the right answer is. She pulls over to the side of the road sharply, making me almost fly into the window, but I grab the handle above it to steady myself. When I look to see where we are, I see nothing but rain, trees, and darkness around us.

"You shouldn't have ever come to my house, Lyla," Aunt Nora says to me in a scolding tone.

"Wh-what are you talking about?" I demand. "How was I supposed to know he would follow me there?!"

She shakes her head. "I don't think he followed you."

Confusion swipes over me. It washes me out for a moment or two. "Wait, what?" I croak out. "Why else would he have been there, then?"

She sighs. And I know what that sigh means. It means she has something to tell me, and it's been a long time coming.

"Aunt Nora?" I ask.

She won't' look at me. She keeps her hands on the steering wheel, gripping it tight, so tightly her knuckles could break and her fingers could just fall right off. For some reason, I keep staring at them.

"Lyla. You have to know the truth. I've kept it hidden for too long now. And after what I saw back there..."

I don't say anything. But I don't think she is expecting me to.

I can feel her eyes on my face now. I can't look at her.

She continues. "I-I know that Carson is alive."

It's like my world has completely flipped. Like I am hanging upside down, attached to some sort of torture device as blood pools in my head. "Oh," is the only sound that comes out of me, barely even audible. Outside, the rain starts hammering down hard. I can hear thunder rumbling in the distance. Lightning lights up Aunt Nora and the interior of her car every few seconds.

"I found him in the woods that night," she continues. "I found him, and he looked dead, Ly. I seriously thought he was. But then... he woke up. He was hurt, soaked from head to toe, and his head was bleeding badly, but he was alive. And he was okay enough to even stand up on his own. I wanted to know what happened to him. I wanted to know who did this to him. But he wouldn't tell me anything. All he said was that he had to stay dead, and that I had to help him do it. And... I didn't have a choice. I had to agree with him. He was hysterical. And I had never seen him like that. But even without the hysterics, Carson could get...well—he could get really scary."

"He hurt you," I say.

She pauses for a moment. Then she nods. "Often."

I swallow.

She keeps going. "All these years, I have kept his secret. I have let him stay on the run. I... I know he has hurt me in the past, and I know what I've done is wrong, but...I loved him, Lyla. I loved him so much. He was my first love. You don't easily get over your first love. You really don't."

I don't know what to say to that. I am plenty over Jackson. But I know he's not over me.

Maybe all those years together, I never even really loved him. How am I supposed to know? What kind of love would it take for me to want to stay with someone who abused me?

"I don't understand," I say instead of one of the five-hundred questions I have in my head right now about all of this.

"I know. I'm getting there. You'll hear me out, won't you?"

I glance at the door lock behind her and see that she hasn't locked it. She's not trying to trap me in here. She's not trying to keep me from running. All she wants is for me to want to listen to her. To understand her.

"Okay," I whisper, a tear streaming down my cheek. Has my Aunt Nora known Carson kidnapped me all this time? Had she even known where he kept me, and she never told a soul?

"I was completely brainwashed by him," Aunt Nora says. "By the feelings I had for him. And he knew that. And he took advantage. He told me we would be together—that we were together, just in secret, because he had to stay dead. But I never understood why. I never got why he couldn't just tell me. He said it was too dangerous. That telling me would put my life in jeopardy. So, I let him keep his secrets. And I helped hide him. For years, Lyla. *Years*. I can't even tell you how much money I've spent—anyway. Eventually, I...I started to go to therapy on my own. I started to understand just how used I was by him. How unloved I was by him. And so... I told him I was done. I didn't want to help him anymore, Lyla. I wanted him out of my life forever. I wanted to act as if he really were dead, just like everyone else assumed he probably was.

"But he wouldn't let me. Sometimes, I would be on the run with him, just so we could spend time together. But once, while we were apart, I told him I didn't want to see him anymore. But he found me. And... it wasn't pretty. He hurt me. Blackmailed me. Made it basically impossible to stop helping him—by wiring him money and whatnot—stay on the run. The more I wanted to be done with him, the more he started acting like he really, truly needed me around. He told me I was the only one in his life. The only one. And that I couldn't just leave him. It was like the tables had turned and *he* was the one who was suddenly desperate to keep *me*. But for what? The company? The money? Was it ever really for love?

"So. Call me naïve. Call me the dumbest, cruelest, most idiotic aunt—*person*, even—in the entire world. But I didn't know he was the one behind all of the attacks on you and your sister. And Warner, even. I think I've been in denial about it. I think I've told myself, 'There's no way he would risk getting caught just to get back at me.' But now... especially after what just happened at my rental... now I feel like there is no way I can keep denying what's right in front of me any longer."

Aunt Nora suddenly clutches my forearm with both of her tiny hands. Hard. Just as hard as she had been gripping the steering wheel. Thunder booms. I jump. Aunt Nora doesn't seem fazed by how terrified I am.

"He's moved on from his threats and attempts to hurt me. He knows they don't work quite as well anymore. He's moved on to my family. And the only family I have is you guys. And I made the mistake of telling him Maddy is like a sister to me, so that's why he's going after her and Warner, too. Lyla. I've been so stupid. This is all my fault. I'm the reason for everything."

She doesn't get it. She doesn't know that she isn't the main reason for Carson going after us. Because even after all of these years, she still doesn't know that it's my mom—her sister—and Maddy who tried to kill Carson that night. That they're likely more the cause of this than she is.

But who am I to rat them out? And why did Carson never tell Aunt Nora about them?

There is still so much that just doesn't make any sense.

Aunt Nora opens her middle console. I have no idea what it could be she's about to pull out. When I see the shiny, black handle of a gun, my heart nearly stops beating.

"I have this," Aunt Nora says, wiping tears from her eyes with her free hand. "But... I don't know if I'm capable. I also don't know what other options I have. I... I don't know what to do here, Lyla. But Carson needs to stop this."

My aunt wants to kill him. To kill Carson to get him to stop.

"We'll... we'll figure something out," I try. The air in the car is *whomp-whomp*-ing around me. Everything feels heavy. So, *so* heavy. "I..."

"There's something else," Aunt Nora says.

All I can think is, *What now?*

I wait. Aunt Nora speaks. "Carson killed Sydney Hutton."

CHAPTER 74

WARNER

It feels like my ribs have been completely crushed, but I manage to get myself back to my feet anyway. I tell Mom as best as I can through the blinding, searing pain, where I am and what is happening.

After Audrey pushed me to the ground, Carson Price, the man in that mask, stomped on me with his huge, steel-toed boots, as hard as he could, to keep me down, before he continued after Audrey.

And now, he is holding her down underwater in the pool.

"Leave her alone!" I grumble through my teeth, trying to sound strong and intimidating as I slowly—much too slowly—make my way to him. Audrey is flailing and splashing and trying to come up for air, but Carson won't let up.

He's killing her.

And when the water stills, that's when I yell out in rage. That's when the pain of my ribs go away. That's when I am able to finally start running at him.

I tackle Carson, flying into him with my entire body. The knife skids away from the both of us. I land a punch, but it doesn't move the mask from his face. And he doesn't make a sound, either. I punch him again. And again.

Then I roll off of him and go to the pool. I reach into the water and use all my strength, screaming at the tops of my lungs while I do it, to heave Audrey's lifeless body out of the water.

She can't be dead. She can't be dead.

But I've forgotten about the knife.

And through my peripherals, I can see Carson going after it.

"Audrey," I sob, having no choice but to leave her there on the ground as I try and scramble backward away from Carson. He reaches the knife and picks it up. He gets to his feet, slowly. Then he turns around and fixes his mask so it's not askew. I keep crawling backward. I don't have any fight left in me. I am in too much pain—physically and mentally—to keep trying to stop him. Or to make my escape. My ribs are crushed. And Audrey is...

Audrey is...

She's...

Carson steps in front of me. He raises the knife.

"Why are you doing this to us?" I know they're likely the last words I will ever say. And he's the only one that will ever hear them.

The knife starts swinging down.

BANG!

A sound so loud breaks through the room, and I feel that my eardrums have ruptured.

"Stop!" a voice yells while my head pounds and my ears ring. I can barely hear it, but when I turn my head, I see Detective Fritz and Officer Wilde, both with their guns drawn, standing in front of the door Carson had entered through. The noise reverberating inside of my head had been a gunshot.

Carson ducks and runs, straight to the doors that lead outside. He bursts through them in a flash, and just as quickly, Detective Fritz is chasing after him while Wilde puts his gun away and runs to Audrey.

Out of everyone in the world, I never thought it would be Freaky Fritz who saves my life.

CHAPTER 75

AMELIA

Finally, we pull into the hotel I booked on my phone when I had pulled into that gas station a little while back during mine and Joey's road trip. The photos of the hotel had made it look much nicer than it really is, but it's too late to do anything about it now. We're in a busy town, on a busy street, and back in the car, Joey doesn't seem like he has any intention of getting out.

"Come on, Joey," I say through my open car door. "What are ya still doing back there? We're finally here!"

"We've been driving for hours. It's late. And this isn't even an ice cream shop," he says, pouting.

I internally wince. Maybe I should have stopped to *actually* get him ice cream on the way here. Maybe he would be happier if I had.

Would Gentry have gotten him ice cream? Would Joey have preferred to go on this road trip with him over me?

I need more meds.

"I know," I say. "But we're going to go to the best ice cream shop there is," I tell him. "It's just closed now because driving here took a lot longer than I thought it would. I'm sorry, Joey."

"I just want to go back."

This hurts me. To my core. He doesn't want to be here with me. He doesn't want me to be the one who adopts him. He wants to be with Gentry. With his father.

I open his door for him. "Don't say that" I try. I just want to change his mind. I *can* change his mind. I'll make him see how much better it is to spend time with me and not Gentry. "Come on. Let's go jump on the bed in our hotel room!"

He's unbuckled his seatbelt at least, so I take that as a good sign, and I gently pull him out of the car.

"Please—stop!" Joey complains. He gets out of the car, but then he yanks his arm away from me.

That's when the smile I've worked so hard to keep on my face finally falls off.

"I don't want to be here," he says, slowly walking backward. "I want my phone back. I want to call Dad. You're not acting like yourself. You're—"

A loud horn blares, and that's when I realize that Joey has backed up right into a busy street, and there's a huge tractor-trailer truck coming straight at him.

"Joey!" I scream, diving for him without a single other thought. I pull him back away from the truck in just enough time, and the two of us fly back onto the sidewalk in front of where I—horribly—parked my car.

"Joey, are you okay?!" I cry out, breathing hard. How did that happen? *How* did that *just* happen? How had I not even seen that Joey had wandered straight into oncoming traffic? What is *wrong* with me?

"I was wondering the same thing!" Joey shouts, getting to his feet.

Wait, had I been talking out loud?

"Yes!" Joey screeches. "You are talking out loud! Something is wrong with you! And you're supposed to be my mom! You're supposed to take care of me! But right now, I'm just scared! I just want to go home!"

I wish that truck would come back and run me right over. I look up at Joey, who seems more mature and alert and in charge of this situation than I, his caretaker, am. How could this all have gone so wrong? How could it all have turned this way?

"Joey," I say, pulling myself up on my elbows, not bothering to try and stand. I'm all wobbly and weak right now anyway. I would probably just fall right back down if I tried to get up. "I don't know how this happened. I don't know what I'm doing. I'm—I'm sorry."

"I want to go home," he demands.

I nod and begin to cry. "My phone is in the front seat. Please. Will you get it for me?"

He does as he's asked. When he hands it to me, the screen is lit up, and I know he's seen how many times Gentry, and other numbers, have tried to get ahold of me.

I already know without having to check what those other numbers are. The police. Gentry found out what I did, and he called
them.

And now I need to turn myself in.

* * *

Gentry isn't going to press charges. Why, is beyond me.

We're at the station. I don't even know where Joey is right now. All
I know is I am in a room alone. Alone until Gentry walks in, followed
by my own mother.

"What are you doing here?" I ask, putting my elbows on the cold
table as she closes the door behind her. They both stand there in
front of me in my chair, neither of them making the move to sit
down with me.

"Gentry called me," Mom says.

"Okay..." I trail off. Why did she need to be involved?

"You could have killed him," Gentry says. I already told him about
what nearly happened at that hotel. I wanted him to hear it from
me before Joey told him later.

"I know," I say. But I don't even want to be here right now. While
I was three hours away, kidnapping my own foster son, one of my
daughters was getting attacked by Carson.

I could have lost two of my kids this evening.

What I don't understand is why I feel so numb about it.

"Honey," Mom tells me. She steps forward like she wants to give
me a comforting arm touch or hug, but then she steps back next
to Gentry, like she'd rather be next to him. She probably doesn't
want to catch my crazy. "Gentry isn't going to press charges, as you
know."

I nod. I feel nothing... nothing... nothing.

"But there's something we need from you," she continues. "Both
of us. And your son. And your daughters."

"Anything," I say, meaning it.

"Amelia, you need help." Gentry's voice isn't as caring and soothing as Mom's had been. "And we'd like you to... to go away to
treatment."

CHAPTER 76

WARNER

It's nearly four in the morning. I am at home.

And I still have no idea where my mother is.

After I was able to answer her call discreetly inside of the pool, I know she heard me, and I know she found out where I was and what was happening to me because it was she who called the police. It was she who sent Wilde and Fritz to save me. She is the reason I am still alive right now.

But after that. Nothing. Mom is missing. No one has seen or heard from her since she made the call to the police.

And I am so terrified of why that is that I can hardly even breathe.

Back at school earlier, after Fritz had left the indoor pool to chase after Carson in his stupid disguise, Wilde had given Audrey mouth to mouth. And she came to. But then she fell unconscious again and was taken away in an ambulance. I went away in another ambulance. I got some tests done. Found out I had three broken ribs. I was given pain meds and told to take it easy for six weeks.

By then, I still hadn't heard from Mom. No one had.

So, I called Officer Wilde, worried. He hadn't heard from her either. I asked if Craig had caught Carson yet. He didn't have an answer for me. I tried to go see Audrey but couldn't. I was advised by Wilde to go home and wait there in case my mom showed up. And Wilde told me he personally was out searching for her. It has done little to ease my nerves, knowing that Wilde is searching. All I know is Carson said he was going to kill my mother, and now no one can find her.

A knock on the door jolts me out of my thoughts, and the jolt sends a stab of pain through my tender ribs. I slowly get up and answer the door, stupidly hoping it's my mom even though I know she'd have no reason to knock instead of just let herself in.

Both Detective Fritz and Officer Wilde are on my front porch.

And they don't look like they have good news to tell me.

Behind them, it's still dark and cloudy out. Lightning still streaks across the sky every so often, but I don't hear any thunder anymore and the rain has stopped.

"Did you find her?" I ask. "Did you find Carson?"

"We haven't been able to locate your mother yet, Warner," Officer Wilde says, looking grim. "But we wanted to both come and tell you some other news. In person."

"What?" My stomach drops.

Please don't let Audrey be dead.

"I did manage to find Carson Price, after over twenty years of searching, in the woods earlier this evening," Fritz says.

"Th-that's good news, isn't it?" My eyebrows go sky high. I don't understand how they can be telling me something so relieving, so monumental, but have these grim expressions on their faces.

"Maybe," Fritz says, looking more tired than I think I have ever seen him. "But the thing is, Warner, when I found him, he was—he was dead."

CHAPTER 77

AMELIA

I'm not even allowed to go see my own daughter in the hospital before Gentry and my mother both drive me to the institute. Maple Meadows Psychiatric Hospital. At least it looks nothing like an insane asylum. It seems as if Gentry and Mom are willing to spare no expense to keep me in here. Maybe I should be grateful.

They walk me inside, which I think might be a nice gesture. Either that or they just want to make sure I didn't try and run for it if they were to just drop me on the curb.

When I am admitted, I give over everything. Even my phone. I am given a hospital-like gown. I'm told it's not what I am wearing the entire time I am in here, it's just so they can run some initial tests on me. Bloodwork and whatnot on top of the many psychiatric evaluations I will undoubtedly be going through while I am here as well.

I feel numb the entire day. Like I am watching someone else's life, because there is no way this is mine. There is no way Amelia Flynn Bailey turned into... whoever this person in the hospital gown with the sunken cheeks and red, bloodshot eyes is.

What has happened to my world?

I don't even know how much time passes after the tests are done, I am given a tour, shown my room, and given the scrub-like outfit to change into. All I know is it's already time for Mom and Gentry to say their goodbyes to me.

"Thank you for doing this," Gentry tells me as we stand in the "community room" with all the other patients visiting with their family or hanging out doing puzzles, reading, or watching something mindless on TV.

"Yeah," I manage to croak out. I don't want to cry. I don't want to scream. I hardly even want to talk.

"It's not forever," Mom says, tilting her head slightly and giving me a kind smile. "And I think it will help. A lot more than you might even realize."

I stiffly nod my head.

Whatever they need me to do. Whatever I need to do so I never put any of my children in danger ever again.

Gentry puts a hand on my lower back, pulls me slightly into him, and kisses me tenderly on the forehead. I look up at him through my lashes. He doesn't look at me.

When he steps back, Mom throws her arms around me and squeezes tight. I wonder if this is how she said her goodbye to Nora all those years ago after she and Dad dropped her off at a similar place.

"Call me tomorrow," Mom says. Then she steps back as well. And Mom and Gentry leave.

I don't know what to do with myself. I retreat to my room; glad I am not forced to have a roommate and that it looks more like a very clean hotel suite than something I would see in a movie about a psych ward. Maybe I can do this. Maybe I can just pretend I am on a little vacation. Somewhere I can rest and recover. Like a retreat.

I sit on the bed, feel how stiff it is, and I hear the frame creak under my weight from the poor quality of it.

Definitely not a retreat.

I don't know how long I sit there, numbly, until there is a soft knock on my door. Then it opens before I can even give the person permission to come in.

It's one of the nurses I talked to earlier. I think her name is Sandra.

"So, I was wondering if you could come into the doctor's office for a chat," she says, her face devoid of any expression that might hint to me what the doctor wants to talk to me about. I glance out the window, wishing I could just leave this place instead.

"Sure," I say, still feeling flat and numb. I get off the bed, and I follow Sandra down some halls, through some locked doors, and to an office with a dark mahogany wood door.

Sandra knocks.

"Come in," says the doctor's voice. The door opens, and I see the man I also spoke to earlier. His name is Dr. Willoughby, and he's in his late sixties with a bald head and a kind smile. "Hi, Amelia, why don't you take a seat?"

I do as I'm asked and look behind me to see that Sandra has closed the door and left us alone.

"I wanted to go over your test results with you," Dr. Willoughby says.

"Okay..." I bite my bottom lip. Did they find some sort of strange, brain-eating disease in my bloodwork, and that's the explanation for why my anxiety meds haven't been working? Why I have felt so crazy lately?

"You stated that the only medication you were on was diazepam."

"Correct," I say.

He gives me a pointed look. It makes him seem less kind than I thought he was earlier.

"Is there a problem?" I ask.

"Your blood work told me otherwise." He holds a small stack of paper in his right hand and reads it over.

"I'm—I'm sorry?"

I barely even comprehend what he tells me afterwards. He goes on about the other drug found in my system. How there is no harm in me coming clean about it, and how I'm not going to be judged here. Or something like that.

But as I sit in that small, stiff chair, the room around me spins and closes in. My chest tightens. I want to crawl out of my skin. All I ever took were the pills prescribed to me.

But I also know I haven't been myself lately. So, I don't think the doctor's test results are wrong. I think I know exactly how this happened.

Carson Price did this to me.

CHAPTER 78

LYLA

My sister nearly died. My sister nearly died, and I hadn't even known she had left my dad's house.

My brother nearly died, too. At the hands of my own mother.

When I learn what happened to Audrey, the same time I had to learn what my mother had done and what nearly happened to Joey, I'm not allowed to go talk to Mom because of where she's being taken, so I head straight for the hospital, where Audrey has been admitted.

"I just don't get it," I tell her. "I should have felt that you were in trouble or something, shouldn't I have?" I sit on the edge of her hospital bed. For now, it's just the two of us in her room. The TV is on, playing a cartoon, but it's muted. It's clear other people have been here based on the flowers, cards, stuffed animals, and additional chairs that have been brought in. I don't know where anyone else is right now. All I know that it's just me and her, and I'm glad about it.

We have a lot to talk about.

"That's what I thought when you were kidnapped" Audrey explains, her voice weak. Her face pale. Her hair in a messy ponytail. "But I guess that twin telepathy stuff doesn't actually work. I think it's just a myth."

I frown. "Carson really tried to kill you."

She nods, and I can tell she'd rather me not talk about it. But I have to talk about it. "He kidnapped me for days, and never tried to kill *me*."

"Lucky you."

"I'm not trying to brag." I shake my head quickly and stare out the window, in deep thought over it. "It's just... strange. I don't get it."

"Tell me about it."

"And Warner," I continue. "Where is he now? Is he okay?"

She shrugs smally. It's like she can barely move her body, and I hope she's just feeling heavy from the pain meds and isn't actually this weak. "I don't know. But no one can seem to find his mom. Maddy."

My stomach dips. "*She's* missing now?"

"Apparently."

I run a hand through my hair and take in a deep gulp of air. "Oh my God. This craziness with Mom. With you. Now Maddy is missing... What is happening, Ree?"

"Hey," she says, and I can tell she's trying to be comforting to me. "I'm okay. Joey is okay. Mom is going to be okay. And I am sure Maddy will be found soon. Don't worry, Ly. Okay?"

Too bad worrying is quickly becoming the thing I am best at doing.

CHAPTER 79

AUDREY

I tell Lyla all about what happened to Warner and me in that pool at Blackfell High. About how Carson escaped and Detective Fritz went after him. How I remember waking up on the floor next to the pool, under Officer Wilde's piercing gaze, before I blacked out again and woke up here with Dad filling me in on how Mom was found with Joey and how they were taking her to a place she could "get better."

When I finish filling her in, I quickly discover that while all this was going down, she was off having quite a night of her own. That she went to go see Aunt Nora to try and figure out where Joey was. And how it led to her learning everything she did about Aunt Nora and Carson. She also told me about how Aunt Nora had a gun. Like she wants to kill Carson so he can't hurt anyone again.

And then I learn about Sydney.

"He... he killed her?" I ask my sister. I should feel relieved to finally have an answer about what happened to Sydney that night. But I don't feel relieved. I feel sick. Confused. "Why? How?"

"Aunt Nora didn't go into specifics. But Carson was there, during the upperclassman camping trip. And Aunt Nora thinks Sydney saw him snooping on us that night—when she had been asking the three of us to meet her. And he worried she was going to say something to someone about it. So, he... yeah."

"Oh my God."

"And he told her about it because he wanted her to know just how capable he was of actually hurting one of us if he really wanted to. If Aunt Nora wouldn't... comply to what he wants."

"So, for the past twenty years, Aunt Nora has just been in this messed up, toxic, quasi relationship with him while he's been on the run for reasons she doesn't even know about."

"Exactly."

"And he wants to hurt us to hurt her."

"Yes."

"So now she wants to kill him."

"*Wants* to. But she doesn't know if she could ever actually go through with it. She did love him once, after all. Imagine Mom trying to decide on if she should kill Dad or not."

I scoff. "Uh, no thanks."

"Fair."

As we sit there in silence, I hear the loud noise of her stomach rumbling. "When's the last time you ate something?" I ask, giggling slightly.

"I don't even remember," she tells me.

"Go get something to eat at the cafeteria. Seriously."

Lyla sighs and gets off the bed. "Want anything?"

My stomach revolts inside of me. I frown. "No."

"Kay. Be right back. Don't go anywhere."

"Ha ha."

She shoots me a wink and walks out. I look over at the yellow flowers on my side table. They're from Ryan. He dropped them off while I was asleep and left me a note that said he didn't want to disturb me but that he was super close by and could come back to see me when I woke if I texted him. I smile thinking about it. But I don't want him seeing me like this. So, I will just see him when I get out of here. Hopefully it's soon.

I pick up my phone with the hand that doesn't have needles stuck inside of it and try texting Warner again.

Me: *Any word on your Mom? Or on you? R U ok?*

I feel anxious since I haven't seen him or heard from him since the... incident. I hope he's all right.

I go to set my phone back down and maybe rest my eyes so that I don't have to process everything Lyla just told me about Aunt Nora, but before I can, my phone buzzes, and on the screen is a TikTok notification.

From Toxeydramaenthusiast.

Great.

In wonder for a second if I should skip it. If I am already overwhelmed enough as it is with what I have just been through and what I've already learned.

But I also don't want to be too out of the loop.

So I watch the video. It's just of a single image. Carson Price's high school yearbook photo.

I turn the volume up so I can hear what the voiceover is saying.

"After twenty years missing, Carson Price was finally found in the woods...right here in Toxey... late last night—technically early this morning. That's correct—you all heard me right. Carson Price has been alive all this time. Or... at least... he was."

My eyebrows furrow. I keep watching.

"When he was found, by Detective Craig Fritz of Toxey Police Department, who was also Carson Price's best friend in high school apparently, Carson Price was dead. *Dead*. Details are still in development, but the cause of death is rumored to be suicide via a self-inflicted gun wound. We don't know how long he had been in the woods, or if he was the one who was behind what's been happening to the Bailey and Carpenter family all this time. Do you think he was the one responsible? And does that mean that it's all finally over if he was?"

CHAPTER 80

WARNER

I bolt for the door when I hear a knock, instead of finally texting Audrey back, because I am hopeful that it's my mom, finally having returned from wherever the heck she's been all this time.

It's not Mom at the door, though. It's Dean.

"Oh," I say in lieu of a greeting, my face falling.

"Hey, Warner," Dean says, looking glum. "I wanted to come by and check on you. If that's okay. I... I heard what happened. I heard no one can find Maddy."

I don't say anything. I just walk away from the door and leave it open, the only signal I bother to offer that I don't mind if he comes inside. He takes the cue and enters my house and closes the door behind him. I walk over to the living room, push all the clean laundry off of the armchair onto the ground, and flop myself into it. Dean stands in the living area, looking unsure if he wants to sit with me or not.

"You haven't heard from her." I don't even phrase it like a question.

Still, he answers me like it had been one. "I haven't. I'm sorry. I've been trying, though. I'm sure she will be found soon."

All I can think is it's another situation like what happened with Lyla. Except this time, my mom is stuck somewhere where Carson can't even feed her trail mix, protein bars, and bottles of water like he did for Lyla. Instead, Mom is trapped somewhere no one will ever find her, and Carson is dead, so he can't even lead us to her.

I say nothing to Dean.

He sighs. He sounds exhausted. I look at him for the first time since he's showed up—like, I *really* look at him. He *looks* exhausted. Troubled. Worried. He doesn't look like the calm, cool, collected English teacher and football coach I have gotten used to knowing. He's different now.

"So," I start slowly. "Did you also hear about what happened with Carson Price?"

He nods his head, and finally, he takes a seat on the sofa. "He... he died."

"Yeah. All this time, he's been alive. Then he just... dies all over again."

"I'm sorry, Warner."

"For what?"

"All of this. It's not fair. What you're being forced to deal with."

I say nothing.

"I think—I don't know how you feel about it, but—it might be best if I stick around until we figure out where your mom went," he continues.

"Oh." I don't know how else to react to what he's just said. What am I supposed to say? My father wants to look after me since my mother hasn't been located.

"I could just stay here," he says. "Crash on the sofa or whatever—if she doesn't show before tonight, anyway. And I doubt that we'll even get to that point. Or, you can crash at my place. I have a spare room. It's totally up to you. Whatever you'd be more comfortable with."

"Yeah." I don't know why I say it. There's no way I can picture myself going to stay at Dean's house. I don't care if he's my father or nor. "Sure."

He pulls his vibrating phone out and checks it. I watch as his face clouds over. Grows dark. His eyebrows lower. His jaw hardens.

"Everything okay?" I ask, my stomach twisting and my heart immediately skipping a beat. Has be heard from Mom?

"Warner. I... I have to go." He stands from the couch.

"I thought you wanted to stay," I say, not meaning to sound like a whiny kid. Why has he changed his mind all of a sudden?

"I do," he tells me quickly. "I am staying. I just have to go check on something. I'll be fast. I promise." He sounds like he's sorry he's letting me down. Like I am the one who begged him to come here. But that's not the case. So I sit up straighter and try to look unaffected.

"Kay," I say.

He stuffs his phone in his pocket, purses his lips, and heads for the door. "I'll bring some food on my way back. Chinese good for you?"

"Whatever."

"I'm sorry, Warner. I wouldn't leave right now if it weren't absolutely necessary."

"I don't care, Dean," I tell him. But what is it that he's finding "absolutely necessary?" Suddenly, I am suspicious.

So, I wait a little after he leaves, making sure to watch which direction he drives his car when he does, and then I get in my Jeep and I...follow him.

Maybe it's wrong. Sue me. Maybe I should have stayed at home in case Mom shows up. Oh well. I have a bad feeling about whatever it is my *father* is about to go do, and so I need to know what it is. It's like my body is telling me I don't have any other choice in the matter.

The drive takes us somewhere outside of the city of Toxey, but we don't go far until Dean pulls into the parking lot of a brand-spanking-new-looking building. Some kind of college? Hospital?

I pull in—keeping my distance and hoping he doesn't see the bright red of my vehicle in his rearview mirror in the luminous, late afternoon sun—and finally see the building's title.

Maple Meadows Psychiatric Hospital.

It sounds familiar, and I am confused as to why that is.

But then it hits me.

And just to confirm I'm right, I take out my phone and scroll to the multiple messages Audrey has sent me since she woke in the hospital. And there it is:

Audrey: *They found my mom and sent her to Maple Meadows Psych Hospital. For kidnapping Joey. This is crazy.*

So that's what this is—Dean is visiting Amelia Bailey in her new home.

My blood starts to boil. Dean said he wants to be a family. With me and my mom. And my mom is currently missing. And what is Dean doing about it? He's visiting his ex-fling—Amelia!

I instantly think everything he's told us about wanting to be a family is a lie. He doesn't want anything do with my mother. He's just been leading her on and saying whatever he can so he can at least get to know me. It's not fair. All my mom wanted when she was younger was for him to step up. For us to be a family. And he brought her that promise, even if it was years later.

And he's a liar.

My phone lights up in my hand with a new text. I figure it's Audrey checking in... again.

But it's not.

The text is from a number I don't have saved:

Unknown: *It's your mom. I just wanted to tell you that I'm fine. And that I don't want you to worry about me. Ok?*

CHAPTER 81

AMELIA

He came.

He actually came.

I don't know how he even knows I am here. All I know is I hope I'm not dreaming. That this isn't another side effect of the drug I've been accidentally taking.

Dean Reeves sits at a table and waits for me to meet him in the community room. He stands when I approach him. I don't know what to do or say. Then thankfully, he steps toward me and envelops me in a hug. A tight one, where he allows me to bury my head in his neck, and he brushes the back of my hair with his hand.

"You okay?" he asks me. We sit in black plastic chairs with metal legs at a round table meant for six people.

"I don't know," I answer honestly. "I just found out that the only reason I'm in here is because Carson Price switched out my...meds... for ones that have made me basically insane."

"He...what?"

"Yeah."

"Your mom, believe it or not, was the one who texted me to tell me you were here. She said she thought I might want to know."

My mom might be nosy, but in this instance, I am a little glad—if not slightly embarrassed still—about it.

"I... I kept taking more pills because I thought they weren't working," I begin to explain, wanting Dean to know there's a reason I have been acting so erratic.

"Mia, it's okay," he says. Then he clears his throat.

"What's wrong?" I ask, able to read his expression. Of course I can read his expression. I've known him since elementary school. I know Dean. All of him.

"They found Carson Price. And... he's dead. Has anyone told you?"

This was not something I was told by my mom or Gentry when they were here. They must have not known. And I was already told the rules about the TVs in here—no news or reality television allowed.

"He—what?" I choke out.

"I guess not," Dean says with a grimace.

I swallow. How is this happening? How is it possible? "Dead? For... for how long?" Do I even want to know? Had I imagined the interactions I had had with him? Has he been dead all this time? How crazy did that medication really make me, and who was the one who gave it to me if Carson is dead?

I think back to that day. The day in the woods when after days and days of searching, I finally found Carson Price.

He was living out of his truck. In the middle of the Boldosa redwoods. In the middle of absolutely nowhere. When I first saw him, he was building himself a fire and hanging some wet, black clothes up to dry. I took photos of him first, staying a good distance away. I had to get the evidence first. Something to show the police. That was what was most important. After I had them, I thought about turning around and leaving. About heading right to Craig and Officer Wilde so I could show them. So they could finally know the truth.

But the more I stared at Carson, the more I felt compelled to stay. The more my anger came over me. The more I wanted to know why he was here, why he had been hiding, and why he was torturing my family.

So I stepped out from behind the tree I had been hiding behind. "Carson."

I was brought back to the class fieldtrip we took when we were in high school. The walk through the orchards to pick some oranges for a science project. When *he* was my partner. Even back then, I had been skeptical about what kind of person he was.

Carson turned to look at me. And it made it that much more real. "Mia."

I hated that he knew right away who I was, like it confirmed everything. It seemed nothing like how he should have reacted if he was seeing me for the first time in twenty years.

I took a step toward him, my heart hammering in my chest. My body begging for more anxiety medication. So I could stop feeling this way. So I could stop being afraid. Right then and there, I was terrified.

But I kept going.

"What are you doing?" I stupidly asked.

"Wh—how did you find me?" he asked back, not moving from his spot by the fire he hadn't managed to start yet.

"Does that really matter right now?"

"Get out of here, Mia."

I hated that he was calling me that. Like we were old friends or something.

"Excuse me?" I kept walking toward him. "I don't think so. Not this time. Not after what you've done."

"What I've done?" His face sharpened. "I haven't done anything, okay?"

"Are you kidding me?" I asked. "Carson. I *saw* you in the woods that night. You... you kidnapped my daughter. You attacked Audrey. You—"

"You don't have any idea what you're talking about," he retorted suddenly. "You need to leave. Now."

"No!" I snapped. Because who did he think he was?

"I—I didn't do anything to your kids, okay?!" he cried.

"Don't even try to deny it!" I cried back.

He took one step. One single step. Then he stopped again. But his face had turned red. It was weird to see how much he had changed, but also how much he had stayed exactly the same. "I've been on the run all these years trying to escape my father, okay?! That's why I've tried faking my death! To escape from him! To run from him so he doesn't kill me! And I need to stay dead. So you need to get. Away. from. me!"

I shook my head over and over. Lies. All of it. It had to be. "No." I was adamant about it. I wanted his admission of the truth. And I wanted him to come with me and turn himself in at the station.

"I don't want to hurt you, Amelia, but I swear to God I will," he told me. "You don't know me. You never did. And you don't know what I will do to keep my secret. I can't be found. My location can't be revealed. I won't risk it. Leave now or you'll regret it."

"You don't seriously expect me to—" I stopped mid-sentence because he had suddenly stormed over to his orange, rusted truck. He threw open the driver's door and was quick to grab something and turn back to face me.

He had a gun. And it was pointed directly at me.

"Run," he demanded. "*Now*."

And so, I did.

But how much of that memory had really even happened?

In the community room of the psych hospital, Dean continues speaking to me. "Oh—Mia, you were right—he was alive this whole time. That much is true. He... he killed himself early this morning after he attacked Warner and Audrey."

And things are just getting crazier.

"Carson... killed himself?"

"You now know as much as I do about it."

Tears instantly stream down my cheeks, and I don't even know why. Because I am relieved? Because it's over? Because he can't hurt my girls ever again? Because he can't hurt me, Maddy, or Nora?

Dean reaches out and takes my hand in his. "Hey. I know it's a lot. Are you okay?"

"I honestly don't know," I say, wiping my cheek. "But I know I will be."

He nods. "Look. I just... I want you to know how sorry I am for how I've been acting toward you lately. I was mad. But more at myself."

I'm still reeling over the news about Carson. Hearing what Dean is telling me now is almost too much to process. "We don't have to talk about it," I say.

He gives my hand a squeeze. I squeeze it back. He gives me a gentle, kind smile, his eyes gazing deep into mine. And suddenly, I know that everything is okay between us.

Maybe even more than okay.

CHAPTER 82

AUDREY

When I am finally released from the hospital in the evening, I get a ride to the school from Dad to retrieve my car, then I tell him I have a quick stop to make before I see him at his house, where I have already told Ryan I want to meet up with him.

I can tell Dad doesn't want me anywhere out of his sight after what just happened to me, but now that Carson Price is dead, I suppose there is nothing to worry about anymore.

Right?

Carson Price's guilt finally caught up with him. That must be it.

I drive to Sophia Key's house. From what I've seen on social media since Halloween when she was attacked by Carson, she's been a bit of a mess. And I still feel deeply inside of me that the only reason she was attacked was because she used to be a friend of mine, and Carson somehow knew that. And when he could no longer get to me... he went for her instead. She had probably been the person nearest to him after he lost track of where I had gone who had a relationship to me.

I knock on her front door, feeling fine other than being a little tired, dizzy, and nauseated about seeing Soph.

Her mother, Yvette, answers with a big smile on her face. "Audrey! What are you doing here? Aren't you supposed to... be in the hospital? And I haven't seen you in so long! My, your hair! I love it, girlfriend!" She's all smiles and happiness like I've always remembered her being. She doesn't care about everything that's happened. It isn't going to prevent her from treating me like a normal person who deserves kindness. I have no idea where Sophia got her mean streak from. Maybe her dad, who I hardly see or talk to.

"Hi, Yvette," I say, knowing she likes to be called by her first name. "Ms. Key" makes her feel old. "Is Sophia here?"

Yvette frowns, showing wrinkles that age her by a lot. "She's not. But she did text me a bit ago that she was on her way home from hanging with a friend. You're more than welcome to wait."

I came all this way, dedicated to saying what I wanted to say. So I should wait. "Okay," I say with a small smile.

Yvette opens the door wide and lets me enter their quaint, slightly outdated midsized two story home. "You wanna wait in her room? I know you know the way!"

"Sounds great. Thank you."

She reaches out and hugs me. "I am so glad you're okay, sweetheart." I let her chest suffocate me for a moment, then I take a deep breath when she finally pulls away.

"Thank you," I say, feeling awkward. She smiles and turns away from me, leaving me to head up to Soph's room. I take the stairs slowly and flick on some lights on my way, since it's dark up here. When I crack open the door to Sophia's room, I have to turn on her bedroom light, too. It floods the pink, girly space, looking exactly like it had the last time I was in here, which wasn't that long ago but feels like a lifetime.

Only, there is a difference in her room now. One quite noticeable. It sticks out like a sore thumb. Sophia's room is usually frilly, girly, and pastel. The bulky metal equipment between her dresser and the foot of her bed are new. For a moment, I don't know what it is I'm seeing. Then I recognize the green backdrop in front of a camera on a tripod.

A green screen.

She was gifted from her dad not long ago. So we could mess around and...film TikToks in front of it.

I step closer to it. I can't believe I forgot about it. I can't believe I didn't even think about it. Question it.

Sophia has a green screen. In her bedroom. She's the queen of Blackfell High. She loves being the center of attention. She loves gossip. She loves knowing everything juicy going on.

I think... I think Sophia might be Toxeydramaenthusiast.

Something moves outside her window, and I move closer to it. Down below, on the street, a familiar car pulls up to the curb.

It's an old gray Mustang. Sophia gets out of the passenger seat.

In the driver's seat is Jackson Mullens.

CHAPTER 83

LYLA

After I returned to Audrey's hospital room from getting a quick bite to eat at the cafeteria, she filled me in on Carson and his apparent suicide. After that, I decided I needed some air. That I needed to go on a walk.

So I did just that. I left the hospital and I walked. All the way to Mom's.

Here now, outside on the sidewalk, I stare up at our house. I know it's empty inside. I know that Mom is at that psych ward, just like Aunt Nora had been, getting treatment because she had tried to kidnap Joey. I know that when I go inside the house, I will finally be able to see the study, and how Mom transformed it into some sort of Carson shrine.

Carson Price is dead.

It's as if it still won't register in me. I don't know how I feel about it. He locked me up in a shed. He drowned my sister. And now he's dead. I almost feel like in a way, it means he got to get away with it.

I walk up the front path and punch the code into the front door handle, then I let myself in.

I want Mom to be here. I want to find that this has all been one, long, horrific nightmare. That I was just getting back from having a sleepover at Trinity's house.

But my whole life has changed since the last time I did that. Trinity wouldn't even recognize me anymore.

I'm almost afraid to go check out the study for myself, especially since Carson is dead now and it feels eerie to look at pictures of him and proof that he's been alive all this time, but I want to see it. It feels like I have to. To know he was real for a moment. To confirm that face under the mask had been him this whole time.

I enter the study. I see the photos. The articles. I read about his Dad. I get on the computer and see the real photos Mom took of

him. The him that was alive just yesterday. The him who tried to kill
Audrey. The him who held me prisoner in a pool shed.

A sob escapes me as I look at the proof of him existing. Then I
scramble to get to my feet and out of this room.

I need more. I want answers. And the only person I feel I can get
them from is the last person who saw him.

Freaky Fritz.

I leave the study and pace around in area between the open
kitchen and living area.

Detective Craig Fritz lives on the other side of Toxey. My bike is
at my dad's. It would take me all night to walk there. And I doubt
Audrey or Warner are in any sort of mood to come and get me and
take me to him. And I can't ask Wrigley. I don't even know how I
would begin to start explaining everything that's been going on to
him.

I stop pacing and go into the mudroom. I stare, long and hard, at
my car keys hanging from their hook.

I pick them up.

How badly do I want to talk to Fritz? What am I willing to risk?
What am I willing to do?

I go into the garage. I see my parked Toyota there, all glossy and
unused.

I feel so lost. So angry. So confused.

I want those answers.

So, I get in the car.

And I drive.

I'm on such an adrenaline high from making it all the way to Detective Fritz's house—in one piece, too—that I barely pay attention to
the cars in the driveway, or to what his house even looks like, as I
walk up the pathway to his screen door and ring the doorbell. Then
I knock on the screen, too, for good measure. My heart is pounding.
I can't believe I just drove a car.

I drove a car.

I *drove* a car!

Detective Fritz opens the door. It's so weird to see him in a casual pair of sweatpants and a gray T-shirt.

"Lyla?" he asks through the screen door. "Wait—you *are* Lyla, right?"

"Yeah," I reply. "I was wondering if I could talk to you. About...about Carson."

"What are you saying about Lyla?" a voice asks behind him. Even though it's hard to see through his screen door, which he still hasn't opened yet, the voice I hear is unmistakable. And it makes me realize I should have paid better attention to the car that is parked in the driveway.

My stomach drops. I read the guilty expression I can make out on Craig's face even through the screen. He says nothing, and instead, opens the door and reveals the interior of his house and who is walking up behind him, their hair in a towel and their feet bare like they've just taken a shower and are quite comfortable here. Like they're here all the time. Like they're Craig's roommate. Or maybe more.

My mouth has gone so dry I am not even sure I will be able to talk.

Somehow, the words come. As strained as they are, I manage to croak out, "Aunt Nora?"

CHAPTER 84

WARNER

I don't want to go back home after I make my discovery about Dean still being into Amelia, because I don't want to risk having to see him again when he comes back and continues to act all fake, pretending he wants us all to be a family when that's simply not true. He wants Amelia as his girlfriend and me as his son. That's two separate families, as far as I am concerned.

Instead, I drive around aimlessly. I try texting and calling the unknown number that was apparently my mother telling me everything is fine. How can I even know for sure it was from her? Why wouldn't she just text me to let me know from her own phone? Why wouldn't she tell the police they can stop their search for her? Why does she seem like she's on the run from something when Carson Price is dead?

I don't know how much time has passed before I finally remember that I never did message Audrey back from the many texts she had tried to send me. Feeling guilty, and wanting to check on her since I haven't seen her since I thought she was dead...I drive to her dad's house.

I park my car on the curb and see that her car is parked on the driveway, so I am confident that she's here. I get out and walk up the pathway to the front door. It opens before I can reach it, and the first person to step outside is Ryan Carpenter. Behind him is a giggling, smiling, looking totally like she didn't just have a near death experience, Audrey.

"Oh," Ryan says, the smile he had on his face from Audrey still half there when he sees me standing there.

"Warner!" Audrey cries, stepping out onto the patio with Ryan. "Um, hi! Are you okay?"

"I just swung by to ask *you* that," I say, giving her a small smile. I try to come off as friendly. I don't want Ryan to see me as some sort of threat. I've had enough of that type of drama from Jackson.

"Hey, I'll text you, okay?" Ryan says, turning toward Audrey and slinking a hand around her waist. She looks up at him adoringly, smiles, and nods. Then he bends his neck and kisses her cheek. Right there. Right in front of me. Then he raises his eyebrows at me as he passes—in what way? Like a "Hey, man" or a "She's mine" kind of way? I don't even know—and then he gets in what I now see is his car, parked also in the driveway next to Audrey's.

A weird feeling comes over me. One I don't recognize. One that feels misplaced. One that's confusing the heck out of me as I stand here on Audrey's porch, feeling her scrutinizing stare.

"Um, I'm good," she tells me slowly, as if she's trying to pretend Ryan was never just standing there kissing her on the cheek in front of me. "I was released from the hospital a little while ago. I've been texting and calling you."

I scratch the back of my neck, trying to shake this feeling but unable to. "Yeah. Sorry about that," I say, my insides feeling hot and uncomfortable. "Sorta a lot going on. But I was in the area when I remembered I hadn't talked to you yet, so I figured it would be easier to just swing by."

She smiles at me.

"Besides," I continue, stepping toward her. I don't hear Ryan's car anymore. He's gone. "I wanted to see you. In person. To confirm that you're really alive. Because the Audrey I saw back at school..." I shudder visibly and can't even say the words aloud.

I thought you were dead.

I thought Carson Price killed you.

Audrey, the incredible girl that she is, risked her life to save Carson from hurting my mom. She did it for me.

She smiles at me. And it does something to me. "I'm alive," she says. "And I'm okay."

I'm glad to hear it. In fact, I am overwhelmed with relief. She *is* alive. She's here. She's right in front of me.

And she always has been.

Out of the blue, I close the gap between us, and I kiss Audrey Bailey.

It's quick. Quick because as soon as our lips touch, as soon as I realize what I've just done, I realize how stupid I am, and I step back.

Audrey stares at me in shock. In complete and total shock. And I get it. I'm in shock, too.

What did I just do?

"Uh, I—I'm sorry," I say quickly, turning away from her.

"Warner," she starts.

"I gotta go." Before she can say anything else, I book it back to my car and get the heck out of there.

"Stupid, stupid, stupid!" I keep saying to myself as I drive away from her house. I can tell in my rearview mirror that she's watching me fade away into the distance. She probably still has that shocked expression on her face. "What is the matter with you?!" I yell at myself.

I kissed Audrey Bailey.

Why did I do that?

Because you have feelings for her, a voice in my head says. *You have for a while, and it took her risking her life for you and nearly dying for you to see it.*

"Shut up!" I yell at the voice, tightening my grip on the steering wheel. My phone rings in the cupholder, and I am terrified that it's Audrey calling, demanding me to explain myself to her. But Wilde's name is on the screen.

I answer it, my breathing heavy. "Did you find her?"

"Warner?" he asks in his deep, professional voice.

"Duh."

"Warner, we—I don't know how to tell you this."

"What?" I think maybe I should pull over because whatever he is about to say isn't anything good. But I don't stop.

"We, uh, found your mom's car. It's... it's in pretty bad shape. Really bad, actually. We found it in a ditch. Upside down. There... there are traces of blood, but... Warner, there's still no sign of your mother anywhere."

And just like that, my world is ripped from under me once again.

TO BE CONTINUED

Up Next

Poor Warner, and well... everybody in Toxey.

But what if I told you that in the next (and final) book in the *"Moms Who Lie"* series, you'll get all your questions answered and everything wrapped up in a nice bow?

"Lying In Plain Sight: Book 5 in the 'Moms Who Lie' Psychological Thriller Series" is just, well, lying there... in plain sight... waiting for you.

All the answers. All the truth. But not without a price.

Warner, Lyla, Audrey, and their families have been through four books worth of sheer torture. They're about to get all the answers they've been looking for, but they're going to have to fight harder than ever to find them.

The person they thought was behind all the threats, attacks, and murders is dead, but the mysterious stalker is still tormenting them worse than ever.

Who will get their "happily ever after" and who will end up paying for the truth with their lives?

Grab your copy of ***"Lying In Plain Sight"*** to get all the answers.

Author Notes by Brett Monk

C an we keep in touch?

Seriously. *Especially if you've now read four or more of my books.*

I'm an independent author and my loyal readers are really important to me. I'd like to know what you like and what you'd like to see more of.

I've gone to a lot of work to create an email newsletter, a private Facebook community, and other ways that I can interact with my fans, and that my fans can interact with each other.

You might want to become an ARC READER. (Someone who gets free e-book copies of my books before they're published in return for feedback to me and reviews on Amazon and other places.

You might even want to become part of my "STREET TEAM." That's for folks who would like to help me share news about my books and movies on their blogs and social media platforms. I provide memes and fun graphics for people to use, and I've been known to send gifts of appreciation to my highly active Street Team Members.

I correspond personally to my emails and to comments in my social media, especially with my ARC readers and Street Team Members.

Also, If you want to learn **all the details about what happened back when Maddy and Mia were in high school, the night Carson disappeared**, you can download the free bonus novella, *"The Lying Begins"* at the link below.

More details are available at this link:
https://www.brettmonk .com

About the Authors

Brett Monk

Brett Monk is an author, movie director, and voiceover artist.

He holds degrees in Communications and Psychology and spent over 30 years writing and directing films for businesses and government agencies in the Washington, DC area before turning his focus to creating books and audiobooks.

He also directed and co-wrote two feature-length murder mystery movies which are in worldwide distribution.

Originally from the Shenandoah Valley area, he now lives in Northern Virginia with his family and a rambunctious Bernedoodle named Merlin.

McKenna Langford

McKenna lives in Arizona with her husband and two goofy Boxador brothers.

Before she dove into the world of ghostwriting and co-writing, she got her bachelor's degree in interior design and published her first five novels. She worked in a boutique interior design firm in the valley for two years, moved to Seattle with her husband to explore for another two years, then moved back to Arizona and made writing her full-time career in 2021.

www.ingramcontent.com/pod-product-compliance
Lightning Source LLC
Chambersburg PA
CBHW032008310726
48972CB00002B/319